"*Cold Spell* is an honest and compelling coming-of-age-in-the-wilderness tale where packing bear meat and scaling a glacier are rites of passage. Sixteen-year-old Sylvie and her family move north and learn that there's the dream of Alaska, and then there's waking up from that dream. Vanasse's characters in the fictional Alaska town are rustic and real and all of them, including the adults, experience growing pains."

—Melinda Moustakis, author *Bear Down, Bear North: Alaska Stories* (Flannery O'Connor Award for Short Fiction)

"In clear, gracious prose, *Cold Spell* tells the story of mother and daughter each caught at the intersection of desire and vulnerability. From the Midwest to the Far North, the story of Sylvie and Ruth shines a light on the complexity of mother-daughter relationships, while examining the trauma of a fractured home and the complications of starting over. *Cold Spell* is an important addition to the growing shelf of Alaska fiction."

—Brendan Jones, author of *The Alaskan Laundry*

"*Cold Spell* will catch you in its icy grip as Vanasse deftly reveals the cracks and fissures of a frozen heart. A love story, a coming-of-age tale, and glimpse into a rarely seen slice of Alaska, the story reminds us that a life without dreams and without love might not be living at all."

—Don Rearden, author of *The Raven's Gift*

Other Books in the Alaska Literary Series

Cold Spell

Deb Vanasse

ALASKA
LITERARY
SERIES

University of Alaska Press
Fairbanks

ALASKA LITERARY SERIES

University of Alaska Press

P.O. Box 756240

Fairbanks, AK 99775-6240

Library of Congress Cataloging-in-Publication Data

Vanasse, Deb.

 Cold spell / by Deb Vanasse.

    pages cm

  ISBN 978-1-60223-242-6 (pbk. : alk. paper)

  1. Women—Alaska—Fiction. 2. Glaciers—Alaska—Fiction. 3. Alaska—Fiction. I. Title.

  PS3622.A585894C65 2014

  813'.6—dc23

                          2013048827

Cover design by Dixon Jones

This publication was printed on acid-free paper that meets the minimum requirements for ANSI / NISO Z39.48–1992 (R2002) (Permanence of Paper for Printed Library Materials).

Printed in the United States

Contents

"I seek the everlasting ices of the north."
—*Mary Shelley*

Isostasy

Displacement from the advance or retreat of a glacier

I am a poem, Sylvie once thought, swollen like a springtime river, light swirled in dark, music and memory. Then her father ran off and her mother became obsessed with a glacier and she realized this was what happened to girls who believed themselves poems, poems in fact being prone to bad turns and misunderstandings.

Before the glacier, Sylvie's mother had been ordinary and dependable, a plain woman with kind eyes, unlike her father who was dashing and quick, with a flair for the dramatic. When he'd come home cursing his boss in the Ford parts department or when he'd blow up at the neighbor for turning his dog loose, Sylvie's mother would massage the base of his neck and speak calm, soothing words. After he left Minnesota for Florida in the company of Mirabelle, a redhead from the dealership, Sylvie cried in long, heaving sobs every night for a week, and because she cried her sister Anna did too, and there was nothing poetic in their sorrow, no words for it even.

With her soft, steady voice and her fingers stroking their hair, Sylvie's mother assured the girls that their father loved them whether he was still in Pine Lake or not. For her mother's sake Sylvie tried to pretend this was so, though in truth she doubted it deeply. She wished her mother would cry, wished she would wail and scream and flail, wished she would rage at something, at someone, at anyone, even at Sylvie.

Instead her mother's smile, always ready, became automatic, as if by the push of a button her lips made their slight upward turn. She roused the girls every day at precisely 6:30, even on weekends. She sliced bananas over their oatmeal and sprinkled brown sugar, one tablespoon each. She sipped coffee brewed in a new pot that made only one cup and ate toast spread thin with peach preserves and deflected Sylvie's complaints that no one else ate oatmeal for breakfast. She rinsed the dishes and loaded the dishwasher, glasses on top, bowls on the bottom, spoons up, butter knives down, and she folded tidy waxed paper over sandwiches cut on the diagonal, peanut butter and apple for Anna, cream cheese and turkey for Sylvie, both on wheat bread no matter how Anna begged for white, the old-fashioned wrapping an embarrassment to Sylvie, who turned her wishes to small things like thin, transparent plastic. The tiniest quiver in her mother's smile hinted at their shared understanding, hers and Sylvie's, of how a single uncontrolled moment could upend everything.

Not long after Sylvie's father drove off, her mother took the girls for their annual physicals. Dr. Temple was the only pediatrician in Pine Lake, and for as long as Sylvie could remember she had been ushered to him for every sniffle and cough. She was humiliated at the idea of the old doctor with his hairy hands and long ears poking her cold naked chest where breasts had recently sprouted. She begged to be taken to Gainesville, to the sprawling clinic where no one would know her, but her mother refused, insisting of course on their usual routine. So Sylvie planted herself in a corner of Dr. Temple's waiting room, apart from her mother and sister, and buried her head in a book as she tried not to choke on the heavy smell that hangs over medical places, part alcohol and part cleaning products, foolishly confident that after her father's sudden departure things at least couldn't get any worse.

From the doorway that separated the waiting room from the business inside, Dr. Temple's nurse called for Sylvie and Anna. When their mother rose to join them, the nurse suggested the girls were old enough to see the doctor alone. "But Anna is only five," Sylvie's mother said through her auto-smile. "She just started kindergarten."

The nurse cupped a milky white hand over Anna's shoulder. "Eleven and five. Plenty old to see the doctor alone." As she steered the girls toward the door, Sylvie's mother blinked hard, like a shutter that closed on an image to save it.

"You're a big girl," the nurse said to Sylvie as she trotted them down the corridor. "Slide right on into this little room and slip off your clothes and put on that gown while I help your sister." The nurse brushed back a strand of Anna's hair, silky and fine like their mother's.

"We always…" But Sylvie had no words for their self-conscious cleaving since her father had left.

"It's okay." Anna's pressed lips turned up like their mother's. "I don't mind."

Since she was in no way a poem, Sylvie did as the nurse said, slipping out of her jeans and her shirt and folding inside them her underpants and her sad little bra. She eased onto the exam table, her slender but big-knuckled feet dangling as her haunches stuck to the vinyl and her nipples stiffened beneath the rough cotton. She had never before had to fully undress for the doctor, and her resentment at this fell squarely on her mother, helpless to insist on a routine when for once one was needed.

She sat hunched under the impossible blue gown, a limp balloon from which her limbs protruded, while Dr. Temple tapped at her knees with his little hammer and pretended not to look as he pressed his cold stethoscope to her chest. Then he started in with the questions. How were things at home, now that it was only the girls? Did Sylvie miss her dad something awful? Were there bad dreams she might want to share?

Sylvie mumbled fine, no, and no as she beat back the dream image of her father sinking in a vast, lapping ocean, and Sylvie paddling with all she had, trying to save him. Finally the doctor gave up with his stethoscope and patted her shoulder, his hand sweet with soap, and pronounced her a good strong girl who would be a great help to her mother during this difficult time.

That's when Sylvie realized that not only a few of the parents but the whole town of Pine Lake was talking about how her dad had run off. If she'd been the good strong girl the doctor pronounced her to be, she might have thought how this gossip must impact her mother. But instead her resentment balled up even tighter, like a leech left to dry in the sun.

Dressed, she returned to the waiting room. On her mother's lap was a magazine, splayed open to a white and blue-shadowed mass that shrugged out from a large range of mountains. Sylvie slid into a chair and waited for her mother to ask what had gone on with the doctor. But her mother only stared at the ice as if it were the most lovely and mysterious thing she had ever encountered. A tingling crept beneath Sylvie's skin, up her arms to her chest, dread at how a mere image could insert itself between them, so that it was no longer just her and her mother, pretending for Anna's sake that everything would be fine.

Sylvie's mother glanced at the receptionist, then pressed the magazine flat and with great precision tore out the glacier, folded it twice, and tucked the photo into her purse. "You're not supposed to do that," Sylvie said. Known by everyone, including herself, to be a compliant child, she was struck by the power in so few words. "The magazines are for everyone."

"What magazines?" From the hallway, Anna came forward.

Their mother pressed a finger to her lips. The way she draped her hand on her purse made Sylvie suspicious of what else might be stashed inside. Sylvie's father was the one to come home with a fluffy hotel towel stuffed in his suitcase or a shot glass swiped from a bar in his pocket. Her mother she'd never known to take anything.

They piled into the car. "I can't believe you ripped out that picture," Sylvie said.

"I want to see," Anna said.

Their mother tucked the purse next to her hip and folded her elbow across it. "Later."

In light of Sylvie's recent exposure, her mother's smug smile was especially hateful. "They're all talking about us," she said

Her mother's eyes shone in the rearview mirror. "Who's talking about us?"

"Everyone." Of all things, her mother was smiling; you could see it in the way the skin crinkled at the corners of her eyes. "Everyone in this whole entire town. And you think it's funny."

"No, honey." The smile stayed. "It's not funny. But there's nothing we can do about it."

"Is it a picture of someone we know?" Anna poked the side of the purse. "I want to see."

"In a minute." Their mother hung a sharp right into the Carson Crafts parking lot, where she wheeled the sedan between a panel truck and a big Suburban.

"You're parked crooked." How had Sylvie not noticed sooner this duty to point out her mother's flaws? "The door of that truck's gonna smack us."

"I'm just running in for a minute." Her neck flushed at the base, her mother pressed her purse between her ribs and her arm.

"I'm coming in." When Anna swung open her door, it clunked against the side of the panel truck.

"Told you," said Sylvie, but already her mother was scurrying toward the entrance, Anna half-running to keep up. Sylvie scooted out of the sunlit square that beamed through the window into her lap. She was used to hanging back, not drawing attention, but she had failed to anticipate this unexpected consequence, that Anna would latch on to their mother in her place.

When they returned, her mother clutched a small bag next to her purse. Anna got in from the driver's side. "It's a glacier," she informed Sylvie. "A big bunch of ice that never melts."

"I know that," said Sylvie, though it was clear no one cared.

Once home, Sylvie's mother trimmed the magazine picture and used a knife to pry back the wires that held cardboard next to the glass. She balled up the glossy photo that came with the frame, a girl plucking petals from a daisy, and replaced it with the glacier. Then she bent the wires back into place and raised the picture between her hands. "This will sit right on my desk."

"I'm never eating oatmeal again." It was the single act of rebellion Sylvie could summon on short notice. "Never."

"Goodness," her mother said. "What's gotten into you?" But her eyes never left the glacier.

Ogive

An undulation formed on the surface of ice

In the flat farm country of central Minnesota where mothers went crazy for things like PTA fundraisers and shoe sales at Henkes, her mother's picture drew attention as it sat on her secretary's desk outside the principal's office at Pine Lake High School, where she used her calm words to soothe students who'd gotten in trouble and their parents who believed bad behavior was all the fault of the school. Photos of Sylvie and Anna were displaced to a shelf behind her. When people asked about the glacier, Sylvie's mother would shrug and say she liked ice. Sometimes she'd balance the frame between her two index fingers and lift the image to her face, as if there were secrets chiseled into the frozen fissures of the glacier.

She passed through her own Little Ice Age. At home she'd pull the shades, dim the lights, draw her knees to her chest, wrap herself in a blanket, and stare for hours at movie footage of glaciers. Docu-voices crooned over snow that fell soft and light, gathering into a mass that turned harder than rock and yet still flowed like water. Calving ice crashed alarmingly into the sea. Cameras tracked climbers who scuttled backwards, clinging to ropes as they disappeared into steep blue crevasses. Helicopters chopped like insects, hovering over glaciers that might one day disappear, if the earth kept heating up.

You couldn't walk past the living room without being assaulted by some cold fact or another. Glaciers trap three times the fresh water that runs free on earth. The pressure inside a glacier builds to one thousand pounds per square inch. Believing ice had a soul, medieval peasants set crosses in front of glaciers, in vain hope of stopping them. One documentary featured a man who claimed that through the sheer power of thought you could infuse ice with beauty. He amassed believers who prayed for pure, crystalline ice, as if the forces that conjured a glacier could be moved by a tiny thing like desire.

The ice drew her mother as it shut out Sylvie, who was helpless to stop it. It was as if once her father packed his belongings into that refurbished Ford and pointed it south, her mother's head had swelled with palm trees and beaches and skimpy swimsuits that a woman like Mirabelle might still pull off, and she needed the big frozen mass to butt those tropical images out of her head. Or maybe she simply aspired to the cold, regal power of ice.

Sylvie grew into her body, the wisp of a bra swapped for a real one. A young woman, her father remarked when Sylvie and Anna flew down for their annual visit, eyeing Sylvie in a way that made her look down at her feet. She sensed the bad things that rattled inside her—anger, unsteadiness, guilt—but she remained an obedient girl, a good student, reliable in ways that would prove no match for ice.

On a cloudy February day during Sylvie's sophomore year, Kenny arrived. Sent to the school to retrieve his cousin's son after he'd gotten smacked with a ball in PE, no one would deal with him until he first signed in and received the required visitor's pass. He'd gone fuming to her mother's desk, directed first by the hall monitor and then by the school nurse. Sylvie's mother had set down her pen and tucked her hair in back of her ear while Kenny went on about the sorts of rules that robbed the last bits of freedom left in this country. Where he came from, he said, a man could do as he pleased. She'd nodded and watched with her plain but kind eyes until at last Kenny jabbed at her photo and said, "I'll be damned. That's my glacier."

By the time Kenny got done explaining how he'd come from Alaska where he lived not far from this same piece of ice, by the time he'd finished saying how the glacier wound twenty-six miles down from the mountains and how the face of it reared up wide as a fortress, he'd calmed himself. In the meantime her mother's obsession had grown to encompass a man, not that she realized it yet. As she escorted Kenny to the nurse's office, she slipped him her telephone number. What were the chances, she would say later. What were the chances a man from that very glacier would walk right up to her desk? And not any man, but one who with the press of his hands and his deliberate speech and the depth of his eyes seemed the glacier incarnate.

The attention she'd lavished on ice, Sylvie's mother now turned on Kenny. He began spending the night. Sylvie could hardly stand the sight of him shirtless in their tiny kitchen, the sun teasing the coiled hairs of his chest as he kneaded her mother's shoulders. The furrows on her mother's forehead softened and her plain eyes turned wide and alert with the mascara and shadow and liner she'd started to wear. For breakfast she set out cocoa and toast—no more oatmeal—and sliced peaches, Kenny's favorite, instead of bananas, and she sent the girls off with money instead of packed lunches. On her shirts, she left so many buttons unfastened that their principal, old doddering Mr. Stanton, could only stammer and look the other way.

Sylvie had just turned sixteen, and though she should have been happy for her mother, the danger locked up in the glacier was nothing compared to this man. One night their eyes met, hers and Kenny's, across the living room, and the look that passed between them was a humming that rippled down Sylvie's legs to her toes, an exquisite and shameful vibration that replayed when she lay down to sleep.

Anna loved Kenny because he took her and their mother to Happy Pete's Ice Cream Emporium, where he bought them waffle cones in flavors like Bubble Gum Mint and Cherry Cheesecake Surprise. He always brought a pint home for Sylvie, Double Deep Chocolate: a reward for staying back with her homework. With a flash of his perfect white smile, he'd set the frosty carton in Sylvie's hand, and with a mumbled thanks she'd shove the ice cream in the back of the freezer behind bags of peas and whole chickens. Only after everyone else was asleep and she could hear the puff-puffs of Kenny's breathing behind her mother's bedroom door would she sneak to the kitchen and scoop spoonfuls straight from the carton, the cold chocolate sliding in accusatory lumps down the back of her throat.

Her only hope was that Kenny would soon leave. The work he'd come to help with at his cousin's was done, and he swore any day he'd head back to Alaska. In the meantime, Sylvie did her best to avoid the yellow-flecked blue of his eyes.

Daffodils poked through the dirt and after them tulips. The yard went dizzy with lilacs. May came, the first day and the next and the next. Still Kenny lingered. Sylvie buried herself in her homework, projects and papers and tests that teachers piled on at the end of the year. But at night she'd catch her tongue running over the edge of her teeth as if they were his teeth and her hand touching her thigh as if it were his hand, and the humming would start all over.

The last day of school came, and still Kenny was there. Sylvie waded the halls to her mother's office where she sometimes sat after school, swiveling in the tall, cushioned chair, enjoying the way the attendance counter cut her view of the hallway, forcing her to imagine the bottom halves of bodies as they passed, the legs of girls who held themselves prim and tight while others self-consciously swayed at the hips, the feet of boys so full of themselves that they swaggered, shoelaces dangling, tempting fate.

She swung through the gate in the attendance counter and strode to her mother, bent over her desk. Sylvie shifted her books on her hip. "I'm going to Karen's," she said. "Right after school."

Her mother looked up. "We're going with Kenny to the lake."

Sylvie dismissed the swell that came from hearing his name. "Karen's filling the pool. I told her I'd help."

"Filling the pool takes one person," her mother said. "And a hose. We'll swim at the lake. And Kenny's renting a boat, to go fishing."

Sylvie's eyes flitted to the hallway, where the crowd was starting to thin, so she wouldn't think of the four of them packed in a boat, her mother and Kenny and Anna and Sylvie, so close their knees would be touching. "It's too cold to swim at the lake," Sylvie said. "And I hate fishing."

"A few hours with family," said her mother. "That's not asking much."

"Kenny's not family." He wasn't. He never would be.

Her mother fingered the papers on her desk as she searched Sylvie's face, looking perhaps for some trace of the child she had been—the wondering eyes, the compliant smile—a version of herself that Sylvie, too, longed for, reaching back to a time before the glacier and Kenny had inserted themselves between her and her mother.

"Family is whatever we make it," said Sylvie's mother, looking satisfied with the cagey truth of her words. "Wherever we make it."

Sylvie shifted her books to the other hip. "But I promised Karen."

Her mother looked down at the red squiggles and lines that crisscrossed the paper on her desk, then up at the glacier as if for fortitude. "You're coming with us," she said. "End of discussion."

There were moments captured on film, when huge chunks of ice fell booming and crashing to the sea. Though these collapses seemed sudden, there was always some kind of warning. Hairline fissures. Downwasting. Icefalls. Shifting you'd notice if only you tried. And Sylvie was trying. She was weary with trying. Queasy and weak, from pushing Kenny aside only to have him thrust back at her.

"You should get rid of that thing," Sylvie said, with the slightest of nods at the glacier. She turned and with a deliberate sway of her hips left the calm of the office for the noise of the hallway, forgetting the way the attendance counter would work, slicing her to half of what she thought she might be.

The lake glittered with the promise of summer. Sylvie's sixteen years were wrapped around the oblong body of water along which the town arranged itself. In this town her father was raised, her grandmother buried. It was where Sylvie had gone to grade school and middle school and where she would graduate high school. She knew every shop that lined Grand Street, the florist and the chocolate store and the six antique dealers that aimed to lure tourists off the two-lane on their way to Minnesota's North Country. She knew every farm yard along County 15, including the one where she'd gone on the hay ride that ended in her first-ever kiss. More times than she could count, she'd biked the four-and-a-half-mile circumference of Pine Lake, sometimes with Karen and sometimes alone, marking spring and summer and fall on the road that circled from the downtown shops to the fancy homes on the north end to the eastside park and back to the old part of town, where the lumber mill had been boarded up and closed three years before.

At the park that stretched along the east side of the lake, her mother lay on the dock, squeezed into shorts and a button-down shirt, her head in Kenny's lap. Kenny swung his feet in the water, stirring up mud, his pants rolled to expose thick, white legs. He lifted her mother's hair in his fingers, then let it fall. Her mother brushed her hand along the edge of his chin, as if Anna and Sylvie weren't there to see, on the hard seats of the rented boat tied to the dock.

Anna traced a finger over the gills of the dead fish that lay at her feet, a perch hardening in the sun, too small to keep. "Stop it." Sylvie whiffed at her hand. "That thing stinks."

Anna clutched her fingers to her chest. "I thought you liked me."

Their mother lifted her head. "You girls enjoy the sunshine," she said. "Before you know it'll be winter all over."

Kenny's fingers snagged in her hair. "You haven't seen winter till you've been at the glacier." He glanced at Sylvie, and the lake shimmered and its edges blurred and the sky shifted, a widening, a falling away. Then he leaned back on the gray boards of the dock, hands locked under his head, and Sylvie's mother arranged herself to accommodate the loss of his lap, her head at his shoulder, her shirt riding up to expose the thin skin of her waist as she fingered a worn spot in his jeans.

Kenny hoisted his head and squinted at Anna and Sylvie. "You kids run and play," he said, as if a merry-go-round were the thing they most needed.

You kids. Sylvie gripped the hot metal seat. From the shore rose the rank smell of lake weeds, from the boat the dead smell of the fish. *You kids.* "Race you," she said, and reached a hand to her sister.

Their feet thundered the dock. "Whoa, Nellie," said Kenny, but Sylvie refused his smile. Gone, gone, gone. Once he returned to Alaska, it would be as if he'd never had any part in their lives.

At ten, Anna was still of the age where a playground got her excited as long as she wasn't with girls who liked to watch boys acting like they weren't being watched. She clattered the worn wood of the merry-go-round and gripped the metal bars and closed her eyes and demanded Sylvie spin her faster and faster. Sylvie crouched, slapping the cold metal of each passing bar with the flat of her hand, until the spin acquired its own whirring force. Anna squealed and flung back her head, hair splayed in the sun. Sylvie might have jumped on and ridden with her sister, but she refused to give Kenny the satisfaction. *You kids.*

Anna dragged her feet in the dust and stumbled off the platform, swaying and staggering like a drunk. She insisted Sylvie ride the swings, the two of them pumping their legs like horses racing the sky. "Look, Sylvie. My toes will touch the trees." She flattened herself as she swung, arms rigid, face toward the sun, fearless. Sylvie half-stretched to pump her swing higher, but the gap between them was too wide to reach.

She left Anna arcing toward the blue-screeched sky and wandered toward Kenny's truck. It was the sort of vehicle her father and his friends at the dealership would have made fun of if someone had been foolish enough to take it on trade. The dull orange-red paint screamed after-market and the right fender was caved in and the driver's door rattled and the tailgate was crinkled so it had to be slammed. She grabbed the roll bar, the one part that still looked shiny and new, and swung herself onto the running boards, the metallic smell of the bar rubbing into her palms as she slid into the driver's seat.

The cab smelled like Kenny, dusty and raw. Ripped vinyl scraped her shoulder, pink from the sun. Stuffed in the visor were pull tabs and pay stubs and torn bits of paper, pieces of him. On a scrap torn from a yellow tablet, she read a handwritten number from some other area code, then tucked it back so it appeared undisturbed. Frowning at her bare thighs flattened against the worn gray upholstery, she leaned forward. Her chest brushed the steering wheel, and she had a sudden strong urge for the keys, though until now she'd driven only their tinny sedan, her mother gripping the seat, telling her when to brake, when to turn, how to watch backing up.

She rooted under the floor mats, gritty with sand and a winter's accumulation of dirt, pawing through crumpled fast food bags and smashed aluminum cans and wrinkled work shirts. The deeper she dug, the more convinced she became she would find them. She thrust her hand in the dark hole of the glove box where she'd seen Kenny lob keys, in where papers were shoved without creasing or care. She rifled through books of matches. Bottle openers. The serrated foil edges of condoms wrapped and ready. A fat pamphlet with a black-and-white sketch of Jesus. Good News, it said. Bits of Kenny that she felt as if blind, with her fingers. Her hopes rose when she came upon a thin looped wire that might have held keys, but it was only the tag from a repair shop.

She eased over to the passenger side and with a sweep of her arm dumped the entire contents of the glove box into her lap. *You kids.* A red matchbook with silver letters read Pharaoh's Den Cairo, Illinois. Sylvie had been through Cairo once, on the way to Missouri with Karen's family. It was a long way south of Pine Lake, down the Mississippi, where people talked in slow drawls. With the matchbook, she could challenge Kenny's claim that he'd driven straight to Pine Lake from Alaska and weaken perhaps her mother's unwavering trust.

She struck a match to the book, and the smell of sulfur and smoke rose. As she hovered the flame over the trash in her lap, a reluctant corner of a damp pink receipt from Joe's Transmission and Body ignited, a thin yellow burn wriggling along its edge. Near the smoldering paper lay a full matchbook that had the potential to ignite. She held that possibility like a full breath before a deep plunge.

Anna pounded the truck. "Whatcha doing?" she yelled at the window. Sylvie snuffed the creeping flame under the heel of her hand, then shoved the papers and condoms and matches and Jesus book into the glove box, slammed it shut, and slid out of the truck. She rubbed her hands on the sides of her legs, leaving a faint charcoaled streak. "Let's get Mom," she said, avoiding Anna's wide eyes. "Let's get Mom and go home." But even as she said the word *home*, she felt it slipping away. Like the glacier, Kenny was part of them now.

⁘

She would later recall the afternoon heat, the prickle of grass through the blanket, the remarkable flatness of land, lake, and sky. The smell of mustard on rye, the hurried clouds blotting the sun, her desire to take Anna's hand, even though Anna didn't need her the way that she once had. The knowing way Kenny had looked at her mother, like she was the only one there, and the loathing that floated like an oily sheen across her desire.

Kenny wouldn't stay. No, that was too easy. With a large smile, Sylvie's mother announced that the three of them would pack into Kenny's truck and ride with him up to Alaska. Not for the summer. For good.

"We'll get to see moose," Anna said.

"Moose. Fox. Wolverine. Wolf." Kenny swatted a slow-circling fly away from the sandwiches, then roughed Anna's hair with the flat of his hand. "Heck, we might even find you a bear."

Her mother reached across the blanket toward Sylvie. "I know what you're thinking. But you'll make friends there just as easy as here."

Sylvie sprang up. Tipped soda gurgled from her can and streamed toward her feet. "You don't know what I'm thinking. And you can't make me leave." Her voice caught on *leave*. She would not cry, would not cry, would not cry. This punishment was beyond anything she deserved, no matter what evil thoughts she'd refused to let go of. She swore it all off. Anything could be denied. She might quite possibly hate Kenny, him and his sorry excuse for a truck, now that she saw where this was going, yanking her straight out of her life. She plucked a single sorry objection out of the jumble of hurt. "You'll lose your job," she said.

"Mr. Stanton already knows." Her mother spoke with deliberate, hateful calm. "I left him a note."

Of course. She must have nestled with Kenny on the front porch swing as she penned in careful script an explanation for this ridiculous turn of events. Creepy Mr. Stanton with his liver-spotted hands and shiny bald head must have nearly keeled over, reading it. Alaska. Of all places. Though what he'd mean of course would be *of all people*.

"Beauty of Alaska," said Kenny, "is you don't need a job." He stroked the back of her mother's hand. "And I've got a nice little place for you girls."

A nice little place for you girls. All Sylvie could picture was ice, bitter and cold.

That night Kenny took her mother to the movies to celebrate. Once his truck pulled away, Sylvie emerged from her room, her belly tight from having refused the mustard-laced ham and cheese. She stirred up mayo and tuna, then rinsed out the can and hid it in the bottom of the trash so no one would know she'd given in to her hunger.

Their house in Pine Lake was small, and even though they'd lived there for years and the landlord was willing to sell it, her mother had never shown any interest, making excuses about how the girls shared a bedroom and how the bathroom paint peeled and how the rusty kitchen sink leaked. This seemed a sign now, that her mother had somehow seen from the moment she tore the glacier out of the magazine the entire outrageous mess Kenny would make of their lives, while Sylvie herself had been too stupid to notice.

In the bedroom, Anna flattened herself on a quilt pieced of sharp-edged triangles, like dishes broken and scattered. "Aren't you excited?" she asked. "Not even one little bit?"

"No." Steam burbled from the iron as Sylvie pressed the collar of a crisp white shirt. "And you shouldn't be either."

"But it's an adventure."

"That's just what Mom says."

Anna rolled to her stomach and propped her chin on her hands. "How come you're so cranky?"

"Zip it," said Sylvie.

Anna looked away. A lump rose in Sylvie's throat as she slipped the warm sleeves over her arms. "What's to get excited about?" she asked. "No more Happy Pete's. No more swimming at the lake."

"I don't care." Anna jutted her chin.

In front of the mirror, Sylvie buttoned her shirt, then undid one button. She flattened the collar and turned to the side, catching the pleasing rise of her breasts. She bent toward the mirror and with her mother's liquid liner traced her eyes like Karen had been forever after her to.

"You look pretty," said Anna. "Prettier than Mom."

"Don't let Mom hear you say that." Sylvie brushed blush over the color that rose in her cheeks. "You'll hurt her feelings." Then she crouched next to the bed, the quilt a warm mess of cut blue and purple. "Tuck you in?"

"No thanks." Anna crossed her ankles and swung her legs, up and back. "I'll go to bed later."

"Someone's getting big for her britches." Their dad liked to say that. Sylvie jumped on the bed. She straddled Anna, who squealed and wriggled and rolled herself over while Sylvie dove for her ribs, tickling. "Uncle," said Sylvie. "Say uncle."

Anna laughed, and Sylvie laughed, too. "Uncle, uncle, uncle," Anna screeched.

"That's better," Sylvie said as Anna quit her thrashing. She tucked her shirt back into her jeans and checked her hair in the mirror. "Now, you want me to tuck you in?"

"Nope," Anna said.

Sylvie's disappointment in this small ritual forgone was larger than it should have been. She retreated to the top step of the porch and tucked her knees to her chin and waited for Karen. The night was starting to cool, a half-moon lighting a tendril of cloud that trailed in the sky. The far edge of town glowed with the lights of the state prison, shot up into the night. She had no sense of who she might be outside of this place, or of what she might become.

When her father first left, she'd developed a fear of the places they might end up if their mother acquired the same sudden urge to take off. Holiday visits to Miami were barely tolerable, between Mirabelle's dangling jewelry and her over-teased hair and the unending sound of traffic below the condo's guest bedroom with its seashell lamp and flimsy curtains, sea green, and its postage-stamp view of the ocean. Coming home to the gray skies and snow of Pine Lake, Sylvie felt as if God had breathed it to earth only for her. She loved the smell of mower exhaust mixed with the neighbor's fresh-cut grass in summer and the smoke-sting of trash that smoldered in burn barrels and the fine powdered smell of grain dumped in the Miller's Feed silo.

Tires scraped the curb. "Sorry I'm late." Karen leaned across the seat to pop the door, which didn't open from outside. "Lecture about good behavior and watching myself and all that. You have no idea how lucky you are. Your mom doesn't nag."

"There's Kenny." Sylvie's pulse betrayed her, quickening as she spoke his name. *"Don't let those boys get all handsy."* She dropped her voice, inflecting the way Kenny did.

Karen laughed. "I think Kenny's cute. In an old guy kinda way. Nice blue eyes."

"I hate how he talks," Sylvie said, so quickly she almost believed it herself. "He's all country music gone wrong. *I ain't never seen no one as pretty as you."*

Karen laughed, fleeting as a snowflake that lands, crystal and perfect, on a patch of warm flesh. "I like what you've done to your eyes."

Sylvie touched the edge of the liner, leaving a gentle smudge on the tip of her finger. She would not cry, would not cry. Karen hit the brakes, stopping hard at the four-way. Having pulled out partway, the driver to the right looked annoyed. Karen flipped him off. Then she started in about Ginny DeLong who was seeing Joe Matthews after dumping Brent Skinner, and about Tracy Larkin who was chasing Charlie Hodges who supposedly had gotten a girl pregnant over in Little Falls. Small-town talk, the indulgence of good girls. Karen might flip off a stranger, but only if there was no chance it would get back to her parents. Like Sylvie, she took honors classes and only copied her homework when the teacher didn't care enough to catch on. They went out to the dike not to be bad but because everyone did, and they only went out there together.

The party was well underway by the time they arrived. Karen eased the car into a dark shrubby spot. The dew on the grass chilled Sylvie's toes, open in sandals. Out here where the prison lights didn't quite reach, stars punched the sky. Beside the dike a bonfire glowed, lighting faces still giddy from the last day of school, fresh with the splat of water balloons and the pained looks of teachers and the plastic smell of silly string let loose in the halls.

Karen stuffed some cash in the bucket and filled a cup from the tap. Sylvie filled hers only to half. She should tell Karen now, but she had no words. They hovered next to the fire, the dike rising behind them, a long bump in a flat place. Near the keg a girl screamed, and a bunch of boys laughed.

Aside from a few out-of-towners, the lit faces were ones Sylvie had grown up with. The half-light made them look changed, but that was only illusion. They were the same, would always be the same, and among them only Sylvie would be transformed into someone she barely recognized.

Along the edge of her tongue, the beer tasted bitter. "What went on at the lake?" Karen asked.

"Not much," Sylvie said. There were things she couldn't speak aloud, even to Karen. How she'd once thought herself like a poem. How she lay in the dark, hanging on to the knowing and wanting she'd felt when her eyes had met Kenny's. How there would soon be nothing to ground her, not her friends or their house or the town she'd grown up in.

She sipped from her cup, holding the plastic rim between her teeth, warming the beer in her mouth. "You're awful quiet," said Karen. She leaned into Sylvie, brushing against her goose-bumped arm. "Kaelynn's gonna break up with Skyler. Maybe tonight. And you always said Skyler was cute."

Sylvie looked beyond the fire to where a truck gleamed the way Kenny's truck must have once. "I see Ricky drove his new truck." Amazing, the way your voice could carry on with the smallest things no matter what else fell apart. Rick Clement had just turned sixteen, and for his birthday his dad, who worked at the bank, had bought him a shiny new truck. Rick had one arm slung over a girl and in the other he clutched a big plastic cup, fresh-headed with beer. "Who's the girl?"

Karen leaned to look. "Dunno. Maybe from Gainesville. Or the Falls." When a Piney Lake boy got his first truck, an out-of-town girl would follow, sure as if she were part of the accessory package. Losers whose parents couldn't afford to buy them a truck got stuck with the locals.

Rick's eyes flitted, anxious, from the girl to the truck, like he didn't know which might escape from him first. The girl pulled out from under Rick's arm and began flirting with one of his friends. She laughed, wide and pretty, in a way that reminded Sylvie of Mirabelle. Rick leaned toward his truck like he didn't know where else to look, like he too needed grounding. "He looks lonely," said Sylvie.

"Rick the Prick?" Karen asked. He liked to strip his shirt, showing off in the gym, and so they'd christened him that.

"Rick's not so bad," Sylvie said. There were worse sins than wanting to be noticed.

Karen nodded toward the group at the fire. "I'm telling you. Skyler."

The girl turned completely from Rick to Pine Lake's football hero, the guy who'd thrown a game-winning pass in the final match of the season. There was talk he might play college ball. Rick wrestled, and while his body was tough and hard on the mats, in Pine Lake and in the towns all around, it was football that mattered, and in football Rick walked off the field in a uniform as clean as the one he'd walked on with. He was already dumped. Anyone could see it.

Sylvie handed Karen her cup and nodded toward Rick. "I'll be back."

Karen sipped first from her own cup, then from Sylvie's. "Really. Rick Clement."

Sylvie ran her fingers along the hem of her shorts as she worked her way toward the fire. *Hey, Sylvie. Hey.* Kids she'd known since grade school huddled close to the warmth, smelling of smoke and beer. She murmured *heys* back as she moved close to Rick, filling the space where the girl's perfume lingered. Next to Sylvie's hand, Rick jittered his leg, like he was weighing whether going after the girl or letting her go would do the least damage.

"That's a nice-looking truck," Sylvie said. She trailed her words one into the other like it might be the beer. In the fire a log popped, the sparks a dizzy swirl in the night. A thin film of sweat glistened on Rick's forehead. Sylvie felt awake without having known that she'd slept, disoriented but alert. Though she'd never been one for bold moves, she walked her fingers over the bulge of keys in Rick's pocket. "How 'bout a ride?"

His eyes fell on Sylvie like she was new and fresh like the truck, and they seemed good eyes and strong. She kept one hand on his pocket and ran the other up the inside of his arm. She would not think of Kenny. "Please," she said in a voice that wasn't quite hers.

She presented herself with enough possibility that Rick quit looking back at the out-of-town girl. Together they moved, shoulders touching, to the far side of the truck, away from the fire. It was cool there, and dark. Sharp-edged grass brushed Sylvie's feet. She moved her hands from the sides of Rick's jeans to his belt and ran her fingers under his waistband. He sucked in a breath where she touched. "Wow," Rick said. "Sylvie."

She took him all in with the truck, plucked from dozens that lined the lot where her father once worked. It was only her eyes but she saw how he liked it. He bent over her, parting his lips for a kiss. She slid underneath him, her back to the truck, palms flattened into the door. "Careful," he said. She spread her fingers and flush with power massaged the shiny red paint as he watched, helpless and panicked and filled with desire. "We should get in," he said.

They sprawled on the seat, Sylvie flattened beneath him, choked by the smell of the new dash and new mats and new floorboards, smells that had rolled over the darkened showroom each time her father would open the door of a new vehicle and hoist her inside, pretending they'd drive home together and surprise her mother.

"God, I never knew you were hot." Rick worked her breasts, urgent and hard. He thrust his hand up her shorts, and for a moment she wanted only the thing she'd vowed not to want. She felt his pants for the keys and eased out from under him and straightened her shirt and her shorts. "Let's go for a ride."

"Aw, Sylvie," Rick said. But his eyes caught the dash, gleamed by the fire, and he pulled the keys from his pocket.

Sylvie grabbed them out of his hand. A quick turn, and the truck rumbled mean and low, the twin mufflers chugging exhaust. "Hey," Rick said. "You can't drive."

"Don't worry," said Sylvie. *Listen,* her father would say as they moved through the lot, turning key after key. *Hear how this baby purrs.* Sylvie wrapped one hand over the stick and shifted the way he had taught her, stomping the clutch and moving the stick up and out. She gave it some gas and the gears caught and she shifted to second. Rick grabbed for the wheel. She jerked it away, and the truck spun a hard left.

Rick gripped the dash with one hand, the seat with the other. "At least get on the road."

She steered around the dark shapes of trees lit up in the headlights. In the mirror, the bonfire became a distant glow as she nosed the truck up and onto the road that ran along the top of the dike.

"Jesus, Sylvie," Rick said. "Take it easy." He smelled of sweat and beer and fear, and she felt his heart thumping as he leaned close, as if by pressing into her he might gain control. On one side the road dropped off into the embankment they'd climbed. On the other it fell toward a sheer wall that held back the river. The tires spit rocks as Sylvie shifted from second to third.

"Not so fast," Rick said as the truck hurtled into the night. She held tight to the wheel and scooted into the steering column as if through it she could pour herself onto the road, which wasn't so much a road as a built-up mound of gravel. There were signs warning kids to stay off, and since it was too narrow to race on and too exposed to go parking, mostly they did.

"Okay, Sylvie," said Rick. "You've had your fun. Let's go back." He flattened his sweaty palm against the bare skin of her leg as the truck lurched over a pothole. "I just got this truck."

She felt a surge of affection for him having said that, so simple and obvious. "A little farther," she said, and then, "please." She flicked off the lights.

"Hey," he said. "I can't bring this home wrecked."

The truck eased along the top of the dike, the half-moon overwhelmed by a jumble of stars and now, in the distance, the prison lights melting into them. Sylvie rolled the truck to a stop, and Rick's hand relaxed on her leg. "See," she said. "You get used to the dark." She longed to believe it herself, that you could get used to anything. Images flickered in her head, layers of ice creeping under their own weight, impervious to water and air. You might be safe, even from yourself, if you could somehow get to its core. It might have been what had attracted her mother.

Rick's hand rode up her thigh. She hugged the wheel, and her breath caught as he probed the hem of her shorts, shivering her leg. "You ever been to a glacier?" she asked, her voice thick.

"Nope." He reached to shut off the truck.

She leaned back. "This place was leveled by glaciers," she said. Rick nuzzled her neck, shifting goose bumps up and down the length of her. "Ice scraped it flat." A throaty whisper, deposited next to his ear. "Dragged out big chunks of land. Carved all these lakes."

"School's out." Rick's lips brushed her cheek. His arm shifted under her back as he drew her away from the steering wheel and into his chest. "Summer's here. No one cares about ice."

But she did. She cared, though she had no way to show it. Rick stroked her skin, his hands skipping down her arms, past her waist, pressing and kneading. She wanted to slow him, to make him back up so she could feel it again, the drift of his fingers, the force of his hands. She yielded to his warm probing tongue and then to a fumble of buttons and snaps, her breasts shining smooth and white in the moonlight, and she saw how she might feel and forget, requiring nothing more than the foil-wrapped package stashed in her pocket.

She closed her eyes and in the patch of darkness Rick's fingers weren't Rick's and Rick's breath wasn't his and it was all Kenny and wrong. She pulled away, smoothing her shirt and her shorts and her hair. Rick hugged the steering wheel, heaving half-breaths. "I'm sorry," she said. "I didn't...I mean, I'm not..."

Rick flexed and unflexed his hands. "Whatever." He turned the key, and the engine surged and then settled.

"Please," Sylvie said. "Don't be mad." This seemed all at once urgent, that Rick Clement not be angry, that she get this one small thing right.

He yanked the wheel and spun a tight circle on the gravel. How could she say that her life was a poem, that her future was ice? "I'm leaving," she said. "I might not be back."

Rick's hands relaxed on the wheel, the truck tamed now and sure. "For real? That sucks."

Sylvie would have leaned close and hugged him, but in her mind she was already gone.

Fracture Zone

A rigid section of ice, moving forward as a single unit

When Ruth first found the glacier, she learned words that rolled from her tongue when no one was listening. *Firns and striations. Cirques and moraines. Adulation. Sublimation.* She fell asleep to their music, and she woke to it. *Chatter marks, eskers, and drumlins. Truncated spurs. Corries and tarns. Kames. Eolian loess. Katabatic winds.*

A glacier was large and unyielding, while Ruth was small and pliable, bending to the needs and desires of everyone but herself. But she believed in the promise of ice, and the words to describe the transformation that might one day be hers she incanted like magic. *Moulins. Plastic deformation. Transverse crevasse.*

She hadn't expected the glacier to bring her a man. She hadn't believed in big sweeping forces like fate. But that was before she met Kenny. The move they were planning was bold and exciting and unexpected. She repeated these words when she woke every morning, *bold* and *exciting* and *unexpected*, to displace the ones that crept in while she slept, *reckless* and *foolish* and *irresponsible.*

For once she would not over-think, and she could care less what anyone else thought, least of all Richard. "Good God, Ruth. *Alaska.*" Richard had a knack for making a word sound like it meant something entirely different. In this case, *disaster.* Ruth steadied the phone and reached across the table for Kenny, his fingers thick and warm and reassuring. "A letter, Richard," she said. "That's all I'm asking."

"The girls will hate it," Richard said. "All that snow and cold."

In the background Ruth heard television voices, an argument escalating. She pictured Mirabelle reclined on a sofa, white leather, a cold drink sweating in her hand, wearing the same silky tee she'd had on the day she drove off with Ruth's husband, a red plunging V-neck. "The girls are excited to try something new," Ruth said.

"Let me talk to Sylvie."

Ruth sucked in a breath. "Sylvie's not up yet." From Kenny's eyes, she drew strength. "She was out late. Last day of school."

"Anna, then." Richard was a master of diversion, having diverted himself right out of their lives.

"A letter, Richard. That's all I'm asking. Permission to take the girls over the border. *I, Richard Sanders, give permission for Ruth Sanders to take our daughters Anna and Sylvie through Canada on their way to Alaska.* One sentence. That's it."

"You're driving? Do you have any idea how far it is to Alaska? A trip like that will take weeks."

She gripped the phone with both hands. "I didn't say I was driving. But for your information, I am. We are."

"We. Who's this *we*?"

"It's been five years, Richard. Five years since you left. And guess what? I've moved on." And she had. She really had.

"Don't kid yourself." The television noise shifted to a plunky tune, an advertising jingle. "You haven't changed."

"And you haven't either," Ruth snapped, though this was the wrong tack with Richard. The slightest turning of tables only hardened his position. "This isn't about us," she added quickly. "It's the chance of a lifetime. An adventure for the girls."

"Adventure," he sputtered. "Honestly, Ruth."

Richard had this special talent, this finely honed way of slicing deep to expose her. Ruth pitied him and his beach and his palm trees, the little life he had carved for himself in the sand. "Anna's already packing," she said. "Sylvie, too." An utter lie, but what would it hurt? "You've got no cause, Richard." She chose her words carefully. "You have to have cause to withhold your consent. That's what the judge said."

"I know that," Richard said.

"I know that you know. I'm just reminding you."

"I don't need your reminders."

"A letter, Richard. One sentence. To Whom It May Concern."

"You know what, Ruth? You've got a real disconnect going on here. What about your job?"

"There are jobs in Alaska." Across the table, Kenny leaned over his folded hands.

"Just like your mother," Richard said. "A total disconnect."

She summoned an image. Unwavering ice, solid and strong. "I'll go to court if I have to. And you know how expensive that gets." Parts work paid even less in Florida than it did in Pine Lake, this Ruth knew from her research. And the upkeep on Mirabelle couldn't be cheap.

"You're really stuck on this, aren't you?"

Kenny brushed the top of her head with a kiss. "Yes, Richard. I am. I'm really stuck on this. If I don't have that letter by Friday, I'm filing papers in court. By Friday," she repeated, and hung up.

"The same old crap." It made her crazy, the way Richard could still get her adrenaline going. "I'm just like my mother. Screwed up from childhood. *You know your family's not right.*" She mimicked his flat, bitter tone.

"You're done with him," Kenny said. "Over and out."

"Of course *his* family's perfect." Ruth's hands flew as she spoke. "Never mind that his mom and dad argue over every little thing. Who should bring in the paper. Whether the dog has been out for too long. You should see them at holidays. Big shouting matches between him and his brothers. But Richard can't point out enough how my dad drinks and how my mom pretends that he doesn't. *You're just like your mother.* That's his favorite line."

Kenny settled her hands in his. "As if my mother would give the first thought to Alaska. If her bridge club switches from Tuesday to Monday, she needs sedation. Telling her won't be any better. It's wearing me out, trying to make people understand."

He teased a strand of her hair in his fingers. "Quit trying then. You know what you want. You're going after it. People are jealous, that's all."

"I don't know why they can't just be happy for me." Martha had looked up the glacier online and pronounced it too far from everything. Doctors. Groceries. Internet access. Why not encourage Kenny to hang around Pine Lake for awhile, Martha said, and get to know him a little? It was almost as bad as when Richard left, when total strangers had looked away, as if Ruth's sudden vulnerability were contagious and yet also somehow her fault. Hadn't she been reliable enough for the both of them? And still she hadn't seen it coming, the sudden wrenching hole of his leaving.

"Screw them," Kenny said. "Screw them all."

She stroked her hair where Kenny had touched it, silky and familiar. "What if he won't send the letter?" Ruth said. "A court order takes money. And time."

"If he doesn't send it, we'll forge one," said Kenny.

The prospect made Ruth feel wild and unsteady. But she knew what she wanted. She was going after it. There was no good reason to linger in Richard's hometown. Already she'd been here too long. Love and adventure. A fresh start at the ice. She owed that much to herself, and the girls.

"What about your mom?" she asked Kenny. "Have you told her we're coming?"

"I will."

She touched a finger to his chin. "You're not ashamed of us, are you?" It was the sort of teasing Richard could never tolerate.

Kenny pulled her finger to his lips. "Of course not. Mom's been distracted, that's all." His lips parted and his tongue wet her finger.

"Mom!" Ruth pulled her hands to her lap as Anna staggered into the kitchen and dumped a pile of books on the table. "I don't know which ones to take."

Kenny hovered his fingers over the books and plucked from the pile a Dr. Seuss title, the cover worn at the corners. "Gotta love *Horton*."

"You'd better bring fat ones," Ruth said. "Since there's no TV."

Anna clutched the book to her chest. "I don't want to sell *Horton*." She twisted toward Kenny the way she once had toward Richard, reaching without using her arms.

Kenny cupped a hand to his ear. "What's that I hear? A Who?"

Ruth brushed the feathery tips of Anna's bangs. "You don't have to sell *Horton*. We'll put him in storage."

Sylvie slouched into the kitchen, gray sweats slung loose on her hips, exposing skin between the waistband and the hem of her tee shirt. Though her hair was mussed from sleep and her face hadn't been washed, she had the glow that even the consistent bad mood of an adolescent can't extinguish.

But then Sylvie had always had fine features, her face a perfect oval, her forehead the right height to accommodate bangs, her skin creamy, her lips full.

"Look what rolled out of bed," Kenny said. "Sleeping Beauty."

"How was the party?" Ruth asked

"Who said anything about a party?" Sylvie filled the teakettle.

"Of course there was a party," said Kenny. "Last day of school."

"We only get one box for our books," Anna said. "You and me. So you better pick yours."

"I don't care." Sylvie leaned against the sink, feet crossed at the ankles, the bottoms of her white ankle socks gray from the floor, which Ruth had been lax about cleaning. "You can have the whole box."

"There's no need to be unreasonable." Ruth summoned the even tone she used on children sent to the office at school. Sylvie's small objections—refusing the picnic, hiding out in her room, avoiding Kenny's eyes—these were nothing, understandable even, since they'd kept her out of their decision, knowing she'd have only said no, and that would have made everything more difficult.

"You talked to Dad," Sylvie said.

"Your father's sending a letter."

"So they'll let you two rascals through Canada." Kenny wiggled his fingers at Anna, threatening a tickle. She squealed and ran from the kitchen, her books still on the table.

Sylvie worked a hangnail on her thumb. Ruth patted a chair. "Have a seat and tell us what you and Karen were up to last night."

"We weren't *up* to anything."

"It wasn't an accusation. I'm just interested. *We're* interested. Aren't we, Kenny?"

"Sure," Kenny said.

Sylvie brought her thumb to her face and studied the little flap of skin. From a young age, she'd been like this—serious, fixed on things, wanting but not letting on. "We hung out, that's all."

"You must have gone somewhere. With someone."

Sylvie tucked her hair in back of her ear. "Seriously. You want the blow by blow."

"Not every last detail. Just the highlights."

Sylvie dumped powdered chocolate into her cup and reached for the whistling kettle. There were things no one warned you about when you became a mother. Not the homework and the shopping and the ferrying in the car but the moods and the minefields and the way that on one wrong word your sweet girl could turn.

Kenny tipped back his chair, balancing on its two back legs. "Who wants to go to the pawnshop?" he asked.

Sylvie eyed the chair while avoiding Kenny. "So now we're pawning our stuff," she said.

It was a big change, all around, but Ruth wasn't about to let Sylvie ruin it, right from the start. "No one's pawning anything," she said. "Kenny's shopping for a gun. He's extending the invitation, that's all. All I—we—expect is a little respect."

The spoon clanked as Sylvie stirred. "As in the respect you gave me when you decided we'd move to Alaska."

"Your mother's doing you kids a favor." Kenny pressed his hands together, fingertip to fingertip. "Maybe you don't see it now, but you will."

"I never asked for a favor." Sylvie's tossed spoon clanged off the side of the sink and into the dishes. "I just want my life back." Her eyelids quivered, a furious blinking.

"There are kids around here who'd die for this kind of adventure," Ruth said.

"Adventure. What's that? Some kind of code for your crush?"

If only Sylvie were still young enough to crawl into her lap. Then Ruth would stroke her shiny hair, thick like her father's, until she relaxed. "Perhaps we should have talked to you first," she conceded.

Kenny pressed his palms to the table. "She wants to be pissy, that's how she'll be. No sense trying to stop her."

Sylvie chucked the mug after the spoon, splashing thick chocolate over the white porcelain. "Sorry I can't make the pawnshop." She wiped her hands on a towel without looking at Ruth or Kenny. "I'm going to Gainesville."

"Gainesville," Ruth said. "That's nice." It was only midmorning, with a long day of sorting and packing ahead, and already she felt tired. "When's Karen picking you up?"

A faint smile. "I'm going with Rick."

"Rick." Ruth shuffled through the possibilities.

"Rick Clement. He's got a new truck."

"A boy with a truck," Kenny said. "A new truck. Even better."

He was nice, the Clement boy. A little full of himself, like his father, but nice. He didn't deserve being hurt, and neither did Sylvie. "This isn't the best time to take up with a boy," Ruth said.

"Why not?" Sylvie flipped her hair over her shoulder. "You did." It could have been Richard, stabbing and slicing with only a handful of words, leaving Ruth not so much shamed or angry as sad.

The moment she'd slipped her carefully worded note onto Bill Scranton's desk, Pine Lake had begun to shrink in Ruth's eyes. The First Episcopal Church receded into the corner of Seventh and Oak along with its sign announcing the weekly attendance in black removable numbers, the sermon topic "Give and Let Give" tilting even more than usual toward the improbable. The high school now seemed made of square sliding parts that in quick shell game moves might be swapped one for the other, the pool with the auditorium, the classroom wing with the library. In the parking lot of the Piggly Wiggly, shopping carts angled like spilled paperclips. Not one thing she would miss. Remarkable, not to have seen this before.

Kenny's truck idled at the lone stoplight. "Sylvie won't give two hoots for Pine Lake," he said. "Not once she gets to Alaska."

"Maybe we should have asked what she thought instead of just telling her." Beyond the traffic light, Sam Brenton swept the sidewalk in front of the drugstore with mechanical vigor. Ruth pictured him still there years from now, working the very same spot.

"If she's that upset about going, you can send her to live with her dad."

"Oh no," Ruth said quickly. "That would never work out. Sylvie shuts down around Richard. She took it hard when he left."

The light changed, and Kenny turned a hard right onto County 15. "She used to try so hard to get Richard's attention," she said. "I swear sometimes he forgot she existed. When Sylvie was six, she had this dance recital. She got all dressed up in a cute little tutu, pink tights, matching slippers, the works. Her big debut, on the stage at the high school. Of course Richard forgot. I called once the performance began, but the shop said he wasn't available. He showed up ten minutes before the whole thing was over, long after Sylvie had danced. But he pretended he'd seen it all, the pliés and the jetés and the pirouettes. You should have seen Sylvie beam. Then he took her to Mac's Mart and bought her this little tiara. 'For my princess,' he told her. Bragged to the store clerk how well she had danced. Sylvie wore that tiara around for a week. In and out of the shop. She'd ride her bike to visit him there. If the salesmen were watching, Richard would make a big fuss over her. But at home, she had to practically fall out a window to get his attention."

Kenny rubbed his jawline. "About time I started my beard."

Ruth ran her finger across the stubble, golden-red like his hair. "Then no one will see your nice chin."

"They'll all think I've turned soft if I go back clean-shaven." He brushed the back of her hand with a kiss. "They'll think I'm whipped."

Had Richard ever loved her like this? Sylvie could pitch fits and Ruth could wake up drowning in doubt, but the fact was that Kenny was everything Richard wasn't. Generous. Lighthearted. Kind. Not reliant on Ruth or on anyone else.

Past a curve, the half-lit sign for Roy's Pawn came into view, the store behind it a squat concrete fortress. "I can't count the times I've gone past here," Ruth said. "And still I've never gone in." The truth was she'd never had the slightest desire. Even when money got tight, she had drawn a line at buying other people's things, especially when they'd been given up in desperation. "I wish Sylvie had come." Sylvie had an eye for possibilities. In Alaska, they'd do things together. They'd have to, with no television or internet. Ruth tried to form an image in her head, based on what Kenny had told her, of how they might spend their days, but the ice, heaving and crashing, blocked out everything else.

Roy's Pawn smelled like damp cardboard and metal. Overhead a fluorescent tube buzzed and flickered. Utility shelves spanning one wall displayed piles of dusty tools, blades and bits configured for purposes Ruth didn't recognize. She couldn't help but think of where each had come from, the reasons they'd been let go. Kenny picked up a tool with a thin-toothed blade, and a coiled orange cord patched with electrical tape dropped like a heaped snake to the floor.

Ruth veered toward the glass cases crowded with knives and watches and jewelry. Propped next to each item was an enthusiastic note penned in what she assumed was Roy's shaky hand: *No Mexican Rolex! Authentic!* Beside a ring set, chipped diamonds set in white gold: *Never too late to get lucky in love!*

A bent, thin-bearded man appeared through a curtain that hung behind the cash register. "Howdy," said Kenny. "I take it you're Roy."

"Most days," he said.

Kenny set the tool back on the shelf, the orange cord dangling. "Where's your guns?"

Roy gave Kenny and Ruth the once-over, like they were something brought in for pawn, then led them through the curtains and down a narrow hallway to a windowless room where guns were displayed in glass cases.

"What sort of weapon you looking for?" Roy asked.

"Hunting rifle," Kenny said. "Something to take to Alaska."

An approximation of a smile lit Roy's face. "Alaska. Well then." With a key, he began unlocking the cases. "Go ahead. Pick 'em up. Get a feel for 'em." To Ruth, he offered a thin-lidded wink. "Lucky you, going north."

Ruth's lips curved on cue. "It's an adventure," she said. Kenny fondled a rifle, the barrel, the trigger, the grip. He held the gun out, straight-armed. Squinting into the sights, he swung it toward Ruth.

She jumped. "Holy Moses," she said, an expression of her grandmother's that until that moment she'd forgotten. "That better not be loaded."

"Of course not." Kenny tipped the barrel toward the floor and worked a mechanism that Ruth couldn't name, click, click, click.

"I suppose some people bring them in loaded," she said to Roy. "I suppose you have to make sure they're empty before you display them."

"You should learn how to shoot," Kenny said. "Then you won't be so skittish."

"I'm not skittish," Ruth said.

Roy cracked a smile, revealing a single empty slot on his bottom jaw guarded on either side by a rusty row of teeth. Kenny set the gun on the glass. "A three hundred's better for bear. Got some big grizzlies up north."

"You never said bear." Roy padded to another glass case. "This here's a nice Browning." He handed over a rifle, its barrel long and black. "Guy said he bought it for deer. Blasted the whole side in on the first one he shot." His rheumy eyes fell on Ruth. "Wish I was headed for Alaska. You're one lucky gal."

"Shoot," Kenny said. "Three hundred's way big for deer." He shifted the gun's bolt up and back. "Nice action." Ruth touched her arm to his elbow. A man she could trust, that's what he was.

Kenny set the gun down, then picked it back up and fingered the etched lines on the stock. Roy flattened his hands on the glass. "Road up there's a bitch. That's what I hear."

"It's not that bad," Ruth said. "Is it, honey?" But Kenny was busy checking the sights—she believed they were called that.

"The wife wouldn't have it," said Roy. "No matter how much I begged. Got me stuck right here in Pine Lake."

"Pine Lake's not so bad." Ruth gripped the glass, overcome with a sudden wave of nostalgia for the shrinking town. She wished herself home, drenched in the morning light that streamed through the windows.

Kenny bent close to the gun, his finger on the trigger. "How'd he do it?" Roy asked. "How'd he talk you into it?"

"Wasn't hard, really," Kenny said.

It must have been a closet once, that room, thick as it was with the smell of old forgotten things.

"Ain't the hunting," said Roy. "I see she's got no interest in that. So it must be the money."

"No," Ruth said. "Not the money." Love and adventure. What would Roy know about that? And what business was it of his, where she went or why? What business was it of anyone's? Hadn't Kenny said as much? She needed him to say it again. Now. So Roy would shut up.

Between the heat of the room and the musty smell and Roy's relentless watery eyes Ruth felt heavy with wrongness, the way she had when Richard first left. She pressed close to Kenny. "What's that gun got that I don't?" The teasing tone she'd intended fell flat.

"The jealous wife." Roy sounded delighted with this observation. "Half the guns that come in, it's the wife that's behind it."

"I'm not that way," Ruth said.

"Love to know your secret," Roy said to Kenny. "How you twisted her arm."

Kenny hoisted the .300 again to his shoulder and pointed it at the wall. "She had it in her head already."

"Stars lined up, did they?"

Kenny's eye squeezed shut, his finger on the trigger. "Not stars." He lowered the gun. "Ice."

Helpless under Roy's rheumy gaze, Ruth said, "There's this glacier. I've always wanted to see it."

"I'll be Double-Dutch damned." Roy slapped the glass. "If that don't take all."

"It's not so odd." She felt ready to gag on Roy's wheezing breath, the stench of onions and bacon that rolled from between his tobacco-stained teeth.

Kenny's hands left the gun, but his eyes never wavered. "How much?"

"Eight-fifty," Roy said.

Ruth grabbed Kenny's sleeve. "Let's get out of here."

He shook loose of her grasp. "They're just over nine hundred new."

Roy trailed a skinny finger along the shiny barrel. "Been shot only once."

"We don't have room." It felt like someone else talking, someone who didn't love Kenny the way she did. "The truck will be jam-packed. That's what you told the girls."

"Must be a bitch up there come winter," Roy said. "Dark all the time. Snow and cold." Across the glass case, Roy jabbed an elbow at Ruth. "Great for rolling around in the sack."

She tried nudging her hand through the crook of Kenny's arm, but he bent it and the space disappeared.

"That's what I heard," Roy insisted. "Dark twenty-four seven."

"Not where we're going," Ruth said, though she had no idea actually. "The ice goes back twenty-six miles. Except it's not really ice. The snow turns to something called firn. It's from the pressure. The age."

Kenny set down the gun. "Seven-fifty," he said.

"The air gets squeezed out." Ruth couldn't stop herself. "The whole thing starts to move. On the liquid beneath it. Plastic flow, it's called."

Roy seemed at a sudden, happy loss for words. "The man didn't ask for a lecture," Kenny said. "Seven-fifty," he repeated.

"That's a lot of money." Ruth felt desperate to steady herself.

"A lot of my money," Kenny said sharply.

From Roy, a perverted smile. "Eight hundred," he said, "and it's yours."

Ruth slipped outside as Kenny began to count bills. Through the thin soles of her shoes, the sun-soaked asphalt warmed her feet as she leaned against the truck. A single bird chirped from the pawnshop's flat roof, a familiar loop of sound that seemed tinged with desperation. Ruth tried the door. Kenny never locked it, and he always left the keys stashed inside. But the door wouldn't give. She tugged on the handle again and again, as if through sheer persistence she could crawl in and hide.

When Kenny came out, he leaned on the door and lifted the handle and popped the latch. Tenderly, he slid the gun across the seat. Ruth reached past it to brush her hand on his jeans. "If they think you want it too much," she said, "they never budge on the price."

Kenny eased the truck onto the highway. He checked the rearview as he rubbed his perfect, beautiful chin. "Guess I did save fifty bucks."

Eskers. Eolian loess. Truncated spurs. Ruth repeated the words to herself as they passed the stoplight and the empty sidewalk in front of the drugstore and the parking lot of the Piggly Wiggly and the sign in front of the First Episcopal Church, repeated them over and over until her faith was restored.

Advance

The forward motion of ice, often cyclical

Your mom's crazy. That's what Karen had said when she learned that Sylvie's mother had called the glacier their destiny, foretold in a magazine. The photo had led her to Kenny, and Kenny would lead them to the glacier. What Sylvie's mother failed to see was that when you conceded to fate, any number of disasters could follow. Mirabelle, for instance, could be chalked up to fate, if you chose to see it like that.

Even though he knew Sylvie was leaving, or maybe because of it, Rick stuck by her. He took her fishing on Pine Lake, where she reeled in a bass so big that the man in the boat next to them snapped a picture. He drove her to Gainesville where they lay on the grassy bank of the river, propped on their elbows, watching the boats go by, and he held her hand all the way through the goodbye party at Karen's when she kept wanting to cry but somehow held it in till they left, and he never tried much of anything else, which was too bad in a way because he became one more thing she could miss. When he held her, the salty smell of his sweat and the freshly mowed grass and the lake nearly did her in, and when he touched her, it was as if the entire town pulsed along her skin. Still, Sylvie could not stop the hateful way she responded when Kenny came near, her skin tingling as she summoned the many reasons to hate him.

Horrified at the thought of Alaska, all that cold, Karen's mother suggested that Sylvie stay behind and live at their house, but Sylvie's mother refused to even consider such a thing. A fresh start, she said. It would be good for them all.

D-day, as Karen called it, their date of departure, was circled in red marker on the calendar that hung in the kitchen even as everything else disappeared, the pots and pans sold at a yard sale, the dishes boxed up for storage. *Tell your mom you'll never ask her to buy you anything ever again*, Karen said. *Tell her you'll do every chore, the dishes, the dusting, the lawn. Beg her to wait till you graduate.*

But Sylvie's mother proved immune to every possibility. I'll run away, Sylvie threatened. Never before had she considered such a thing. But the threat seemed to barely register with her mother, who must have realized that running away was exactly what Sylvie was trying to escape.

As the house emptied, Sylvie did too. She felt alone, on the outside of her mother and Anna and Kenny. She wished she'd gone all the way with Rick that night at the dike. But it seemed wrong now, to use Rick like that, when he'd been so kind.

Early one morning when sunlight cut through curtains of fog that steamed up from the grass, Sylvie climbed after Anna into the back seat of Kenny's truck. "Goodbye, Pine Lake," Anna said. She fogged the window with a circle of breath, wiped it with the heel of her hand, then pressed her face to the glass. Filtered through the fluttering leaves of the big maple tree, light washed the broken-slatted porch swing. "Goodbye forever."

"Quit being dramatic," Sylvie said. It came out harsher than she intended. "It's not forever."

"Is too." Anna pressed her lips in a pout. "Mom said."

"Right," Sylvie said. "It's an *adventure*."

"Girls," her mother said, but her eyes were on Kenny.

Anna kicked the back of Kenny's seat. "I'm squished back here."

The engine rumbled to life. Kenny glanced in the rearview. "Maybe you girls should switch places."

Anna scrambled over the duffel bag their mother had strategically placed between them, landing almost in Sylvie's lap. Kenny's eyes followed in the mirror as Sylvie slid to where Anna had been, the space still warm and smelling freshly washed like her shirt, and she felt again how he must sense what she couldn't erase, her hateful longing.

He swung the truck from the curb and onto the sleepy street, away from the house and the porch and the swing. Tied down with a blue tarp in the back of the truck were the thinned-down possessions chosen to make the trip. Though pretending not to care, Sylvie had packed her half of the book box with dog-eared titles she'd outgrown, *Charlotte's Web* and *The Bridge to Terabithia* and *The Indian in the Cupboard*. Among her sweaters and jeans she'd tucked a framed photo of Karen plus a card Rick had clumsily signed and the cheap tiara that she'd first tossed in with the yard sale items but later went back and picked up.

Karen's mom had loaded Sylvie up with mittens and gloves and scarves and jackets she'd gotten from the off-season stock at a friend's boutique. She'd also dragged Karen and Sylvie to the bookstore and wouldn't let Sylvie leave till she'd chosen a stack of new books to keep her from going crazy. Because Kenny had warned they'd have no TV or mobile phone or internet service, Sylvie's electronics had gone into storage, the most egregious of losses. Who in this day and age went without cell phone and internet, Karen wanted to know, but Kenny claimed lots of people in Alaska lived off the grid, and they liked it.

Pine Lake receded in the mirrors as they rolled down the highway. The quick route was to veer west through Grand Forks to Minot and then to Great Falls, but Kenny said he preferred going north through the woods and then west across Canada. Northern Minnesota reminded him of home, he said, even though it lacked mountains and grizzlies and glaciers.

Because she'd refused the facts Karen looked up, their destination to Sylvie consisted only of ice, huge frozen masses with chunks that peeled off and crashed as she'd seen in the films. She shut her eyes to the back of Kenny's head, his sun-glinted hair curling delicately over the band of a hat that proclaimed *Alaska, Home of the Free*. She dozed but woke at every bump to some new thing she'd miss, lazy cows that twitched their ears as the sun burned dew from the grass, yellow buttercups that bobbed along barbed-wire fences. When they stopped, she got gas station coffee, burning and bitter, consumed while her mother recounted for their amusement the conversation she'd had the night before with her parents. Sylvie's grandpa had gone on at some length about how if he'd headed north like he'd wanted when the oil pipeline was under construction, they'd all be rich. Then Sylvie's grandma had grabbed the phone to inform Sylvie's mother, as if she needed reminding, that the bourbon was talking and that what Sylvie's grandfather knew of Alaska could be scratched on a toothpick.

Sylvie's grandma had said how they'd better be careful—she had a friend whose car had gotten two flats on the Al-Can, the highway for which they were headed. Then she'd rolled right over her daughter's big news to complain about how hot it had gotten already in Phoenix, how she'd had to hose down her four greyhounds so they wouldn't get heat stroke. All of this Sylvie's mother retold using large gestures and an animated voice. *You do get the strangest notions*, she repeated in Sylvie's grandma's schleppy Boston-Minnesota accent. *Did I tell you the trick I taught Henry? He holds a little kibble on his nose, and when I snap my fingers, he tosses it up in the air and then eats it.*

Kenny planted a kiss on the back of her mother's hand. "Your mom sounds like a hoot."

"Today she'll ask Dad where it was I said we were going, and if he was really into the bourbon he'll swear it was Arkansas or Alabama, and there will be no convincing him otherwise." She glanced back at Anna and Sylvie. "You know I love your granddaddy. And Grandmom. They've just got their quirks."

"We won't see them again," Anna said. "Not for a long, long time. Maybe never."

"My mom's gonna love you." Kenny held her mother in a gaze so long that Sylvie feared they'd drift into the ditch.

At last Kenny looked back at the highway. Sylvie's mother cocked her head and tucked her Akeley Gas-N-Go cup at her feet. Her eyes flitted to the passenger door, which had begun to rattle. "This door isn't latched."

"Give it a tug," Kenny said. Her mother pulled on the door, but the rattle continued. "Like you mean it." Kenny leaned across her lap and yanked it, hard.

She nudged the door. "It still feels loose. Like it's almost shut, but not quite." She groped the place where the door met the frame. "I feel air coming in."

"It's shut," Kenny said.

Anna pulled her seatbelt away from her chest. "This thing hurts."

"Let's pull over and check," said their mother. "Just to be certain."

"The mechanic said the truck's fine."

"The mechanic's not here to see whether the door is shut right."

Kenny hit the brakes. From underneath came the sound of sliding gravel and pinging rocks as he maneuvered the truck onto the shoulder. Without looking at their mother, he got out and went around the front of the truck to the passenger door.

"Unlock it," he said, louder than necessary. Sylvie's mother hit the release and grabbed for the handle, but Kenny was quicker. He popped the door to the smell of fresh-cut weeds in the ditch, then slammed it shut. He ambled back around the front of the truck, climbed in, and steered onto the blacktop.

For several miles no one spoke. Anna hummed the refrain from an old TV cartoon that featured two crows, cycling over and over the song as she smeared circles on the window, then polished them off with the edge of her fist. Sylvie willed her mother to speak, to defend herself even though she'd been foolish. But she only folded her hands in her lap, lips pressed tight, like a child who'd been scolded.

An ongan fyrene fremman feond on helle. Against the whirr of tires on asphalt, Sylvie mouthed the words. She'd had a small crush on dark-eyed Joe Karstens, her sophomore English teacher who'd shouted the *Beowulf* lines like curses at kids who acted out in his class. Sylvie had demanded he translate: fashion evils, fiend of hell. She committed the ancient words to memory, which was easy enough because in sophomore English there was always *an ongan fyrene fremman feond on helle*. She loved the fiend Grendel, the poem she herself might have been. *Wæs se grimma gæst Grendel haten.* Disturber of the border, who crushes and grinds.

At last Sylvie's mother perked up. She admitted she'd make an awful mechanic, fixing things that weren't broken. In profile, her smile quivered ever so slightly. She proceeded to comment out loud on their route, using *The Milepost*, self-proclaimed bible of the North Country. They would cross into Canada, traveling west through Alberta and Saskatchewan, and then veer north at Calgary and west at Edmonton until they reached the Al-Can Highway.

"After Edmonton, you don't want to break down," Kenny said. "That's where repairs get expensive." *March-riever mighty.* Smooth and warm, Sylvie's lips rolled over the sounds. A dangerous place.

The towns along the two-lane thinned out and shrank, Northhome no more than a café and a gas station and a hardware store, Mitzpah even less, a sprinkling of tired houses. Her mother's eyes flitted between the truck's doors and its windows and dash. As the odometer clicked away miles, she tilted her head like she was listening for a lapse in the engine's low rumble. She began again to worry out loud. Flat tires. Failed brakes. Gaskets blown, though she admitted a blown gasket was something she'd heard of only in passing.

Kenny rubbed his hand on his chin, rough and unshaven. *Fen ond fæsten.* Maybe they really would break down, and that would be enough to make Sylvie's mother retract her talk of adventure. *Adventure* and *mother* still sounded wrong, sharing space in a sentence.

By the time they reached the squat building surrounded by pines that marked the Fort Frances border crossing, Sylvie's mother was twisting her hands in her lap. "Don't make them suspicious," Kenny warned. "They'll tear everything out and we'll have to repack." He glanced in the rearview. "Remember—no one mentions the gun." Packing the truck to go north, Kenny had stashed the gun he'd bought at Roy's Pawn Shop in a pile of blankets. No need to mess with Canadian customs, he said. It was his gun, bought and paid for, and since they were only passing through, it made no sense to declare it.

The uniformed border agent stepped out from his booth. "Glasses," he said, with a curt nod at their mother, who extracted her hand from her lap and tipped her sunglasses back on her head, then looked sideways at the floorboards.

Through the window, Kenny handed over the passports and the letter from Sylvie's father, yet another betrayal. The immigration agent leaned close to the truck. "Time you'll be in the country?"

"We're moving," their mother said. "To Alaska."

Kenny smiled. "I'm headed home. And believe it or not, I talked these three lovely ladies into going there with me."

The agent peered in the back seat at Anna and Sylvie. "Hope you like cold."

"It's an adventure," said Anna. "We're going to see moose. And bears. And we're going to live right next to a glacier."

"A glacier. Lots of cold, then." The agent passed the papers back to Kenny and with his assurance that they had nothing to declare, he waved them through.

Kenny glanced at their mother as he slowly accelerated out of the customs area. "Next time let me do the talking," he said.

A grown woman. She could talk if she wanted. There were plenty of responses to Kenny's instructions. Sylvie's mother offered none, although neither did she reach to rub Kenny's neck.

The road cut through stratified rock, the pine forest still and expectant. Anna slept, her jacket padded between her head and the window. Sylvie stared into the woods, knowing and dark, a place to hide and be hidden. She felt strangely glad for Kenny's old truck and how at least it contained them.

They turned west at Kenora, the sun a screaming ball straight ahead, barely shut out by the visors. Sylvie's mother began with a new list of worries; in her silence, she must have been storing them up. She zeroed in on what she believed was a wobbling wheel. When Kenny paid no attention, she went on about how the wheel would fly off and the crippled truck would skid on its axle, plunging them off the road to their deaths. With every imagined detail, she grew more and more agitated: the thunk of the axle hitting the highway, the fury of sparks, the uncontrolled weaving.

Kenny teased her. He reasoned. At last he gave up. He pulled over and pried off the hubcaps and pounded, unamused, with the lug wrench while Sylvie's mother paced the side of the road. Sylvie helped Anna out of the truck and steered her toward a tangle of brush so she could pee. Humming mosquitoes lit on the exposed skin of their wrists, their ankles, their hands. Flailing her arms, Anna plowed up the side of the ditch and headed straight for the truck.

Once they were all back inside, Sylvie's mother apologized and promised it wouldn't happen again. Kenny half-smiled, but his jaw was set tight. "Maybe you should drive," he said. "So you quit second-guessing."

"I'll drive," Sylvie offered.

"Not on your life," said her mother. "You've never driven a truck."

"I drove Rick's."

"Your permit might not be good here. And you don't know the roads. Tomorrow," she said. "Tomorrow, I'll drive. Once I'm rested."

They rolled out of the woods and onto the prairie, endless and flat, farms set apart with long fields of green. Sylvie dozed. They skirted Winnipeg, and the prairie emptied, the space between barns growing longer. Anna complained of leg cramps, of boredom, of Sylvie taking more than her share of space. Bent on getting through Manitoba before nightfall, Kenny refused to stop.

Clouds crowded the sun as it lit the sky orange. Though they were still a hundred klicks from Saskatchewan, Kenny finally declared they'd gone far enough and wheeled the truck into the parking lot of a motel that promised clean, affordable rooms.

An entire day lost. Sylvie climbed out of the truck to the smell of cut grass and dirt. She stared at the asphalt, avoiding Kenny as in the fading light he locked up the truck. In the room she lay down without undressing next to Anna on the hard bed. Before closing her eyes, she glanced at her mother, stiff as straw next to Kenny. She wished she'd taken the other side of the bed so she wouldn't know after the lights went out whether her mother softened and eased herself into his chest, or whether he wrapped his arms over her.

She thought of Rick, not his frenzied fumbling at the dike but the way he sometimes ran his finger from her elbow up the inside of her arm and then let out a little sigh, as if her skin were too delicate for words, and how the new smell of his truck would burn in the back of her throat, so unlike Kenny's, which was musty and old. She clutched her arms to her waist and rolled to her side, her back to her mother and Kenny. It was hateful, all of it.

Each morning Kenny woke at sunrise, anxious to get on the road. He liked to log six hundred miles in a day, so they drove almost from sunup to sundown, though as they snaked north, daylight stretched into more hours than even Kenny could manage in the pickup. Red Deer. Onoway. Dawson Creek, where an odd little monument topped with three flags marked the official start of the Al-Can Highway. Dusty towns broke the monotony of the road with over-priced gas stations and restaurants that smelled of old grease.

Kenny retrieved their box of books from the back so the girls would have something to read. Sylvie turned page after page, her lowered head bobbing with the pavement as she shut out the landscape, which had turned sprawling and wild. Dulled by motion, she developed an aversion to stopping, the known danger within the truck better than what might lurk in the dense roadside forests. She hadn't counted on the air spiked with spruce or the snowy mountains, the sun no match for their cold. Her memory of Pine Lake shrank to a peephole.

As the truck labored north, it became harder and harder to ignore what lay beyond the windows, limestone cliffs that rose up alongside the road, or a batch of wild roses, or the white-papered birch. Sylvie made postcards of the scenes in her mind, to contain them.

Kenny continued to do all the driving. Reading aloud from *The Milepost*, her mother provided a running travelogue, tidbits like "turnout with litter barrels to the east" and "long straight stretch of highway northbound." Despite getting to read Sylvie's old books and eating ice cream at every meal, Anna whined about the hard seats and the cramped space. Finally Kenny told her to shut up, which drew a sharp look from their mother, because *shut up* wasn't something they said at their house.

The blur of trees and mountain-punched sky made Sylvie feel small. She had once thought there was nothing so large that its flaw couldn't be found, its weakness revealed. But the wilderness suggested something altogether different, how without the truck and its windows to shield her, her desires would be exposed.

Kenny's beard began coming in, bristles that erased the memory of Rick's smooth skin. She fixed her eyes on the back of his sun-reddened neck. Tucked near the base of his skull was the reptilian brain, which Sylvie had studied in bio. For hours she attempted to penetrate it with subliminal thoughts about turning around or even depositing them alongside the road.

No matter how tense things got, Kenny warmed up at night, tucked between cheap motel sheets. The second night she heard him whisper how her mother was a brave woman and strong, doing right by her girls to give them a fresh start in Alaska. He talked of how they'd chip ice from the glacier and bottle water to sell to the tourists. The next night over a dinner of fried chicken and salty mashed potatoes, he announced his plans to build a big eight-wheeled all-terrain vehicle, a sort of personal tank, taking from his wallet a creased photo of the thing, torn from a magazine. Naturally this pleased Sylvie's mother, given what a magazine photo had accomplished for her. Pushing her potatoes into a puddle of chicken grease, Sylvie refused to look.

On the fourth day, as they were getting ready to load into the truck, Sylvie's mother grabbed the keys from Kenny's hand. "I'll drive," she said.

If this surprised him, he didn't show it. "Good deal." He stretched both arms and yawned. "I'll sleep."

But he didn't, not right away. He warned Sylvie's mother of potholes and speed bumps and loose gravel and narrow shoulders. "I'm fine," she said. "It's not like I haven't driven before. Go ahead. Shut your eyes and relax."

Legs spread, hands on his knees, Kenny finally leaned back. Head tipped toward his shoulder, his eyes closed. Though Sylvie had not the least enthusiasm for their so-called adventure, she was glad at least to see her mother let go of her manufactured distress and take charge of something.

Her mother glanced back in the rearview. "You girls doing all right?"

"I'm hungry," said Anna.

"You should have finished your breakfast."

"The sausage tasted funny. Like fish."

"When we stop, I'll unload more snacks from the back." Their mother began to dig in her purse. "I've got a granola bar."

Sylvie leaned forward. "Let me look."

"It's in there somewhere." Her mother gathered the fat leather bag, more satchel than purse, and hoisted it over the top of the seat, toward Sylvie.

"Mom!" Anna screeched. "Mom!"

"Jesus." Kenny sat straight up. They were thrown forward, all of them, against their seatbelts. The truck slid sideways and skidded to a stop, its front end angled over the center line. Aside from the low rumble of the engine, there was no sound.

From the edge of the road, a moose stared down its long nose at them, ears twitching and cupped toward the truck.

"Jesus," Kenny repeated.

Their mother let go of the wheel as if an electric shock had gone through it. She began to sob. "It was just there," she said. "Just there."

Sylvie clutched her arms across her belly. Even when her father had left, her mother had not cried with such outrage.

"It's okay, Mom," Anna said. "We're all right."

Gangle-legged, the moose clomped around the front of the truck, across the road, and into the ditch, where it disappeared into the trees.

"Honey." Kenny didn't seem to know what to do with his hands. "It's only a moose."

"I didn't see it. I should have seen it. But I didn't." With these simple statements of fact, she began to compose herself. From the floor, Sylvie retrieved her purse and the things that had spilled from it and handed her mother a tissue.

"I could have hit it." With the tissue, she blotted her cheeks. "I could have killed us."

"Damned moose don't have one lick of sense." Kenny climbed out and squatted in front of the truck, inspecting for damage. Sylvie's mother edged out from under the wheel to the passenger seat.

"Seen a wreck one time where this big bull slid past the hood and busted clean through the windshield, antlers and all," Kenny said as he climbed in. "Whole windshield exploded into a bunch of little pieces."

"That moose didn't have antlers," said Anna.

Kenny backed up the truck so it once again pointed forward. "Big cow can do just as much damage." He began to accelerate. "Lucky for us, this baby ain't got one fresh dent."

"I should have seen it," said their mother. "I shouldn't have taken my eyes off the road. Not for one second."

Keep your eyes on the road, Ruth. Sylvie had heard it often enough, riding in the back seat, when their father was with them. *Don't slam the brakes. Quit hugging the shoulder. You don't know the first thing about how a vehicle operates, do you?*

The way her mother reached across the seat to squeeze Kenny's hand set Sylvie on edge. Or maybe it was the way she kept piling on blame, as if she herself had somehow conjured the moose from the forest, or the way she'd erased Sylvie's small hope that some piece of the woman she'd been before Kenny, before the glacier, might yet survive in the ordinary act of steering a truck down a road.

The trees along the highway turned skinny, the effect of permafrost, Kenny said. Roots had a hard time taking hold in soils that were frozen year-round, so a black spruce might take a hundred years to grow only as tall as Anna.

"No way," Anna said.

Kenny glanced sideways at their mother. "Bet you can't guess how old your mom's glacier is."

"Three hundred thousand," Anna said.

"A lot older than that."

Sylvie's mother reached across the seat to take Kenny's hand. "That ice has been around since almost the beginning of time."

"Stupid glacier," Sylvie said. *An ongan fyrene fremman feond on helle.*

"Mom," Anna said. "Sylvie's making—"

Sylvie jutted an elbow across the duffel bag. "Shut up."

"Sylvie," her mother warned.

"Kenny says it." It shamed her, to stoop to Anna's level, and with so little to provoke her.

Her mother's face reddened. Sylvie averted her eyes from Kenny's pink lips as he warned she'd better listen to her mother. She had every reason to hate him, him and her mother both. Especially her mother. This whole situation was her doing.

Because of the permafrost—reading from *The Milepost*, Sylvie's mother confirmed this—the highway began to heave and dip. Yee-haw, Kenny said each time the road tossed them into the air. The travel guide slid from her mother's lap as she gripped the dash with one hand and the seat with the other, her lips pressed tight in a smile.

As they jolted and bounced, Sylvie made pacts with the snow-dusted peaks. If they turned back, she would quit comparing her mother to Karen's. She would warm up to her father, no matter how badly he'd failed. She would cast off the image of Kenny that pulsed in the darkness whenever she closed her eyes. She cranked her neck and peered up through the window, pleading with the sky that domed like a cup overturned, spilling blue beneath a faraway sun.

"When do we get there?" Anna asked.

Her mother ran calculations out of *The Milepost*. "Five hundred twenty-six miles."

Not a half-hour later, Anna asked again. "Four hundred ninety-eight miles," their mother calculated.

"I want Alaska," said Anna.

"You know nothing about it," said Sylvie.

"Do too."

"Do not. Now shut up."

"Mom!" When their mother turned, Anna rubbed her arm and glared at Sylvie as if she had punched her.

"I won't stand for this bickering." This her mother directed at Sylvie, though it was clear she would stand for almost anything, having allowed the glacier and Kenny and the entire stripping away of their former life. Sylvie scooted close to the window. She thought of how it felt to lie on one of Karen's thick towels, the concrete warm by the pool, the sun baking her back, the air spiked with chlorine. But the memory was sketchy and faint, like a shadow undone by twilight.

That night they checked in to a motel on the outskirts of Whitehorse, which with a population of just over 26,000 was the largest town in the Yukon Territory, according to *The Milepost*. Their mother sent Anna with Kenny for ice cream while Sylvie lay back on the bed, hands folded under her head, and stared at the flickering TV. From her overnight bag, her mother unwrapped her framed picture and set it on the nightstand. In the semidark, the drapes closed and only one light on near the bathroom, the glacier's image glowed white. Half-curled on the bed, Sylvie felt small and uneven.

Her mother grabbed the remote and muted the sound. "I've had about all I can take," her mother said in her plain, firm voice. "Of your cold, silent treatment."

Sylvie fixed her eyes on the pebbled ceiling. "We've got a chance to start fresh," her mother said. "And you're determined to spoil it."

Sylvie turned, not quite facing her mother, who fingered the smooth metal frame of the glacier. "There's nothing wrong with Pine Lake," she said, though already their home seemed so distant she could barely recall it, the road having spun her remembrance into something shapeless and whirring and endless.

"There are people who'd kill for an adventure like this."

"It's not an adventure," Sylvie said. "It's a stupid glacier." *Fen ond fæsten.*

Her mother paced between the two beds. "There's nothing for us back in Pine Lake," she said. "Kenny's got—"

"What about Anna and me?"

She stopped pacing. "There's no need to be jealous of Kenny."

Sylvie stuffed her hand under the pillow. "I don't care about Kenny." Her cheeks burned. "I just want to go home."

"We're not going home," said her mother, firm and simple.

Sylvie flung her arm at the glacier. To prove it meant nothing. To show how it was all a big crazy coincidence, the way her mother met Kenny. To push it out of her mind, and him, too. Her sleeve caught the edge of the frame. Her mother pitched herself forward, but before she could catch it, the frame hit the floor, a crack skidding through the glass from one corner to the other.

Her mother snatched it up, and with tenderness she began to rub the glass with the edge of her shirt, as though it were a child's tear-streaked face. "I've had enough of your attitude." Her voice shook. Fearing she might again cry, Sylvie looked away.

Her mother grabbed her by the shoulder. "I'm talking to you." But she said nothing more, only rubbed the cracked glass again and again, as if in doing so she could restore its magic. Finally she wrapped the frame in a pair of sweatpants and stuffed it back in her overnight bag. Sylvie turned from her mother, helpless against her longing for something too distant and large to ever be hers.

Beyond Whitehorse, the road descended toward Kluane Lake. Sylvie's mother read from *The Milepost* about how in the eighteenth century the Kaskawulsh Glacier had surged here, closing off the lake and causing its waters to rise until the Yukon River had been forced to change course, following a longer and much more difficult route to the ocean. Along the lake, they passed one boarded-up building after the other, paint peeling from weather and wind, the landscape having bested every attempt to contain it. Kluane Lake Lodge. Mountain View Motel. Kluane Wilderness Village. Burwash Landing Resort. The vacant windows and flapping signs and windswept porches proved that the wilderness would have its way.

At first the landscape quieted even Anna, but then she started in as usual about how she couldn't get comfortable, how she was bored, how she had to pee. Finally Kenny pulled into the cracked asphalt parking lot of what had once been the Bayshore Motel, and they took turns relieving themselves in a patch of tall weeds where wild roses fluttered their faint sweetness and lupine leaves cupped raindrops left by an earlier shower. Skirting horsetail ferns, the wind bore down hard and fresh, stirring the stripped-down smells of water and rock flushed from ice. Along the far edge of the lake, the Kluane Range rose like a saw-toothed grin, taunting clouds that piled at its peaks.

Sylvie dipped her fingers in the lake but pulled them out fast, stunned by the cold. Her resistance was futile, the wilderness too expansive, the waters lapping and long, the mountains jagged, defiant, aloof. In this desolation Sylvie felt complicit, as if the landscape understood what she did not, who she was and what she longed for. She could no longer turn away. The whine of the tires, the spell of the road, none of it could hold back a land that was both filled up and empty. Her eyes ached from zooming out and in, green blurring to granite, *march-riever mighty*, and the water deeper and bluer and more dangerous even than the dream-ocean that threatened her father.

As they drove on, the lake fell away, but the wildness remained. Nothing had prepared her for it, not her mother or Kenny or the droning documentaries. Nothing had suggested the size of the landscape. Nothing had warned that this was a place where anything could happen.

"Border crossing ahead," Kenny announced. "Beaver Creek." This time her mother remembered her sunglasses, and they passed without incident.

In the small town of Tok, Sylvie passed the night in fitful spurts of dreamless sleep. At 3:40 a.m., Kenny pulled the drapes and announced that if they got on the road right away, they'd be at his mom's house for breakfast. Half-asleep, Sylvie trundled to the truck. Anna bundled her coat under her head and fell immediately back to sleep. Their mother nestled against the door she'd mistrusted. Sylvie closed her eyes, shutting out the pink-streaked sky.

"Beautiful sunrise." Kenny jolted her out of the half-lit place that he also inhabited. The sun inched over the line where the earth met the sky, streaming through the dusty window onto Kenny's new beard, soft as a boar-bristle brush. On a pond, two large white swans floated from mist rising out of the nighttime chill. Sylvie waited for Kenny to point out the birds, but he said nothing. As the highway cut through a broad valley, an expanse of trees and water rose toward another set of impossible mountains that commanded a long stretch of sky.

"On the other side of this range, we'll be home." Kenny spoke softly, a promise meant only for her. From behind the wheel of a showroom truck, her father had once leaned toward Sylvie and whispered like that. Soon, very soon, they'd drive this truck home. Each time she believed him, certain that with her father, anything was possible.

Sylvie fixed her ears on the familiar hum of rubber on asphalt and her feet on the vibration of the wheels. Out of waist-high willows rose a patch of black spruce, stunted trees staggered like chess pieces.

"I remember the first time I left home," Kenny said. "Scared half to death, but I made sure not to show it." He tipped his chin and with his hand stroked his beard. "Guess it's like that for you and your sister." He downshifted to accommodate the climbing road. "But then you go to your dad's." He glanced again in the mirror. "Home away from home, right?"

Sylvie stared at the curled hairs on his neck, the worn collar of his green flannel shirt. She thought of Rick at the fire, his truck and the girl, how easy it had been, and how unexpected. She drew her arms tight, hugging her waist, and waited for Kenny to ask whether she was cold, to offer his jacket. But he only leaned into the steering wheel, as if that might help the truck in its struggle uphill.

The morning hit its fullness, sunny and bright. They skirted bald mountains, sheer rusty slopes and rocky cliffs streaked black by dynamite. Signs warned of rock slides, and as proof they passed a boulder as tall as Anna, knocked from its place by some whim of nature. As they wound down through the pass, the size of the rubble shrank. From pebbles quarried alongside the road, some enterprising person had arranged the rocks in a declaration of love, *Todd + Lisa* on the sloped granite.

"Almost home," Kenny said.

They were all awake now. "Almost home," Anna repeated as she bounced in the seat.

Sylvie started to say she was way too old for that kind of behavior. But behavior seemed now up for grabs, the rules off. Her mother pressed her hand into Kenny's as Sylvie leaned toward a sweep of snow-topped mountains.

The truck rounded a bend, and in the distance a band of white stretched the length of the road, crooked fingers of ice crawling over piles of black rock. Their mother leaned toward it. "The glacier!" said Anna.

The truck's rumble slowed as Kenny pulled off the road. With a broad perfect smile he helped their mother out of the truck, and Anna behind her, then held a hand out for Sylvie.

She couldn't find where to settle her eyes. Not on his face or the glacier or her mother.

"Suit yourself." Kenny shut the door, not quite a slam.

Sylvie held her fingers to quiet the trembling. Nothing—not her mother's framed picture, not the documentaries on ice—had prepared her for this thing that spread like a crouching beast from one end of the green valley to the other, cragged and folded, ancient in wanting and knowing.

She slipped on her jacket and let herself out of the truck. Despite the sun warm on her face, cold rushed up her arms. She tugged her sleeves over her wrists, not wanting to look and yet unable to stop herself. The ice was scarred with dirt, spoils of battle. Yet the edge of it curved like the hip of a woman, fragile and slick and ready to thrill to a tickle of breath.

Her mother twisted the toe of her shoe in the gravel. Kenny slung his arm over her shoulder as Anna edged up beside them. Wind whipped her hair so it circled her face. "Wow," she said. "When will it melt?"

"Never, baby," said Kenny. Their mother gazed up as if he'd said something new and profound.

This was no place to stay. Sylvie belonged where the boundaries were certain, where the landscape sank obediently into flat lines. Yet she could not look away.

Icefall

Ice that drops from a steep precipice, resulting in breaks and crevasses

At age five, Ruth had been chosen to play the bride in a pageant, to parade across the kindergarten stage in a white gown and a veil with a boy who squirmed in his starched shirt and tie, a peculiar torture masquerading as a reward for good behavior.

Her mother remembered it differently. You played a princess, she insisted. But Ruth knew they had dressed her up as a bride, clutching flowers and dragging a slip of white tulle, a train that someone's mother had chopped to her size and restitched. Mostly she remembered the clear conviction that she wasn't up to the task, that someone had made a mistake in selecting her, though she'd come to this realization only after the bridal march had begun to play, as the teacher's fingers teased the corners of her mouth. *Smile, honey. Smile.*

With fate it should have been different. No one plucked you out for special treatment, deserving or not. You followed. Yielded. That was the point. Yet from the moment Kenny's truck pulled away from the curb in Pine Lake, doubt had nudged Ruth toward an unanticipated edge. No matter how often she repeated to herself that she'd found what she wanted, that she was going after it, that she deserved love and adventure and a fresh start, she had fought a sense of foreboding as they plowed north into the unhemmed landscape, the ever-lengthening daylight no relief. She found herself longing for any sign of human intrusion: a trash barrel, a mile marker, a gas pump.

The moose made it worse, though in a way the near-miss was almost expected, once she got past the shock of it. Driving wasn't her strength. Richard had made sure she knew it. No one was good at everything, he liked to say, which made her feel as if she'd directed her effort at all the wrong things.

And the moose was nothing compared to the ice, unframed and spilled out over the landscape. Even from a distance, the glacier made her want to draw the girls close, to huddle in their shared warmth, not that Sylvie would allow such a thing.

There were signs. Warnings. Sylvie's refusal to allow for even the smallest possibility that something good could come of their leaving, Roy's scoffing at her in that windowless room, the rope rubbed tight on plastic when Kenny cinched the tarp over their stripped-down belongings, making her flinch.

No. It was the road that had rattled her. She had to settle in, that was all.

"Mom likes you." Kenny bumped Ruth's knee as he shifted from first to second and angled the truck onto a rutted dirt road.

She didn't. The fact that he felt compelled to say so was proof. Lena Preston was a large woman whose cheeks swallowed her eyes when she grinned, as she had at the sight of her son in the doorway. Taking in Ruth and the girls, the smile faded.

"I've never been to a Bible study," Ruth said to Kenny. "I hope they don't ask lots of questions." Lena had invited her, and though Ruth had little interest in church, she'd accepted. A new experience. You could start fresh and still try to fit in.

"You're smart." Kenny massaged her kneecap. "You'll impress them. Just don't impress them too much. Get them thinking you're some know-it-all from Outside."

"You sure liked those pancakes," Ruth said. Once Lena set the plate down in front of him, it had been as if there was nothing else in the room. *Best hotcakes a body could ask for*, Lena said, though it was only a packaged mix. The sodden, syrupy taste of them clung in Ruth's mouth.

"Mom loves to feed us." Kenny patted his belly, taut and tight compared to his brother's. In a red flannel shirt and a blue baseball cap, Steven had risen from Lena's table to slap Kenny's back while only half-acknowledging Ruth and the girls. *Glad to see you didn't bust your neck building that barn.* That was his greeting. Steven's eyes shrank in a face that was wide like his mother's, and his smile, unlike Kenny's, was guarded. Together their talk was all guns and bears. He had a rifle torn apart on the table. It wouldn't sight right, he said. He fiddled with the metal parts in his hands, as if through them he might confer healing, and between him and Kenny there had been all sorts of ideas about how he might fix it. Kenny had given him a hard time about not taking care of his guns, and Steven had given it right back.

He showed Kenny a magazine photo of a big limp bear, a grizzled hunter kneeling beside it. "From Taylor Ridge," Steven said. "Twenty-eight Boone and Crockett."

"Spring bear's not over yet," Kenny said. "We've still got our chance." That launched a debate over the best bait for bears. Dog food was cheap and grease from restaurants was great, but every Joe down in Palmer had that market locked up, Steven said.

"Day-old bakery," said Kenny. "Bears love that stuff."

"Fish oil," said Steven.

"Doughnuts," said Kenny. "Glazed. Chocolate long johns. Jelly-filled. Especially jelly-filled."

"Fish," Steven said. "You gotta have fish. You watch. That barrel of fish guts is gonna bring in the biggest bear this side of the Yukon." Ruth was still getting used to this idea, that large animals would be slaughtered, their pelts and heads preserved and mounted as on Lena's living room wall, where a bear complete with teeth and claws already hung. Circling the pelt were shellacked plaques, praying hands and crosses, and pictures of Jesus that said things like *Give your troubles to God, he's up all night anyhow.* Whatever the bear's troubles had been, it was clearly too late for God's help.

Lena's house was half-finished, the wide living room an open cavity with a long, low sofa and a big vinyl recliner and an assortment of rugs that hid most of a bare plywood floor. The low-pitched ceiling was dry-walled but not taped or mudded, so all the seams and screws showed. Aside from one paneled wall, the rest of the room was painted a bright robin's-egg blue, as if to draw attention from the unfinished parts, and it smelled like coffee and bacon and the jumbled shoes at the door. The windows felt small for the walls, naked without curtains or blinds to soften the edge between indoors and out, where in addition to Steven's barrel of rotting fish and five cars in various stages of disrepair, Lena's yard was littered with gas cans and garden hoses and the rusted guts of some sort of motor and three snowmobiles with their engines exposed and a four-wheeler with a big rack on the back and an old boat on a trailer with a flat tire, half-covered with blue tarps.

In all, Lena seemed able to accept quite a lot, so maybe getting used to Ruth would come more easily than Ruth feared. She couldn't fault Lena completely. Kenny could have phoned sooner, given her time to get used to the idea that they were coming. The short notice—he'd called only last night from Tok—presented an extra challenge. Church, Ruth hoped, would be a way to make up for it, though she'd already gotten off on the wrong foot by claiming to have attended St. Patrick's back home, which they had, though only on Christmas and Easter, and then only because Anna's friend Jill had convinced her that every person with a pulse had to visit church on those days. But as it turned out, Catholics were something less than true believers from Lena's perspective, and so Ruth's feigned allegiance had worked against her.

"You could go with me," Ruth said to Kenny. "To church."

"Those old biddies would shoo me out of their Bible study fast as a weasel out of a woodpile."

She nudged his ribs with her elbow. "Who you calling an old biddy?" The skin around Kenny's eyes creased when he smiled, one of the little things she had fallen in love with. "Your mom would be thrilled."

Kenny laughed. "Mom's just mad that me and Steven settled out on the island with the heathens."

Anna folded her hands over the back of the seat. "How much farther?" she asked.

"Almost there," Kenny said. "Almost home."

To hear this made Ruth woozy, like she'd stayed too long in the sun. Sylvie leaned toward the window and pressed her face to the glass as the truck clattered over a one-lane, wooden-planked bridge. Beneath thrummed the river, fast and wild. "Here we be," Kenny said. "The island. Home to misfits and outlaws and everyone else that stays home Sunday mornings."

The road turned up the island, skinny and long and caressed by the river. Graying houses showed here and there between trees, not only spruce but aspen and poplar, trees Kenny had taught Ruth to identify as they were passing through Canada, white spruce by the bluish-gray needles, black spruce by its top-heavy crown, aspen by leaves that twisted in the smallest of breezes, poplar by its gray, furrowed bark.

The island yards weren't yards in the sense of cut grass and flowers, but places of extended storage, like Lena and Walter's. Kenny said you never knew when you might need a distributor cap or a spark plug or a tire rim or an empty fuel drum.

He rolled his window down, letting in dust and a blast of cool air, and waved at a skinny man in jeans and a flannel shirt. The man, without showing much interest, waved back.

The idea of neighbors on top of Lena and church and the ice made Ruth want to lie down and sleep. She summoned what people back home said, that she was resilient, self-possessed.

The road curved, and there again rushed the river, fast and full. "How come the water's gray and not blue?" Anna asked.

"The glacier grinds rocks into powder," Kenny said. "Flour, they call it, or silt. Not much water's blue, when it comes right down to it."

Anna rested her chin on her hands. "My dad lives by the ocean. It's blue."

"If you say so." Kenny swung the truck down a dirt driveway, wind-rippled grass rising up on either side. "Hope you girls like to mow."

"Mom never lets me," Anna said.

"That's not true," Ruth said.

Set off to the side of the driveway was a large, flat-roofed building with an overhead door. "That's the reason I bought here," Kenny said. "Gotta have a big shop."

What drew Ruth's attention was the house, a plywood structure half the size of the shop and painted the same blue as Lena's living room walls. Kenny took her hand. "Nothing fancy," he said. "But it's home."

The tiny house seemed inevitable, the culmination of all Ruth had taken on faith. Anna bounced on the seat. "There was an old woman who lived in a shoe," she recited. "Had so many children she didn't know what to do."

Kenny pulled the truck close to the house, which was in fact shaped like a shoe. "We'll put the girls upstairs," he said as he shut off the engine. "They'll have a dead-on view of the glacier."

In the back seat, Sylvie tipped her head toward the second-floor window. Kenny climbed out of the truck and stood spread-legged in the tall grass. He stretched, hands to the sky, as he breathed large. "God, I missed this."

Ruth clutched the seat. You might think you expected nothing, that you were ready to let life surprise you. You might think this was freedom, and that in your trust you'd be spared disappointment. But the surprise was that you did expect things, whether you meant to or not.

"Come on, Mom." Anna was already out. A fresh start. That had to feel different from simply holding things together, for the sake of everyone but yourself.

On the small landing that topped the concrete-block steps, Kenny wriggled a key in a rusty padlock. "Steven was supposed to check on the house while I was gone." He tugged on the door and the hasp opened. "Guaranteed he never set foot in here once."

Inside was one long room, musty with trapped air and framed mostly in plywood—the walls, the floors, even the kitchen countertops. A square of light hit the floor as Kenny nudged to one side the brown towel tacked over the door's window. A mantle of fake bricks topped a forced-air furnace set into the wall near the stairs. A strip of carpet, brown flecked with yellow and curled at the ends, covered the floor in front of the furnace. Nailed to the far wall and supported by angled lumber was a slab of wood, the kitchen table she supposed, a sheet of yellow-sprigged vinyl tacked over it.

It wasn't what she'd have wished for. But every place had potential. Pushing past Ruth, Anna bounded the stairs. "Sylvie!" she called down. "The glacier looks gigantic from here."

Sylvie directed an accusing glance at her mother, then plodded the stairs, the sound of her sneakers echoing off the bare walls.

Kenny nudged Ruth toward the kitchen, tucked at the end of the living room opposite the stairs. The worn cabinet doors clacked one into the other as he flung them open. "Plenty to eat," he said. "It's dry up here. Stuff doesn't get stale, so you don't have to go running to town every week."

Ruth peered into the cupboards. A tub of oatmeal. Boxes of cereal. Hamburger Hash. Tuna Delight. In another cabinet were gray plates painted with indeterminate white flowers and plastic mugs printed with gas station names, Holiday and Quik Stop and 7-11. She ran her fingers over the unfinished plywood countertop, rough and unstained, wishing the cupboards empty because town, wherever it was, had a sudden appeal.

"We'll need meat," she said.

"Bear, baby. Bear." Kenny's arm slid round her waist. "Bear's the best meat there is, and free for the getting."

She ducked from his arm and bent to a cupboard that held a garage sale assortment of pots and pans, some Teflon, some stainless. Under the sink an open pipe emptied into a white five-gallon bucket. Kenny tapped the bucket with the side of his foot. "Gray water," he said. "Don't let it run over, or you'll have a big mess."

Ruth knelt, balancing with her hands on the open cupboard doors. "There's no pump? To get it outside?"

"Honey, I warned you. There's no sewer."

She flushed. "I know. I just thought..." What had she thought? She hadn't paid real attention, back in Pine Lake, when Kenny had explained how they'd live. Getting by without running water had at the time sounded adventuresome and romantic, something she mentioned in a casual way to her friends. No running water, she'd say, and then she'd study their reactions, the proportions of admiration and horror.

But here was this bucket, gaping and soiled. "Just fling the water out back," Kenny said. "In the weeds."

Ruth clutched the counter and pulled herself up. In a hopeless gesture, she flipped the faucet handle. She meant to smile but instead bleated, "I don't see how we'll stay clean."

"We'll run to Mom's," Kenny said. "Every couple of days. Alaska-style showers, so Dad won't get cranky about having to haul extra water. Wet down, water off, suds up, quick rinse. You'll get the hang of it."

"She won't like it." Heavy in Ruth's stomach, the pancakes had seemed imposition enough. And Lena had made a point of saying, when they'd only washed their hands, how the water mustn't be wasted, since it had to be brought in the big tank in the back of Walter's truck, to fill another tank that sat in the garage, from which it ran to the faucets.

"Don't worry about Mom," Kenny said. "She's easy."

Ruth flicked a switch, and a round fixture cast a dull glow over the sink. "Least we've got power," Kenny said. "Up the island, you have to fire a generator just to make coffee. Power company offered to come in, but folks there didn't want it."

Think of the things you won't miss, Ruth reminded herself. No more rising at 5 a.m. to shower and dress and trundle the children to school. No more tense calls to parents whose innocent darlings had somehow landed in in-school suspension. No more of Mr. Scranton's tobacco breath half-masked with mints as he leaned over her desk, mildly and sadly flirtatious. No more crawling into bed alone, wondering how she could face another day of the same old routine.

Besides, she'd loved fixing up the old house she and Richard had bought on the west end of Pine Lake when Sylvie was still in diapers. She'd filled dozens of trash bags with junk left by the former owner, an old bachelor who'd gone off to live with his daughter. She'd polished the wide oaken woodwork and sanded the floors. Shined the tarnished door knobs and hinges. Retiled the bath.

"We could tile." She ran the flat of her hand over Kenny's plywood countertop. At a pinprick of pain, she pulled her hand to her chest. A splinter. She rubbed the pad of her thumb, resisting the urge to examine it.

"Tile might be nice," Kenny said. "Hugh never got around to the finish work. Crashed his plane up on the glacier, and that was the end of it."

Anna skipped down the stairs. "Who crashed his plane?"

"The man that built this place." Kenny tousled her hair. "He wasn't paying attention and ran his little old plane right into that big hunk of ice." He extended his hand, strong and thick-veined. "Come outside. I'll show you the prop."

"From the crashed plane?"

"The very same one."

She slipped her hand into his, familiar in a way that roused in Ruth a genuine smile. "This house might be haunted," Anna said.

"Naw." Kenny glanced back at Ruth. "I reckon Hugh's ghost is still up on that glacier."

Ruth thudded the cabinet doors shut. "Sylvie," she called up the stairs. "Come on down." She waited, one finger worrying the splinter, but there was no response. With children, it was all about knowing when to push and when to leave things alone. Kenny seemed to have a natural instinct for it, whereas Ruth tried too hard.

Leaving Sylvie to sulk, she went outside and stood as Kenny had, legs solid beneath her, breathing the scent of roses and sharp, ginny juniper. The grass undulated in the breeze, smelling of freshly cooled earth. Beyond the yard the river crashed, restless and free.

Across the driveway from the shop stood a wood-slabbed shed, its low-angled roof made from chicken wire and rolled roofing paper. Behind it, Kenny nudged a mangled airplane prop with the toe of his boot. "That's what happens when you don't pay attention," he said.

Anna crouched to touch the twisted metal. "Watch out," Ruth warned. "It's sharp."

Anna straightened. "I want to play by the river."

"No," Ruth said, quick and firm.

"Why not?" Anna shielded her eyes. "It's not that far."

"Yeah, Mom." Kenny grinned. "Why not?"

"I'll be careful," said Anna. "I'll stay back from the edge."

"You don't know your way around yet. And we need your help with unpacking."

"Let her go," Kenny said. "She'll be fine."

Ruth squinted at the river, sprung from the ice. "There's no one to play with," she said. "And the river's not like the lake. It's dangerous."

Kenny nudged Anna's back. "Go on," he said. "Run quick, so your mom doesn't worry."

Anna bolted through the weeds, leaping and laughing. "Wait," Ruth called after her. "I'll have Sylvie go with you."

"Never mind about Sylvie," Kenny said. "Let her go for five minutes. Enjoy the freedom."

Freedom. Wasn't that the point of a fresh start, to let go? "Stay where you can see the house," Ruth yelled.

"The shoe," Anna yelled back. "Stay where I can see the shoe."

Kenny set a hand on Ruth's shoulder. "This place is a playground. The kids are going to love it here."

"Not Sylvie." The words squeezed past the tight place in her throat.

"Especially Sylvie." He wrapped his fist around the bottom of a crumpled blade and hoisted the prop. "Might hang this thing up. A tribute to Hugh. Above the door. Like a horseshoe." He said this with hope, so earnest that Ruth had to look away.

She settled her gaze on the shed. She'd start with these structures, the shed and the shop and the house. Become familiar with one and then move to the other. The river would be just another noise in the background, the ice an anomaly in the landscape, signifying nothing.

She tugged on the shed door, but it resisted. Kenny reached to help, but she braced her feet in the grass and pulled with both hands, and the door gave all at once. From the dark rolled the smell of damp wood, logs cut and stacked. Sideways on the wood pile, lit by light leaked from the doorway, a pair of panicked eyes leered from the head of an old spring-loaded rocking horse, brown faded plastic with a molded white mane, its saddle horn worn, its plastic neck cracked, its hooves frozen mid-gallop.

Kenny's hand on her back made her jump. "You look like you've seen old Hugh's ghost."

She shut the door, fast. "Where'd that rocking horse come from?"

Kenny rubbed the back of his hand along the edge of his beard. "Hugh had a kid. And a wife. They went south. After, you know."

Ruth leaned against the door, hands pressed against the rough wood. It wasn't Hugh's specter she feared but his wife's, how she must have tried and yet failed to make herself known here.

Kenny took her arm and led her away from the shed, and it required all the resolve Ruth was known for not to break away and run for the river, to rescue her daughter.

You took one step and the next, things you did without thinking. This Ruth knew from the days and the weeks and the months after Richard left, expanses of time that she'd tried to imagine as squeezed and pressed like dried flowers between the pages of a dictionary. She sent Sylvie to retrieve Anna while Kenny uncinched the tarp from the truck. They hauled boxes inside and sorted them in piles on the floor. The girls carried their belongings upstairs, while Kenny lugged a bundle of blankets into the bedroom and peeled them back to expose his new gun.

Ruth set her overnight bag on the laminate nightstand. She had read in a magazine that rooms could be designed around a single inspiring piece of furniture. She studied the possibilities of the nightstand and decided there were none. She ran her finger over the bumpy chenille bedspread, yellowed like an old paperback page. Towels to fold, a crisp shirt to iron—these she craved. "I guess we'll wash clothes at your mom's."

Kenny lowered the gun. "There's the river."

She rebuked sadness, not to be squandered on small inconveniences. "The water's too cold. And the silt. Nothing would come clean."

"Babe." Kenny settled the gun on the pillows. "I was kidding. If it bugs you that much, we'll get a wringer."

A wringer washer. She had only the vaguest idea that such a thing still existed, with a tub of some sort and rollers that clamped down to press out the water. Perhaps that was what was required for hope, a full and complete wringing. She shifted her bag to the bed and ceremoniously unfolded the sweatpants that covered her picture.

"The glass is cracked," Kenny said.

"It must have gotten bumped." She dug in her make-up bag for her tweezers and began to pick at the place where the splinter had entered her skin. Kenny reached for her hand, but she clasped it to her chest, protective of the small punctured place.

"It's no big deal." She poked hard at the splinter, but the blunt ends of the tweezers only drove it deeper into her reddened skin. "It'll work its way out."

Kenny returned to his gun, pumping a mechanism that went up and back, a piece with a name and a function he had once explained but which now Ruth couldn't recall. She picked some more at the sliver, then tossed the tweezers aside. The frame looked wrong on the nightstand. She pressed it into a drawer, pushing aside scraps of paper and matchbooks and foil-wrapped condoms.

Kenny let go of the gun. He wrapped his arms around her waist and nuzzled her neck, his breath warm against her ear. "Let's go to the glacier. I want you to see it up close."

Alarm thrummed, quick and full. "Not yet. I want to wipe down those cupboards. You've got . . . we've probably got mice."

"Time for that later." He took her hand and led her out of the bedroom, the new Ruth, the one who meant to be someone else here, extended beyond all demands. "Anna. Sylvie," he called up the stairs. "Your mom and I are going for a ride."

Anna appeared on the landing. "I want to come."

"Next time," Kenny said. "Your mom gets to go first."

Anna folded her arms against her chest, a stance Ruth herself took to let the girls know she meant business. "There's a dog running by the river. I want to bring it home."

Ruth flushed at her brashness. "Absolutely not." They'd had a dog once, though Anna would have been too young to recall it, a little brown-and-white terrier that padded dutifully behind Ruth. Whenever Ruth left her sight, the dog had whined and yapped, evoking predictable complaints from Richard. The more attention Ruth gave her, the more the dog clung. "Stray dogs can have rabies," Ruth said. "You keep your distance if you see it again. And I don't want you anywhere near that river unless Sylvie's along."

"Sylvie won't do anything," Anna said. "She just sits on the bed."

"Give her time." This Ruth said loudly, for Sylvie's benefit.

Kenny steered Ruth toward the door. "Tell your sister she's got till we get back to get her stuff put away," he said.

It was easier in the end to give in, which Sylvie would surely learn soon. Ruth climbed in the truck next to Kenny. "A dog," she said. "I don't know what's got into Anna."

As they pulled away from the house, the glacier filled the windshield, sudden and solid. Ruth pressed her damp-palmed hands into her jeans.

"Dad might be at the campground," Kenny said. "If he's done at the mill." Walter was busy cutting lumber, Lena said, for someone whose house had burned down. "He's quiet, but don't let that fool you," Kenny said. "It was pure genius, how he got the land at the glacier. He and Mom had something like twenty bucks between them when they first got to Alaska. That was back before the pipeline went in, and still people figured up here you could make your way pretty much just by breathing. There was homesteading, forty acres, but you had to improve it. You could trap and hunt or farm a little like they did at Mat-Su. That's what most people did. The glacier was only a novelty. But Dad saw its potential."

He turned from the highway onto a dirt road that dropped toward the river and wound around a tall cliff. "Used to be the ice went from here to the ocean," he said. "A hundred miles." The films came to Ruth, the roar of a glacier as it calved and crashed to the water. "Now Dad's got the access tied up. You want to see it up close, you gotta pay. Not you, of course. But everyone else. Folks still complain, after all these years, about the Prestons and their glacier. But Dad thought of it first."

The bumpy road made Ruth reach for the dash. Where it dropped off, the river roiled, frothing white.

"You wouldn't know it," Kenny said. "But the ice moves." She did know this, of course, from the documentaries. "Slow but steady," he said. "Forward and back. Back and forward. Grinds up everything that gets in its way." Ruth tugged her jacket tight. "The tourists don't care," he continued. "They pull off the road and take pictures. Then they get back in their cars and move on."

"But if the buses came down here, like Steven said."

"Dad hates those big outfits," Kenny said. "The buses. The cruise ships. They herd folks around like they're cattle, and they don't give the locals squat out of what they charge." He strained toward the windshield and pointed to where a moose stood up to its belly in the middle of the crashing river. In its eyes Ruth saw panic. A wrong choice, with no turning back. "Must be half-froze," Kenny said. "That water never gets more than thirty-three degrees, thirty-four tops."

As he steered the truck onto a one-lane bridge, the glacier dropped out of view. The bridge had wide slats for the tires to travel, but between were gaps where the water showed through, a small but precarious passing. "Dad built it himself," Kenny said. "Tricky, with the water moving so fast. No engineer could've done better, considering what he had to work with."

Ruth let out a breath, once the road was back underneath. A stenciled sign announced *Preston's Glacier Park. Private access to Resurrection Glacier. Admission paid here.* Between two metal posts a rusty chain stretched. Kenny set the brake and got out to unlatch it. "These days Mom and Dad don't open up much," he said as he climbed back in. "Not enough traffic."

They passed a small shuttered building with yellow siding and another stenciled sign, this one reading *Preston's Glacier Gifts.* "Nobody goes for this stuff anymore," Kenny said. "Mom and Dad gotta start thinking outside the box. This was supposed to be their retirement. But they can't sell. Not enough cash flow."

On the gravel, the truck bumped past primitive campsites, each one numbered with a hand-painted sign, each one empty. Close to the road crept the forest, crowded with low, scraggly spruce and slender aspen. Oddly, the glacier had disappeared from their view.

Past the campsites, the trees dwindled. They rounded a corner, and Ruth's breath caught at a sudden mass of white. Black rocks, sharp and gleaming, were mounded in front of the ice. Kenny pulled the truck next to the rocks and shut off the engine. Wind squealed past the truck windows, pressing in. "All that rock, that's moraine," Kenny said. "Hauled around by the glacier."

Ruth knew how moraines were made. She understood isostacy, how the weight of the glacier could alter the very shape of the earth. She knew about icefalls that formed within fracture zones, and about a glacier's mass balance, the sum of its accumulation and ablation within a single season.

Kenny cracked the door, and the wind sprang it open. Cold poured from the ice. Ruth zipped her jacket to her chin. The wind whipped her hair as she stood by the truck, the ice towering larger than any photo could capture, rubbled and scarred, stubborn and old, wrinkled, pored, pocked, a lumines-cent blue escaping from its densest parts.

"Those black streaks, that's dirt," Kenny said. "The larger ones, crevass-es. Big breaks in the ice that can swallow you whole. If you climb it, that is."

As cold swelled her throat, Ruth clamped her lips to shut out the dust. The silence felt heavy. At a clatter, she jumped, then saw it was only pebbles streaming down the face of the ice, unleashed by melting, and she was re-minded of how easily fear filled the gap between knowing and doing.

"Get this," Kenny said. "You dig ice from the middle of the glacier, and it explodes when you drop it in water." Bergy seltzer, that's what it was called, the cold sizzle of air bubbles released when glacier ice melted, but Ruth didn't say so.

"My Aunt Judy told me about it, when I was a kid," Kenny said. "She had a thing for the glacier. Read all about it, hung out here all the time. Dad used to tease her, that no man would have her, the way she'd fallen for ice."

This was the woman Ruth wished to know, a woman who'd not shied from the ice, unlike Hugh's phantom wife, who'd scuttled away at the first opportunity. She and Judy might come here together to laugh at the grit and the throat-swelling cold and the smell of the ice. Through Judy, Lena might even grow to like Ruth. "I'd like to meet her," Ruth said. "Your Aunt Judy."

"She's gone," Kenny said. "An accident. Don't bring it up with Mom. She took it hard."

Rocks clattered again down the face of the ice. Ruth could barely feel the tips of her fingers, the end of her nose. "Hard to believe," Kenny said. "It's just snow piled on snow. Little flakes, one on top of the other. But at the core, it's hard as rock." Harder than rock, Ruth knew, but she didn't correct him.

She required little. To love and be loved. To act, rather than be acted upon. She turned from the glacier, full of longing for her girls. Kenny took her hand, and she squeezed his fingers, large and warm, wishing she knew how the ice had called her, or why.

When they drove off, Ruth refused to look back. When they got home, she found a needle, lit a match, and burned the point till it glowed red. Then she thrust it into her flesh. The splinter came out in pieces, and though her finger throbbed, this small accomplishment pleased her. From the first-aid kit she'd stashed in the glove box, she wrapped a bandage around her thumb and continued unpacking.

Anna had made short work of setting up her half of the girls' room, but despite Kenny's mandate, Sylvie's unopened boxes still lay heaped on the floor. She sat by the window, staring out at the ice, an old children's book open in her lap, one Richard used to read aloud from, as he'd done most every night in his booming voice, before Mirabelle claimed his bedtime attentions.

For supper Ruth made macaroni from a box, mixing in tuna and canned peas, soothed by the ordinary act of preparing a meal. She envisioned a quiet domesticity, concocting new blends of canned vegetables and macaroni, sauces mixed from ingredients found in the back of the cupboards, tomato paste and black beans and chili powder, a real cloth on the table and a new rug in front of the furnace and a real curtain on the door and if not tile then something to spruce up the counters. There could in time be a well, and pipes that brought water, in and out, and down the road, a washing machine, the regular kind. The glacier would be only a hunk of white in the background, and she'd laugh to think of the hold it once had.

Erratic

An aberration, transported and deposited by ice

Sylvie woke in the usual way from the dream of her father, startled and angry and ashamed. Though the house held the quiet of night, there was no darkness to hide her. Blue spilled in from the window, twilight that would soon shift toward dawn. A not-in-Kansas moment, as her dad used to say. When Sylvie was young, she'd sit beside him on the couch, right as tornado season was gearing up in the Midwest, and they'd watch *The Wizard of Oz*, Sylvie squealing as the spiraling storm shifted Dorothy's vision from black and white into color, just like that.

One day had passed. One day and half a night, if you could call it that. An eternity already, and every bit of it worse than she'd braced for. Lena's pancakes. The sorry shoe of a house. Anna's rush to unpack. Her mother's smug pleasure over canned peas. This room that opened wide to the glacier, its sheer silent power shored up against the river and mountains and forests and sky.

In the other bed, Anna's breath rose and fell, untroubled. Sylvie resented her sister's easy sleep, and her acceptance of any lure dangled in front of her. Ice cream. Pancakes. Adventure. Not so long ago, their father's leaving had drawn them together, the two of them cleaved to their mother.

She rolled out of bed, a thin throw rug cushioning her feet. Dim silhouettes rose in the dark, Anna's shirts and pants a sloppy stack on a shelf—there was no dresser—and beside them her books. Shoved next to the bed were Sylvie's boxes, still taped, waiting for her to unpack the photo of Karen, the card signed by Rick.

Despite the closed window, she heard the steady roar of the river as it pulsed from the ice. Beyond that, the night was empty of sound. No whirring tires, no buzz from a streetlamp. No steady click of the Regulator clock in the hall, the clock having been assigned to storage.

She moved slowly, breasts brushing against her shirt as she buttoned it. She slipped on sweatpants and sandals, then a jacket, unzipped. From the landing she looked down at the fake brick mantel over the furnace, the vinyl-covered table built into the wall, the tiny kitchen with its all-but-useless sink. To call it home would be as pointless and silly as any poem.

She descended the stairs, half-hoping her mother would rise and confront her. But no sound came from beyond the closed door where she lay next to Kenny, flesh against flesh, no sound except his breathing, which Sylvie seemed to hear preternaturally, the way a fish hears through water. With a few steps she could cross the living room and turn the knob and expose them, her mother and Kenny, naked under the musty sheets, tee shirts and jeans cast to the floor. But she had never been that kind of girl.

With a light shove of the door, Sylvie released herself into the night, the air cool and dry and scented with juniper, hard little berries clustered on prickly bushes spread low to the ground. She went to the shed, which her mother had looked on with terror—this Sylvie had seen from the window. But inside was nothing remarkable, only stacked wood and an old plastic horse, one like Sylvie had ridden for countless hours as a child. Eventually her mother had taken it away, saying it took up too much room, and even after Anna was born the horse did not reappear.

She turned toward the river, wishing for the impossible clacking of Dorothy's red shoes, magic that would transport her back to the thick-barked maple in their yard, the chatter of squirrels, the dip where the sidewalk met the driveway, common things Sylvie had taken for granted. Sand-like gravel sluiced over her sandals. Clumps of weeds suffered up from the compacted earth, an old riverbed, Kenny said. In the dim light, clusters of tiny white flowers swayed like little galaxies held up on thin reddish stalks. Closed tight, giant dandelions anticipated a darkness that had never arrived.

The crashing water evoked a memory from when Sylvie was nine. On a crisp September evening, after the dealership closed, her father had turned the key in one of the shiny new trucks and driven it off the lot with Sylvie beside him, peering over the dash, delighted as much with the joy in her father's eyes as with the idea that they were about to really surprise her mother this time by bringing home a shiny red truck with chrome hubcaps that spun like pinwheels—this she'd seen when her father peeled the truck across the lot as she jumped up and down, hollering for him to stop and let her in.

But they didn't drive home to her mother. Her father commandeered the road along the south end of Pine Lake, driving fast, grinning and glancing again and again in the rearview. He reached over and clutched Sylvie's hand, so tight that it hurt her fingers, but she didn't complain. "This is our little secret," he said. "Remember that, Sylvie."

He pulled into a long driveway with big stone pillars on either side, toward a sprawling brick house with a white-columned porch, going so fast it seemed they would smash into the four-car garage, but as one of the overhead doors loomed in the windshield, her father hit the brakes and shut off the truck. He blinked hard, his eyes unable to settle on any one thing, the house or the dash or his daughter, Sylvie not daring to move as he breathed shallow and fast, and for a moment she'd thought that through some sleight of hand her father had purchased not only the truck but this big fancy house.

"Don't dawdle," he'd said, almost scolding, as if she were the only reason they sat there, and so she'd scrambled out of the truck and half-run to keep up with her father's quick, long strides, around the end of the four-car garage and across the big green backyard toward the lake, where the setting sun streamed orange rays so bright they turned the windows of the dark, silent house into mirrors. She recalled then staring out from one of those windows onto a wide swath of snow glimmered by a pale moon, clutching a bag filled with chocolates and peppermints.

"Mr. Fenton lives here," she said.

"That's right." Her father's mouth twitched at the corner. "But he's gone to Key West."

She hadn't know then what Key West might be, maybe someplace where even more keys hung on the wall than they did at the dealership, but before she could ask, they'd reached the water's edge, the sun a low-hanging ball, the lake glassy and expectant. Tied to the dock, a huge motorboat bobbed. Her father glanced left and right, at the neighboring docks half-hidden by trees, their moored boats half the size of this one. He held out his hand as if she were a princess. "Hop in."

She'd gripped the seat, the leather cool on her legs, while her father reached into cubbies and ran his hand under the dash and pried up the floor mats. He'd squatted down and peered under the captain's chair and under Sylvie's seat and then, appearing inspired, he'd run his fingers under a strip of metal trim and produced a magnetized key.

The motor hummed, and a low burbling came from the back as the prop started to spin. Her father untied the boat and, with one knee on the seat, steered away from the dock. Across the lake, a sliver of orange skimmed the trees, the day fading fast. A light topped a pole in the back of the boat, but her father seemed not to know that he should switch it on. He punched the throttle and the boat lunged forward. "Hang on," he'd said, and Sylvie had gripped the seat even tighter as the boat smacked the water, speeding over the lake. Water sprayed Sylvie's face and dribbled into her lap, her father a dark silhouette laughing, and her laughing too. "Now this is the life," he'd shouted over the sound of their splashing and then, in the same breath, "Don't tell your mother," at which Sylvie had felt a surge of conspiratorial delight.

_____

Now in this new place the river splashed as the lake had then, the spray of it cold on her face. The bank fell away toward waves that blanched back where they struck submerged rocks, Sylvie so close that she had only to take one step and the water would sweep her away.

The sky expanded with waiting, too light for stars. From the far shore came the cry of a hawk, an alarm, sharp and shrill. The noise reverberated in the back of Sylvie's throat, or perhaps she herself formed the noise, out of the terrible understanding of where she'd come from and what she might come to, the knowledge that at her core she too might be ice, more spare even than verse, and there was nothing she or anyone else could do about it.

She clutched her arms to her waist as before her the water rushed and moaned. Her mother was right about Kenny. He was like the glacier, hard and strong, a willful presence that refused to retreat. She shivered, fearful and full of longing, as she thought of Kenny's lashes, his beard, his slow way of talking, his laugh. Up the river the sky began to ripen over the glacier, yellow to red like a peach, the sun ready to flood her with light.

In silence was power. She had never let go of that secret.

Foliation

Layers that develop as ice is transformed

We are warned of Earth's unnatural warming, the byproduct of our collective desires. But even as glaciers retreat, some advance. Propelled by such weight that the earth under them sags, these follow the routes of least resistance, their bottom halves shaping the land as their top parts turn brittle. Where the ice meets obstacles too large to crush, crevasses shoot through to its core, its oldest and darkest and most secret place.

The dangers are many. Crevasse walls are prone to collapse. Flimsy snow bridges hide plunging gaps. And the course of a glacier may change without warning, retreating where it once had advanced. If the ice falls back too quickly, melt fills in behind, a dam that may at any moment erupt, releasing a rush of water that floods the earth clean.

Not that these things mattered to the people of Resurrection. Like the boarded-up sawmill back in Pine Lake, the glacier only occupied space in the landscape. And so in the days following her arrival, Ruth made a conscious effort to set aside what she'd learned about ice, facts about eskers and cirques and moulins and moraines. She embraced the familiar, routine being the best remedy for over-thinking. Each morning she dressed and made breakfast and warmed water for dishes. She flooded the dishpan with water, steam teasing the ends of her hair. With a dirty fork—you always used something dirty, to make the most of water that was hauled with a bucket—she stirred the soap, coaxing suds. She refilled the kettle from the blue plastic five-gallon container, plucked a dishrag from the barely sudsed water, balled and squeezed it, her palms red and hot, then stretched it to cool before wiping the table. When the dishes were done, she hauled the gray water out to the yard and, with only a sideways glance at the glacier, chucked it into the weeds.

She made lists of the things she most craved. Apples. Carrots. Celery. Onions. Bananas. Orange juice, fresh squeezed. Romaine lettuce. Endive. A whole chicken, for roasting. Portobello mushrooms. Leeks. Fresh whipping cream. Chocolate. She was eager for Kenny to drive her the ninety-eight miles to town, but he was busy with his bear-baiting plans.

Time, that's all she required. Time and trust and routine. Fate demanded a certain submission, which Ruth welcomed after the effort she'd made to hold things together with Richard. Church fell into this category, a harmless submission to Lena's desire. There was nothing better than a fresh start for showing how open-minded you could be about such things, and besides, where else if not church would the girls make friends?

Ruth had grown up with corn, miles and miles of fields squared off by roads that crossed the farmland in grids. Every so often a town appeared as if by accident, like the one where her father sold farm implements and where her mother shopped every Tuesday at the Piggly Wiggly, and where the two of them sat every summer night on the concrete patio, sipping Manhattans, their glasses dripping from where the waning heat met the cold. As a child she'd taken comfort in the clacking of ice and the chirping of crickets and the voices that filtered from the neighbor's open windows.

In their small town were three churches, a Baptist, a Methodist, and a Roman Catholic, each tucked quietly and inconspicuously onto a residential street corner, none drawing any special attention to itself. Where you went and whether you went was known but not noted especially. Real faith rested in the plows and the roads and the drinks with their clinking ice. Ruth was drawn to the vague idea that a greater truth might lie behind the heavy wooden doors of one of the churches, but having never seen any compelling evidence to that effect, it was easy enough to stay away.

A tidy box with vinyl siding, Lena's Church of New Beginnings sat alone atop its own hill, looking more like a larger version of Kenny's shop than a place of worship. The sign outside said *The Best View's of Heaven*, and indeed, by the way the church angled toward the west, it snubbed an otherwise spectacular view of the glacier.

Come Wednesday, Lena insisted on transporting Ruth and the girls to church. Naturally Sylvie resisted. Then Kenny confided how when he was in high school, he'd snuck off with a girl in the Loft, the upstairs room where the youth met at church. After that, Sylvie relented. She and Anna and Ruth piled into Lena's car, a wide sedan that floated over dips in the highway—as a mother, Lena made clear, she had long ago drawn the line against driving her children around in a truck.

In the church parking lot, Lena grabbed a teenaged girl by the arm and more or less forced her on Sylvie. The two of them disappeared to the Loft, where Ruth hoped by some miracle Sylvie might be restored to the girl she'd once been, dependable and kind and, if not outgoing, at least not using her silence like a weapon against her own mother. She blamed herself for a lack of vision that had caused Sylvie to draw into herself. If only she'd constructed an image of what her daughter might become and then nudged her toward it, Sylvie might have negotiated her circumstances with more grace, using to her advantage her natural beauty and quiet intelligence.

Anna needed no encouragement to go off on her own. Without shyness or hesitation, she followed a girl her own age to a room behind the sanctuary where Lena explained there was a club of some sort, Glory Girls. Kenny was right. In her new surroundings, Anna was growing into a sense of herself.

The Ladies Circle met in the basement, in a big room with long rows of folding tables that ended at a kitchen. A group of women sat at the table nearest the coffee pot, next to a television on a metal cart. As she settled next to Lena, Ruth fought nerves. These women were no different from any in Pine Lake, talking of children and a dry spell and the church's annual barbecue, except that as they spoke, they slid their Bibles onto the table, like bowls set out discreetly for supper.

Ruth had once owned a Bible, with small print and pages so flimsy you could almost see through them. Its origins were a mystery—maybe a gift from a distant aunt or uncle on graduation or a birthday or some other occasion. She had never done more than shuffle the pages for the grassy smell of the paper, but a Bible wasn't the sort of thing you got rid of, unless you were going as far as Alaska and had to pack everything you owned into the bed of a pickup truck. At the yard sale, she'd stuck a preprinted one-dollar sticker on the front and let it go for fifty cents.

Under the table, Lena slipped Ruth a fat, worn Bible that she accepted as a portentous gift, signaling approval. As a lull struck the chatter, Lena rubbed her fingers over the cracked leather cover of her own Bible and said, "Ladies, this is Ruth. She and her girls drove up from Minnesota with Kenny, to try their luck in Alaska."

In the car driving over, Lena had been frank about the matter of how to introduce Ruth to the ladies. It wasn't ideal, the way Kenny and Ruth were shacking up on the island. Shacking up was a problem and so was the island. But everyone would know soon enough, and the church got plenty of grief about hypocrisy without Lena pretending things were any different than they were. Embarrassed by this blunt talk around the girls, Ruth had quickly agreed that Lena's thinking made sense. When you weren't entirely sure what you were up against, it was better to agree than, say, to point out how it had been Kenny who had encouraged Ruth to come north, and to live with him on the island.

The women around the table introduced themselves one by one, welcoming Ruth to the church and to their group and saying in one way or the other how they hoped she'd be back. Ruth listened and smiled and repeated the names to herself. When they were done, she'd impress Lena by recalling each one in a casual way. Remembering names showed you cared. She recalled reading this somewhere, or maybe Martha had told her. It showed that you were outside of yourself. She hoped Sylvie was learning names, up in the Loft.

Marie, with those twins, I don't know how you do it, Ruth would say. *My girls keep me running, and they're six years apart.* Thin with limp hair and stooped shoulders, Marie looked too young to have any children, much less twins. Cherise with her odd name—she pronounced it "chair-ease"—wore a lace camisole that plunged lower than what Ruth would have thought right for wearing in church. Of course she wouldn't comment on the low-cut lace but rather on Cherise's bright smile, how it made her look energetic and young.

Ruth was doing fine with Marie and Cherise and Patricia who spoke shyly of her new baby up in the nursery, but then Roxanne got Ruth off track by asking about Pine Lake, which Roxanne thought might be close to Gull Lake, where she had some Minnesota cousins. In that strange and persistent human habit of forcing weak and absurd connections, Roxanne wondered whether Ruth might have crossed paths with these relatives. She grilled her about whether she knew this store or this restaurant or that lake. For Ruth it was too much sudden remembering, and the names began slipping away.

Finally the next woman took her turn. Ruth struggled to collect herself. Marie and Patricia, yes, but who was the one sitting between them? She turned her attention to the woman now talking, gray hair pulled back tight from her face, penciled eyebrows harsh under the fluorescents, thin hands folded over her open Bible as she peered over her glasses at Ruth. "Lovely name. My favorite book of the Bible, the Book of Ruth. Think of all that she did." Murmurs went around the table. "I wonder," the woman said, "would we do the same?" The woman—had she even offered her name?—seemed to ask this directly of Ruth.

Every other name vanished as Ruth was reminded of her own plain and old-fashioned name, a blight on her life. Befitting her flat, straight hair that could only be thought of as mousy. To blame for the way she'd hung back in school, deferring to girls with names like Yvonne and Claire, girls who knew about make-up and fashion and boys. If she'd had a middle name other than Lois, Ruth would have put it to use. No one named Ruth could compete with a woman like Mirabelle, though Ruth had made a respectable stab at it in college, long before Mirabelle herself came along, a period that ended with Richard and Sylvie and the need to live up to her calm, steady name for their sakes.

Still, Ruth had never before been directly held to account for her name, called on to explain something she clearly should know but did not. She turned to Lena, who surely knew that given her lax association with a church that Lena considered not really a church, Ruth couldn't possibly be familiar with the Bible story in question. Her fingers dipped along the scalloped edges of the Bible where the various books were marked, Deuteronomy and Leviticus and Job, as she summoned Lena's good will, but her face looked as expectant as the rest.

The right answer concerning the Ruth of the Bible must lie in whether what she'd done was virtue or vice. It being the Bible, the odds leaned toward virtue. "Maybe," Ruth began. She found the friendliest face, though she could attach no name to it. "If I was in her same situation," she said, to cover the possibility that this other Ruth had succumbed to her circumstances and hadn't made the right choice at all. "Maybe in her situation, I'd have done what she did."

"Ruth's choice wasn't easy," said the woman who first posed the question. Her eyes pressed Ruth to say more.

Ruth shifted in the hard plastic chair, her thin cotton pants damp with sweat from the back of her knees. "It wasn't easy," she agreed. Agreeing was a trick Ruth had learned from living with Richard. A way to stall, to ease out from the corner you were being backed into. But agreeing could also snap back at you, like a rubber band stretched too tight. Ruth had learned this from Richard as well. In the press of eyes around the table, she felt herself failing as she had with her husband.

Marie—or maybe her name was Patricia—came to Ruth's aid, though perhaps not so much from compassion as from a desire to show off what she knew. "Ruth may have lain down at the feet of a man," said Marie who might be Patricia. "But she did it for love. Not for the man but for Naomi. Not even her real mother. Her husband's mother, and he was dead."

"Ruth obeyed," Lena said.

"Yes," Ruth agreed in a rush.

That seemed to satisfy everyone. Faces relaxed. The introductions continued. Ruth focused again on the names. Exhausted all at once from the travel and the glacier and the unpacking, she found at least the strength to thank Lena for the invitation to church. "I—we—feel so welcome already. My daughter Sylvie is upstairs with the youth group. Lena introduced her to Cara, and I think the two of them are going to hit it off." Her hope swelled, as if speaking this might make it happen.

Cherise—the name returned to Ruth now—threw her hands toward the ceiling. "My Cara," she said. "Lord have mercy. I hope your girl pounds some sense into her."

Murmurs and smiles prodded Ruth to continue. "My youngest is excited about Glory Girls," she said. A banner on the wall saved her from having to recall the name of the program. *Honor, Truth, Purity: Glory Girls*, it read. The white cloth threaded with gold shimmered in a square of summer light that shot through one of the windows.

Lena too was caught in a swath of light that illuminated her pink lipstick and the blush on her ample cheeks. "We've only just got here, and Lena's helped us so much," Ruth said.

"This church runs the best Christmas bazaar this side of Anchorage, thanks to Lena," said Cherise, who spoke with a twang, like a cousin of Ruth's from Missouri.

"You should have seen how Lena got these ladies together when Joey was born." Patricia brushed a straggled curl from her forehead. "We got home from Anchorage and found we had meals for a week. I believe there's still some of Marie's goulash left in my freezer."

Marie set one fist on her hip with exaggerated exasperation. "I'm not sure how to take that, Patricia. But I'll tell you this." She wagged a finger at Ruth. "You want anything done, you put Lena in charge."

Lena tucked her chin and looked down at her hands like she deserved none of the praise. "The grace of the Lord," she said.

The stairs creaked, and the women turned almost as one, drawn up together in their admiration for Lena. "That better not be Felicia," Marie said. "I'll tan her hide if she's snuck out of the nursery again."

It wasn't Marie's little girl but a grown woman, not overly tall, square-built though in no way plump, a red scarf wrapped around her head. With effort, Lena launched from her seat. She scooted a chair from the wall and wedged it between her and Ruth. "Darla," she said. "I thought you were going to stay home and rest."

Darla's laugh shimmered like a lake lit with sun. "And miss seeing you old birds?" She folded into the chair and extended a hand toward Ruth. "You must be Kenny's friend. Welcome."

In her own moist palm, Ruth cupped Darla's hand, her skin translucent and blue-veined, like bone china held to the light.

"You're looking better today," said Marie.

"I look like shit," Darla said. Roxanne looked down at her Bible.

"That's no way to talk," Lena said.

"Cancer." Darla spoke squarely at Ruth. "Hideous disease. Why God allows it I'll never know."

"His ways aren't our ways," Lena said.

"I'm not looking for pity," Darla said.

"Of course not." Lena dabbed at the edge of her eye, as if a bit of dust had caused it to water.

"Ruth's got a girl the same age as Cara and Brody," said Cherise.

"They're living out on the island," said Roxanne.

"I see Nancy Slattery's letting those kids run wild now that the snow's gone," Marie said.

"Not to mention the dogs," Patricia said.

"Michele's thinking of leaving Larry," said Cherise.

"Again?" The older woman lifted a penciled eyebrow.

"Now Trish," Lena said. "It's not our place to judge." Nevertheless the talk grew lively over the bad state of things on the island, where apparently no one took care of their children or dogs and where leaving your spouse was commonplace. Though both her boys lived on the island, Lena nodded and murmured and offered her own complaint about someone called Fong who did who-knew-what behind his tall fence.

"I heard the troopers were asking about him again," Roxanne said.

"Last week an investigator stopped at the lodge," Cherise said. "Magda got all riled up."

"*You mind-a your-a busy-ness!*" Trish shook a finger in the air to go with the accent that must have been meant to be Magda's.

"She wouldn't," Marie said. "Not to a trooper."

"Maybe not," said Patricia. "But you know she wanted to."

"Tommy had to talk her down," Cherise said.

"Tommy," said Marie, with derision.

"Say what you want." Cherise twirled a finger around the inside of one of her big gold loop earrings. "Tommy can get Magda off a rant."

"You'll see, once you meet her," Marie said to Ruth.

"Tommy thinks she's just a little bit better than everyone else," said Patricia. "But then that's the island."

"A free spirit." Roxanne's sly laugh was like a contagion. Ruth laughed, too, while Darla looked into her coffee.

Finally Lena announced they'd better get started or the kids would be left waiting again after their groups let out. Twenty minutes had passed and though each Bible lay open, no one but Roxanne had glanced at the pages. Trish said a quick prayer and Roxanne punched the buttons on the TV, and Minerva Jones appeared on the screen, a smartly dressed woman who looked like she might have sold blenders.

Around the table the women seemed to relax into the authority of her voice. The theme of the lesson was the God of Second Chances, Minerva announced, and then launched into a prayer that went on for some time, a prayer in which she outlined for God's benefit the main points the lesson would cover. As Minerva prayed, Ruth ran once more through the names. Marie with her twins, one of them the nursery-sneaking Felicia. Patricia with Marie's hot dish languishing in her freezer. Trish with her eyebrows and her mocking of Magda, who owned the lodge on the highway. Cherise, who seemed young to be Cara's mother. Roxanne, who said *free spirit* like it was a curse. And Darla. She'd have no trouble with Darla, who with amused eyes nodded her scarf-wrapped head in time with the clack-clack of Minerva's high heels as she trotted across the screen.

The wet smell of ink, fluorescent hues streaked from felt-tipped pens, rose up as the women, other than Ruth, who had no highlighter, and Darla, who seemed indifferent, marked verse after verse at Minerva's direction. God was generous not just in second chances but in third, fourth, and fifth ones, she proclaimed. Then in a small TV miracle, she turned and looked straight at Ruth. "For someone who knew how to grab onto the chances God gave her," she said, "one need look no further than Ruth."

Ruth straightened, impressed by the smart way Minerva had said *one need look*. "Ruth had her husband," Minerva said. "And then he was gone. So God gave her Naomi. And through Naomi, God gave her Boaz, a wealthy man who would care for Ruth and Naomi all of their days. After gleaning what was left of his harvest, Ruth had only to lie at his feet. And then Ruth beget Obed who beget Jesse who beget David, and thus was the lineage of our Lord."

Ruth followed Lena's plump fingers, her nails painted pink like her pen, as she inked broad lines across the *begets*. A simple story, but it presented complications. Ruth wasn't sure how one gleaned, and the only picture that formed of her namesake was of a woman curled like a dog at the bottom of an old man's bed, content with the scraps he might toss.

This was a new concept to Ruth, the conscious decision to lie at the feet of a man. She had certainly never considered such a thing with Richard. Perhaps matters would have turned out differently if she had. But she'd been too busy scraping by, working all day and at night fixing up the big old house they'd purchased for a song. And then there was Sylvie, the reason they'd married in the first place, though of course they'd also fancied themselves in love. Richard quickly turned restless, unhappy with his job supplying parts to testy owners who took personal affront at the poor performance of their vehicles. His boss didn't appreciate him, and there was no upward mobility in Pine Lake.

Richard's dissatisfaction with his job seemed to roll straight onto Ruth. He complained she lacked the spark she once had. She no longer met his standards in bed, though when pressed, Richard couldn't say exactly what else he wanted except that she spice things up between the sheets. At odd moments he'd blow up at her, with Sylvie and later with Anna tucked into bed and Ruth wanting only to sleep. He'd shout about how she didn't wear the baby-doll things he bought her for Christmas, flounced and see-through and red. She tried to point out that his criticism did little to help her feel sexy, but she'd get tangled up in her words and most often it ended with Richard calling her frigid, at which point she'd dissolve into tears. And sometimes she was just so tired. Bone tired. Dog tired. Tired in the most unoriginal ways.

Though Richard's accusations were mostly predictable in their content, Ruth never got good at seeing them coming. Once in awhile he'd add a new twist. "Maybe somebody tried something with you when you were little," he suggested one night. "Maybe you suppressed it."

When Ruth said no, nothing like that had ever happened, he accused her of denial, saying if she'd own up maybe she could be a real woman in bed. That brought on tears, which fueled Richard's anger. Eventually he'd move on to sex, the kind intended, she supposed, to be both raw and healing. It seemed to do the trick for Richard but left Ruth feeling hollowed out like a pumpkin, her flesh scooped and tossed, leaving only limp, sticky strings.

The tirades increased. Still they never failed to surprise her. Richard complained when she wouldn't trade him helping with housework for sex, an idea he'd heard on talk radio, one that made her feel cheap. He brought home magazines with articles like "Twenty Ways to Multiple Orgasms" and "Fifteen Ways to Blow Your Guy's Mind—and Other Parts" and got mad when she shuffled them to the bottom of the magazine rack. She took to wearing old nightshirts and flannels to bed, putting them on in the bathroom to avoid Richard's stares.

The problem was that she had tried, really tried, with Richard and also with the children, researching the safety of car seats and walkers and jump-up toys and grinding cooked carrots and beets, shunning processed baby foods. As she clutched Sylvie fiercely to her chest, she'd discovered unexpected devotion in her dark little eyes, devotion that sustained Ruth through a long run of challenges that included paying a good share of the bills, because parts work wasn't exactly a gold mine. Ruth developed a knack for concealing her doubts, not that it mattered in the end.

As Minerva Jones expounded on the virtues of the Bible woman who had submitted to Boaz, Ruth pictured Mirabelle, curvy and blonde, knees scrunched to her breasts, her head nestled up against Richard's toes. With the girls, Ruth had made a firm pact. Mirabelle's name was not to be mentioned. It wasn't Sylvie but Anna who questioned this. What about their father, she wanted to know. Ruth said of course they could mention their father whenever they liked, but Mirabelle wasn't part of their lives, and sometimes it was necessary to shut certain doors on the past. For the rest of that day, Anna had created reasons not to say Mirabelle's name, stopping with Mira- and Mir- and then looking to her mother to make sure she'd noticed.

Before Ruth could shuffle her thoughts back to Boaz and the Ruth who lay at his feet, the TV credits were rolling. Lena pressed a button and the screen went blank. "Isn't it glorious, the way God never gives up?" she asked.

Ruth straightened, afraid she was about to be called to account, quizzed on verses she would never be able to find. But the TV magic of Minerva Jones had made her invisible. Lena and Marie, Patricia and Cherise, Roxanne and Trish, even Darla—they chattered back and forth across the table like Ruth wasn't there, about second chances and third ones and fourths, and there was no laughing or mocking of people Ruth had yet to meet. They read from the notes they'd jotted in margins between highlighted verses and flipped from chapter to chapter, restating the ways in which God was ever-patient and present and ready to wander in search of lost sheep. Ruth envied them all their answers. It seemed their God had assembled himself right there in that room, invisible and yet large in his ability to work everything out for the best, regardless of how bad things might seem, a mighty force that could muscle through any sort of difficulty.

"God is good," Cherise said.

"Amen," Lena said, and around the table, Bibles thumped shut.

Ruth relaxed into her chair. Perhaps her name was less problem than promise, for what was God but a better-formed version of fate, one that in wisdom had set things up so a woman had only to lie at the feet of a man and she'd be cared for all of her days. Ruth might not have considered such a thing, but she could. She could do anything, be anyone here.

"Hugh's wife—what was her name?" With a start, Ruth realized Marie was speaking to her.

The rocking horse loomed large in her remembrance. "Kenny never mentioned it," Ruth said.

"She was young," Darla said. "Sweet and pretty."

"She and Hugh fought like two moose in rut," Marie said.

"Never believed for one minute those two were married," said Roxanne.

"The little boy was a doll," said Patricia. "Even if she let him run wherever he wanted. Always some scrape on a knee or an elbow. It's a wonder he didn't end up in the river."

"Cynthia," Darla said. "That was her name. She grew quite the garden out there."

"Zucchini like trumpets," said Marie.

"Fat round cabbages, up to your knees." Cherise held her hand from the floor, to illustrate.

"Leafy red kale," Darla said. "Mounds of potatoes."

"Who's got potatoes?" A tall woman with short hair descended the stairs, a red-faced toddler on her hip.

The girl reached for Marie. "Mama."

Marie took the child, who stuck her thumb in her mouth and collapsed against her chest. "You remember Cynthia," she said. "On the island. Hugh's wife. Had that big garden."

"Used to bring around baskets of lettuce," the tall woman said. "That garden kept her out of Hugh's hair, which was blessing enough."

"I don't blame her for complaining," said Cherise. "Hugh's plane ate up all his money and time."

"She might have felt different," Darla said. "Once he was gone."

The tall woman thrust a hand at Ruth. "Kate," she said. "And you must be Ruth." She had dark hair, blunt-cut at the neck, and fast-blinking eyes. "Yes, everyone's talking. That's Resurrection. If you want to spade up that garden, I've got leftover seeds."

Marie unlatched Felicia's fist from her shirt. "A garden's the thing. Gets you out in the sun."

"*Lift up your eyes,*" Roxanne said. "*And look on the fields, for they are white already with harvest.*"

Where Ruth came from, white fields meant frost, and the harvest had better be already in. But she liked that the garden had caused Cynthia to be remembered with some fondness. She pictured Kenny's tall grass turned to dirt, fecund and black, and plants tamed in rows. She told Kate she'd love some seeds, and Lena offered to take her by on the way home from church to pick them up.

In the car, Anna named the Glory Girls she'd befriended, Mila and Hannah and Rachel. Ruth dragged from Sylvie a handful of one-word responses—yeah, no, and maybe—regarding what went on at youth group. Lena talked about having taken Darla to her most recent doctor's appointment in Anchorage, the horror of the oncologist's waiting room, silver-foiled wallpaper shot through with pale purple stripes, chairs the shade of a cheap Easter dress, carpet tinted like plastic lilacs baked too long in the sun.

"Her appointment was for two o'clock," Lena said. "We waited till forty-three minutes past. The receptionist could have cared less." The girl was too young for the job, she said, shiny black hair falling over a silk scarf tied like a headband, the silk also lavender, as if her primary function was to enhance the decor. "I told her we'd driven over two hours to get there. 'Good care can necessitate waiting.' That's all she said. She had no business working with the sick."

Ruth murmured her agreement.

"Scott would have blown a gasket." According to Lena, Darla's husband liked everything to line up his way, right now, and Darla's cancer threw a wrench into that.

Lena swung from the highway toward a big vinyl-sided colonial that with its white pillars and wrap-around deck and three-car garage could have been plucked from the east end of Pine Lake. "Kate's high-strung," Lena said as she shut off the car. "Maybe Kenny told you. Steven and Kate got married right out of high school. It only lasted two years. Kate wouldn't set foot in church back then. Now she's running the nursery and printing the bulletins and hanging begonias. She only converted for Roger. He's got the road contract up on Horn Mountain, and believe you me, they've got no shortage of cash." She relaxed into the seat. "Let go and let God, that's what I say. Steven's a lot better off. Kate always had some chore to keep him at home."

"Let go and let God," Ruth repeated.

Kate beckoned Ruth through the garage, past four snowmachines and two boats. The smell of gasoline seeped from red plastic jugs lined up along one wall. "Boys and their toys," Kate said.

On the far end of the garage was a work space hung with twice the cabinets Kenny had in his kitchen, sleek and tall, of shiny maple. Kate rummaged in one of the drawers. "I know those seeds are here somewhere." Her nails were slick and rounded with pearly pink polish, and her hair bobbed obediently at her neck, unlike Ruth's, which splayed at her shoulders, flat and untamed.

Ruth ran her fingers over the top of the workbench, smooth and slick with Formica. "Funny what a person takes for granted," she said.

Kate thrust a fistful of seed packets at Ruth. "I suppose Kenny's got plywood."

"We're thinking of tile," Ruth said.

Kate laughed. "I'm sure Kenny will get right on that. After he's shot his bear and the fish have quit running and the moose aren't in rut and he's tired of trapping."

No wonder she'd gotten on Lena's bad side. "Let go and let God," Ruth said. It slipped out like she'd been saying it all her life.

"That's one way to put it. Though I'd chalk it up mostly to the Prestons and their priorities. First and foremost, Mama's boys must have their fun." She grabbed a packet of sandpaper from the workbench and handed it to Ruth. "Sand, stain, and varnish. That's what I'd do with those counters. At least that way the plywood will clean."

Before Ruth could object, Kate had thrust on her a quart can of stain and a pint of varnish. "Keep you occupied while you wait on the garden to grow," she said. "Idle hands and all that."

"That's generous," Ruth said, "but I expect Kenny can find some."

"The trick's in the brush." Kate rummaged in a drawer and produced one. She feathered the bristles. "Ox hair. The best. You can bring it back Sunday."

She tucked the brush in Ruth's pocket. "Just don't let on that you expect Kenny to help. No sense getting off on the wrong foot with his mother."

Accumulation

The addition of ice and snow to a glacier system

I saw how Brody Prince looked at you." Cara snapped her gum and wore several layers of eye shadow, pink transitioning to purple, and she had a tarantula tattooed on her instep. In Pine Lake, Sylvie's mother would with one stern look have discouraged a friendship with someone like her. But here she couldn't say enough about Cara and her mother, who dressed in low-cut shirts like the ones sold at Flirty Girls in downtown Pine Lake, shirts that tried too hard to be trendy.

Sylvie sat beside Cara, high on a big erratic, a boulder left behind by the glacier. Fireweed bloomed at its base, bright fuchsia flowers halfway up the stalks. When it fully flowered, Cara said, winter was only six weeks off.

Sylvie tipped her face to the sun, warmth soaking into her skin. Beyond the rock, the river surged swift and relentless, thick with fine-grained silt.

"Don't tell me you haven't noticed," Cara said. "The way Brody stares."

"I guess." Sylvie rubbed her arms, dotted with goosebumps.

"You don't know how lucky you are," Cara said. "The new girl."

Don't get used to it, Sylvie wanted to tell her. *I won't last.* None of them would. You had only to see her mother's wariness around ordinary objects—the tea pot, the furnace, the stove—as if she'd lost the ability to detect danger and so had to watch for it in the most benign things.

Sylvie had begun coming each day to the river, where she felt no need to pretend that she was part of the church or the island or anything else. She traveled the rocks, her eyes on the glacier, not like her mother who turned quickly from it, as she did from Sylvie. She walked as far as she could along the bank, to the place where the river bent toward the ice and the path ended in a tangle of willows. She wanted to see the ice, up close. She wanted Kenny to take her. She imagined him shadowed by the glacier, the chill of it begging them close.

She blamed Nick for this. Barely out of high school himself, the youth group leader talked circles on the topic of purity in a way that made Sylvie almost wistful for health class and the smart-ass remarks about woodies, which the teacher ignored as she made every student roll a condom over the end of a broom, to feel how it was done. Poor earnest Nick had caused Sylvie to stare at the table while Cara traced suggestive images with her finger and Brody Prince messed with his bangs, acting like he could care less.

Nick urged them to come to the altar, where they might offer themselves up like the glassy-eyed mounts on Lena's wall. What he read from the Bible seemed suggestive. *The Word became flesh. As the deer panteth. I will lift up mine eyes to you.*

Cara tapped a pack of cigarettes against the warm, smooth stone and offered a smoke, which Sylvie refused. Cara drew in hard and blew smoke that disappeared in the sunlit air. She pointed the cigarette toward the wide, flat place where Anna ran with the dog. "Your sister sure likes that pooch." She flicked ashes into the water. "My mom never let me run like that when I was a kid. It was church and more church. Sunday school. Kids' Church. Sunday nights. Glory Girls."

"My mom's been busy," Sylvie said, not sure why she felt she had to defend her.

Cara laughed, showing strong, straight white teeth. "I wish mine had been busy."

A raven rode a thermal up the face of a cliff. The land felt more spare with each passing day, the forests and mountains and sky. *March-riever mighty.* The silt that thickened the river hid its depth. *Fen ond fæsten.*

Cara puffed on her smoke, then snubbed it out on the rock and tossed the butt in the water. "Thinking of Brody?" she asked, her smile sly.

Sylvie hugged her knees to her chest, cupping their warmth. "I don't know about Brody."

"The rest of us bore him. Like we're just on in the background. For noise. But you're different. A novelty."

Sylvie laughed. "Like an ice cream bar."

"It's an advantage." Cara jittered her fingers over the rock, her head tipped sideways toward the water. "I know you can't wait to get the hell out of here, but you might as well have some fun till you go. Besides, you can't leave too soon." Her mouth spread again in a smile. "Not till I make a church girl out of you."

Sylvie leaned back, exposed to the sky. "What's it like at the glacier?"

Cara swung her legs, thunking her heels on the rock. "Cold."

"I want to see it up close."

"Have Kenny take you," Cara said. "The rest of us, we have to pay." There were hard feelings all over about how Walter and Lena had tied up the one road to the glacier and then failed to draw enough tourists to benefit everyone else.

"You ever been up there?" Sylvie asked.

"On the ice? People die doing that. They get wedged in big cracks with no way to get out. A couple years back this one kid got stuck down so deep his clothes got torn off. Bare skin on ice." Cara shimmied, an exaggerated shiver, and pointed across the river at cliffs that weren't rock but hardened clay. "Used to be, there was a shortcut. You could cross the river right here, then hike to the glacier. Till some lady died."

She slid from the rock and set off through the brush, head down, searching. Sylvie liked this in Cara, how she did things without needing to talk them through first. Sharp-tipped branches scratched Sylvie's legs, their saw-toothed leaves hardened to a summer green, as she trudged behind Cara, trampling low oily-leafed plants and their tiny pink flowers, twin flowers, Kenny called them, because they hung in pairs, silent little bells. He knew things like that, the names of flowers, which plants you could eat.

Cara waded into a thick patch of willows. "It's here somewhere," she said. "The tram broke. That's how she fell."

The dog dropped its stick and bounded toward them, tail wagging wildly. Tess was its name, and its owner was Tommy, or so Kenny said. Except Cara, who worked with her at the lodge, no one had much good to say about Tommy, or about her dog.

"I always think I can find it," Cara said. "But it's never that easy."

Tess crashed through the willows, ears alert, muscles flexed. "You go around," Sylvie told Anna, who followed close on the dog.

Barrel-chested, Tess loped sideways toward a wide hunk of timber. "There it is." Cara nudged the dark, weathered wood with her toe. "What's left of the tram. They tore it down after she fell in."

"After who fell in?" Anna asked.

"It was a long time ago," Cara said. "Before you were born. This lady was trying to get to the glacier, which was stupid, because you can get there from Preston's, and I think she was some kind of relation, so she would've gotten in free."

Sylvie ran her hand over the rough grain of the wood. The timber was wide and deep and ten feet long at least. Bolts stuck out from one end. The other end was sheared off.

Anna held up a frayed cable. "What's this?"

"There were two of those wooden things, one on each side of the river. That cable stretched between them. There was a seat. And a pulley." Cara reached her arms, demonstrating how it worked. "You sat in the seat and pulled yourself along the cable and that's how you got across the river."

Had the woman dangled helplessly over the water, or had her fall been sudden and swift? Had her last sensation been cold or peace? Sylvie wanted to know.

Tess nudged Cara's hand with a stick, smoothed by the water and bleached by the sun. Cara grabbed onto it, but Tess refused to give up her hold.

"Stupid dog," Cara said in the affectionate tone Sylvie sometimes used with Anna. She let go, and Tess bolted off. Cara shielded her eyes, watching her run. "I better get home," she said. "Before Mom gets on my case."

Tess zigzagged back, high-stepping over clumps of weeds. "Sister Jean says you're a Glory Girl," Anna said.

"Sure I am." Cara grinned. "White dress, the works. You working on badges?"

"I'm starting with Memory," said Anna. Tess prodded her hand with the stick. "I have to learn fourteen verses. Then I'll work on Helper, and Attitude."

"Attitude. Good thing I wrapped that one up when I was your age," Cara said. "Mom wouldn't sign for it now."

"Sister Jean says if I work hard to catch up, I can get crowned with the other girls."

"That's cool. Then you and me, we'll have one on your sister."

"Sister Jean says you're never too old to be holy and pure," Anna said. Cara ground her toe in the dirt, squashing a half-dozen pink flowers.

They walked together to the bridge. Cara retrieved her bike, stashed under a tall leafy birch. "Keep at those badges." She thumped Anna's back, then straddled the bike. "There's no hope for your sister."

"We better get home," Sylvie said as they watched her ride off.

"I want to stay out here all day," Anna said.

"You know how Mom gets." It was always something. The glacier. The river. The bears.

Tess dashed in circles while Anna plodded after Sylvie. Out here she could barely recall Karen's laugh or Rick's smile or his shiny truck or the lake with its placid warm water. She kicked at the gravel, swirling up dust that caught in the light. Even when you had your back to it, the sound of the river never faded. Tess found a hunk of driftwood, not a stick but a branch, weathered and gnarled and nearly too big for her mouth. She latched onto it, trotting ahead, the branch off center, pulling her head to one side. Wings wide, a hawk spiraled overhead, square-faced and speckled brown. Tess dropped the branch and jumped and snapped at the air.

With a slow whoosh of wings, the bird turned toward the river. Tess stood, tail erect, muscles twitching, and whined as it disappeared. "Come on, Tess!" Anna called.

"Don't encourage her," Sylvie said. "Kenny hates it when she follows you home."

"Kenny's not the boss," Anna said. Tess planted herself in front of Anna, ears up, expectant.

"It's his house," Sylvie said.

"You like Kenny better than me."

"Don't be stupid," Sylvie said. "I feel sorry for him, that's all, stuck with us. Now tell that dog to go home."

Anna screwed up her face, ready to argue. "Attitude," Sylvie said. "What would Sister Jean say?"

Anna hesitated, then raised her hand and pointed up the road. "Go home," she said sharply. "Go home."

Tess jumped and snapped at Anna's pointing finger. "Go home," she repeated.

"Never mind," Sylvie said. "Let's go."

"I don't want to get Tess in trouble," said Anna as the dog bounded toward Kenny's driveway. "Do something," Anna pleaded. "Make her go home."

"I can't make her do anything."

"Please." She looked ready to cry.

"It's your fault she's here in the first place."

"I can't help that she likes me."

"Of course not," Sylvie said. It was always like this with Anna. Half-heartedly, Sylvie called to the dog. To her surprise, Tess trotted toward her, though she stopped well out of reach, daring Sylvie to make her come closer.

Sylvie crouched, extending her hand. "Come on," she urged in her sweetest voice. Tess moved toward her, stepping high, eyes wary. "That's a good girl," Sylvie coaxed, feeling almost affectionate, since the dog seemed to trust her. Her markings were beautiful, streaks of black against brown, tiger-like. "That's a girl, that's a girl." Sylvie made a rhythm of it, the way she had as a child, her secret way of wishing.

Tess hesitated, head down, and then slunk almost within reach. Sylvie lunged, hoping to grab her by the neck.

The dog took off. "Bitch." Sylvie got up and brushed her hands on her jeans. "Get yourself shot, for all I care."

"Kenny wouldn't shoot her," said Anna. "Would he?"

"I didn't say he would." But he did kill things. *As the deer panteth.* Sylvie grabbed Anna by the shoulders and steered her toward the house. "Ignore Tess. Don't look back."

Anna shook out of her grasp. "You hate me."

"I don't hate you." She was about to point out that such accusations weren't fit for a Glory Girl when Tess barked, urgent and loud.

Sylvie grabbed Anna again by the shoulders. "I said don't look. She just wants attention."

The barking exploded. "Something's wrong." Anna twisted to see.

"She's got a squirrel or a vole." Sylvie nudged her sister forward. "That's all."

"She never barks like that," Anna insisted.

"Attitude," Sylvie said.

"It might be a bear."

"Bears hang out in the woods. Not on the flats by the river."

"Maybe no one told that to the bear," Anna said. Tess lunged and jumped, fixed on a big bush, a tangle of branches. "She's gonna make it mad."

"There's no bear," Sylvie said, though the bush looked large enough for a grizzly to hide in, teeth bared, claws ready to swipe.

"What if it gets Tess? What if it comes after us?"

"I told you, there's no bear." She let go of Anna and started for the bush.

"You're not supposed to do that," Anna said. "You're supposed to leave bears alone."

From the river, wind thrummed Sylvie's hair across her face. "Stay there," she said. "I'll distract her."

A musky smell came from the bush, like autumn back home, leaves ground into dirt. "Tess!" Sylvie called. "Tess! Come here. Good girl."

Tess nosed the bush and barked louder. The smart thing would be to walk backward, slowly, to the house, to get Kenny and his gun.

Threads of salvia dangled from Tess's bared teeth. She lunged at the branches, then yelped, springing back.

"Do not run," Sylvie called back to Anna. It was all she knew for sure about bears, that running switched on their predator instinct. She moved backward, slowly, one step and then another, arms out, shielding her sister.

Tess whined. She trotted around the bush, eying it. She shook her head side to side and whined again.

"Stay here," Sylvie warned her sister. She moved slowly toward Tess.

No blood. No torn flesh. Only what looked like a fresh set of whiskers. "Porcupine," Sylvie said.

Anna ran to Tess and flung her arms around her neck as the dog wagged her tail, the picture of obedience. She shook her head back and forth like she had a tic, and when in a burst of affection she tried to lick Anna, Sylvie saw a quill was stuck in her tongue.

"I'll take her home," Anna said.

"Tess can take herself home."

Anna clung to Tess's neck. "She won't go by herself." Again Tess shook her head, so violently that Anna was forced to let go. The dog trotted at an angle, away from the house, twisting and flicking her head.

"Tell Mom I'll be careful," Anna said.

"Fantastic," Sylvie said as Anna trotted after Tess. "Lovely." An interrogation would follow, from her mother, about the bears and the river and now Anna off to see Tommy, of whom not even Kenny approved.

Scuffing rocks, Sylvie glanced at the house, and then at the shop. When she'd left the house, Kenny had been out in the shop, cleaning a fifty-five-gallon drum to use for his bear bait.

He'd laugh when she told him what happened, how the porcupine had fooled her into thinking it was a bear. Sylvie had every reason to tell him first, before her mother found out. Every reason.

Mass Balance

The sum of accumulation and loss

W ell before time to wake, an insistent pounding roused Ruth, a steady, primal beat. Rain, she lay thinking, but then she opened her eyes to the morning sun pouring across Kenny's chest and onto her pillow, and she realized of course it was only the river thrashing about at its banks. She threw one arm over her face and curved her back against Kenny so she could feel each breath drawn and exhaled, little puffs of sleep.

Pivotal moments played through her mind, moments from which there had been no second chances. Her response to Richard's first kiss, eager and willing. Giving in when her mother insisted daisies were too simple for weddings; to this day, the heavy smell of lilies made Ruth feel sick. The ice, sucking air from her lungs.

No, not the ice.

Kenny rolled to his back, dreaming she imagined of bear, rooting and scrounging in his barrel of sweets. She edged out of bed, quiet so as not to disturb him, and slipped on her robe. In the kitchen, she mixed pancake batter, the same brand Lena used, requiring only water and mix. It bubbled in circles on the griddle, releasing the sweet smell of flour and grease.

Hair tousled from sleep, Kenny came downstairs. "Morning, sunshine." He wrapped his arm around her waist and kissed her cheek. "Those look delicious." He slathered butter and doused the pancakes with syrup and proclaimed them just like his mother's. Though Ruth didn't care much for pancakes, she poured two little circles for herself.

She'd never thought herself especially important in her work. The women she'd known in college—not that they were close friends, once she and Richard were married—got jobs as accountants and teachers and engineers. But at the school, Phil Scranton had depended on her, and the teachers had, too, to keep things running smoothly. She'd been someone there.

She doused the hotcakes with syrup and washed them down with coffee. "I thought we could start on the countertops." She took Kenny's plate. "You sand, and I'll stain."

"I've gotta get up to Magda's." Though he wiped a napkin at the edges of his mouth, a drop of syrup still glistened in his beard. "She's been saving old pastries. Forget Steven's barrel of fish guts. The trick is fresh bait. By tonight my stand'll be crawling with bears. Be a sweetheart, would you, and fill one of those go-cups with coffee."

Of course he could pour his own coffee. She could say so.

She filled a Qwik Mart mug and snapped on the lid. He pulled away in his truck, stirring up dust from the gravel. She felt foolish and sad, clinging to a vision of the two of them lingering over their coffee like two old married people.

She pumped water from the well, working her arms, feeling strong, then poured water from the blue plastic jug into the kettle and lit the burner, an easy routine. Change presented opportunities. This was what Sylvie had to learn. An entire day ahead, with any number of ways to fill it. A book, a walk, the countertops, the garden.

She took her time with the dishes, and when the leftover water had cooled, she poured it from the kettle over her head in a rush, then sudsed and rinsed until her hair squeaked clean. She dumped the gray-water bucket in back of the house, the wind scattering her damp hair. An adventure. That's what she'd told everyone back in Pine Lake, though Gloria, the attendance secretary, had refused to believe it. Caught up as she was in who was absent for which reasons and which notes had been forged, she couldn't understand why anyone would leave their little town, and if they did, why they'd go someplace as cold and remote as Alaska.

Birds flitted tree to tree in a flutter of wings, flashing red, brown, white. She listened for the calls Kenny had taught her, the thrush and the wren and the kinglet, but the birds all sounded different in the mornings. Though the sun shone bright, the shadowed cliffs on the far side of the river seemed to accuse her, and the trees huddled in an unwelcome way.

You had to let go. Trust fate. Learn the comfort of your own company.

Overhead, the shudder of a small plane broke the quiet. She wondered what Marie might be doing, or Patricia or Cherise, though they were hardly her friends. She longed even for cable news, the same channels she'd once shunned, indignant at the righteous banter.

She had never considered herself a social person, certainly not an extrovert of any kind, and yet as she hauled from the shop freezer a hunk of frozen salmon, its skin dull with frost, and set it to thaw in the sink, she hungered for the gossip of the faculty lounge, for Phil Scranton's slow drawl even, and for the Piggly Wiggly, where you could brush past other adults, with no need to converse, only to share the same space.

She woke the girls, their schedules warped by the light that never fully went away. She made more pancakes, cracking the window to free the house from the smell. Anna announced that she'd get to work on her Glory Girl badge, right after breakfast. "Mila has ten," she said. "It only takes twelve to get crowned."

Crowning was the ultimate goal of a Glory Girl. They earned badges, and when their sashes were full, they walked the aisle at the church to receive their tiaras. Each chapter of the Glory Girls workbook featured a virtue—diligence, cheerfulness, manners, helpfulness, grace—followed by a checklist of Bible reading and projects, like Girl Scouts, but with religion. Indoctrinating, yes, but who could argue with diligence, cheerfulness, manners? And Ruth herself had a workbook, the *Minerva Jones Life Study*, with a lesson to be prepared in advance of the next meeting of the Ladies Circle.

"I need a white dress," Anna said. "For the crowning. Mila's mother made hers."

"When the time comes, we'll get one in town. First, you work on your badges." With a fresh start, you had to be open to new things. Plus there was this day to fill, and the next, and the next.

Sylvie came downstairs, still in the sweats she had slept in, her hair untouched by a brush. Ignoring the pancakes, she poured reconstituted milk over a bowl of corn flakes.

"You don't understand one word of that." This she directed at her sister, bent over the Bible she'd borrowed from church.

"Do too." Anna pointed to her open workbook, an illustration of a blue badge with a flame embroidered at its center. "*There appeared tongues like fire, that sat upon them.*"

"Like anyone believes that."

"Mom," Anna said. "Sylvie's interrupting."

Ruth wiped the last bowl from the dish drainer and deposited it in the cupboard. Once she'd let the dishes drip dry. There hadn't been time for anything else.

"Explain it. How fire sits on you without burning you up."

"I don't have to," said Anna. "I just have to remember. It's in Acts chapter two, verse three."

Sylvie lifted her bowl delicately, like a tea cup, and drank the dregs. "This powdered milk's nasty."

"It just takes getting used to," Ruth said. "In some ways it's better. Less fat."

"Better like washing my hair with a bucket?" Sylvie asked. "Like taking a crap in the outhouse?"

"That's enough. We're all in this together."

"That's not how I remember it," Sylvie said. "I remember being told. *We're moving to Alaska.*"

It was one of Richard's favorite maneuvers, bringing up old accusations. "You can choose to resent that forever." Ruth spoke in a deliberate, firm tone. "Or you can choose to let it go."

Because Anna's workbook advised that activity aided memory, she ran up and down the stairs like she was at boot camp, repeating "The Lord is my strength," and "In whom shall I fear?," a terror of motion that dizzied Ruth. She thumbed the pages of the Minerva Jones workbook as she considered sanding the countertops, mowing the yard, planting her garden. Tomorrow, she resolved. Or the next day, or the next. They marched before her in endless succession, a little army of days.

When Kenny came home, Sylvie slunk from her room and perched on the top step, watching as he toed off his boots and shrugged off his flannel shirt, revealing a sweat-splotched tee shirt beneath. At the sink he poured water from a pitcher and scrubbed his hands and splashed water over his face, then wiped his hands, leaving large wet streaks on the towel. "Screw Steven and his fish," he said. "Every bear in this valley's gonna come in after my pastries." He swung Ruth into his arms. "You and me, we'll kill us a bear."

Giddy as she'd felt on their first date, Ruth slid into the truck next to Kenny, leaving the dinner dishes behind. The wind-rippled grass, the weathered walls of the shed, the curve of the driveway toward the road—all of it spoke encouragement. From the highway, Kenny turned onto a narrow road that turned quickly to dirt. Growing tall between the wheel ruts, grass and weeds thumped underneath as the truck rolled over them. Fresh-leaved branches brushed the windows and dust filtered in through the vents, swirling in sunlight that flickered in and out through the trees.

Where the road ended, Kenny parked in a forest of aspen and spruce, and together they tromped up a muddy four-wheeler trail. Kenny talked again of the all-terrain vehicle he planned to build, once he got his bear. With eight wheels, it would go where four-wheelers couldn't, riding easily over slick mud like this in which Ruth had already slipped, catching herself on the branch of a willow. As the trail rose, her sleeves clung sweaty to her arms. She peeled off her jacket and tied it around her waist, determined to prove herself both tough and flexible.

Mosquitoes poured from the woods, enticed by her glistening flesh. They hovered in fierce swarms, pricking at tender spots on her wrists and her forearms and at the base of her neck. In front of her face she waved the baseball cap she'd borrowed from Kenny, but that only encouraged the mosquitoes to regroup and attack from new angles. She slapped her neck and her arms, leaving streaks of blood where the fat ones had lingered, too bloated to make their escape.

While she scrunched her eyes and held her breath, Kenny sprayed her up and down with repellant that smelled like paint thinner masked over with pine. After that the mosquitoes hovered at a respectful distance, and Ruth determined they would not spoil the evening. Chickadees called from the woods, one of the birds she recognized by sound. Other calls she'd never heard. A buzzed nasal, *seek-a-da-da*. A sharp whistle. A deep-throated cackle that seemed almost human. Kenny named them for her, the dark-eyed junco, the king's thrush, the raven.

They veered off the trail and hiked through the brush to the top of a hill. Wedged next to a thick, gray cottonwood tree was Kenny's bait barrel. "Had a hell of a time getting it in here," he said. "Steven drives right up to his stand. But you watch. I'll get my bear first."

Ruth leaned over, hands on her knees, panting and warm but exhilarated. Nowhere near Pine Lake could you hike for an hour without hearing a truck on the highway or coming up on a barbed-wire fence. She climbed up the tree behind Kenny, on weathered slats nailed to the trunk, the sweet smell of pastries wafting from the barrel below. Kenny helped her onto a plywood platform braced by branches and wooden struts. There they huddled, backs against the tree, breathing the scent of spruce mixed with sugar. A trill pierced the low-slung sky. "Kinglet," said Kenny. Ruth touched the back of his hand. *Kinglet.*

"Nothing feels quite like a bear coming up on your bait." Kenny rubbed his hand over the top of Ruth's thigh. "Your heart pounds and your skin tingles and you get dizzy, thinking what might happen next." She saw how the sun caught his lashes and half-whispered she knew something like that, and he bent to kiss her like he knew it too.

At a rustle he straightened and lifted his .300 magnum, scanning it slowly like a searchlight from one end of the horizon to the other. He breathed hard and deep, and it seemed to Ruth that the forest breathed too. A shuffling came again from the weeds, causing her breath to catch. But it was only a quivering hare, haunches still half-white from winter. Kenny fixed his sights on it, then lowered the gun as the hare bounded out of range. "Tasty," he said. "But stringy this time of year." She let this knowledge sink in, of hares and their texture and taste.

After an hour of watching and waiting and slapping mosquitoes, the smell of old doughnuts and grease from the drum began to make feel her queasy. Forgetting how a bear could sneak up anytime, she asked Kenny when they might leave. He glanced at her sideways and whispered she'd better be quiet or the bears would be spooked.

Chastened, she sat as the sun shrank behind the white-streaked mountains, knees stiffening, legs chilled through her jeans. She stuffed her hands in her pockets and as Kenny stared into the woods, she considered all she had fallen in love with. The edge of his chin. The blue of his eyes. The way his hands made her feel young.

There had been others, after Richard. Not bent on proving anything to anyone other than herself, she'd dated slyly, outside of Pine Lake. There was

Leon, the crop-dusting pilot she met in a coffee shop after a doctor's appointment in Gainesville. Dark-eyed, thick-skinned, smelling faintly of the chemicals he dumped from his plane, he was lean and hard and a little rough in
bed. He expected nothing from Ruth, though he said it might be nice to see
her again. So she feigned a half-dozen doctor's appointments, scooting out
of school after the last bell had rung and getting herself home in time to fix
the girls a late supper.

After Leon came James, a lanky runner she met at the park by the
Gainesville River, and Charles, who manned the Gainesville Library ref-
erence desk and coddled aspirations of writing a novel that would expose
Midwestern life the way Sinclair Lewis had. These were casual relationships,
the kind Richard would never have believed her capable of, and yet each one
in its own unfortunate way brought Richard to mind: the limp lips of Charles
when he kissed and the way James complained about work and Leon's eager
eyes as he watched her clothes slide to the floor. Kenny had none of these
flaws. He kissed hard and he had no boss to hound him and he liked making
love in the dark.

Ruth drew her knees to her chest and shifted quietly on the cold planks
of the wooden platform as the shadows merged into one dark mass and the
mosquitoes fell away in the cold.

"Guess they caught our scent," Kenny said finally. "You ready to go?"

She nodded slightly, so as not to give away her large longing for bed, the
sheets tucked at the corners, the blanket heavy and warm, the old chenille
bedspread a comfort even. Kenny stood, a dark silhouette against the trunk
of the tree. "Let them feast a few days." He reached his hand to help her up.
"That grease will make them slow. Lazy."

It was past midnight by the time they got back to the truck, with Ruth
never so glad for the forced warm air from a heater, though proud too that
she'd never once complained of the cold.

Arete

A jagged, narrow ridge of ice, like a backbone

It was a time of waiting, driven by Kenny. They all got caught up in it—Sylvie, her mother, and Anna—watching as his truck rattled down the driveway each evening, and listening for its return hours later, materializing out of the blue twilight. The only one who'd been allowed to go with him was Sylvie's mother, and that happened only once. Baiting bear was serious business.

Sylvie was lying awake, listening to the rush of the river, when Kenny's truck returned earlier than usual. Looking down from the window, she saw the huge lump of fur in the back. She felt as she had at the bonfire, on the edge of something, a tight ball forming in her stomach. She put on her jacket and ran her brush through her hair, the bristles prickling her scalp.

Across the room, Anna stirred. "What time is it?"

"Late. You should be sleeping." A bird warbled from a birch branch that swayed near the window. A junco, or maybe a kinglet. Kenny knew them, the birds, by their songs, which were different at morning and night, like he knew the bears, what they liked to eat, how they grunted and sniffed, their poor eyesight.

As Sylvie slipped outside, her mother rushed past her to roll up the overhead door. Kenny backed the truck close, then hopped out and dropped the tailgate. "No more freezer-burnt fish," he said, and though the light was dim it seemed he winked, not so much at her mother as at Sylvie, who only that evening had shoved to the side of her plate the baked salmon that her mother had fixed with dried onions and parsley, an attempt to disguise the stale freezer taste.

The mound of old pastries and the .300 magnum had worked like a dream. While the bear wallowed in sweets, Kenny said, he'd sighted in on its chest and fired a clean shot straight through, the bear staggering twenty yards before it hit the dirt.

"It's beautiful," Sylvie's mother said, though she leaned away from the bear as she said it. *Beautiful* wasn't the right word at all, though it might once have been, when the bear was alive, lumbering through the brush, snout in the air, enticed by the pastries.

Having followed Sylvie out, Anna scrambled onto the truck's bumper and leaned over the tailgate to stroke the bear's claws. "So big," she said.

On tiptoe, Sylvie reached to set her hand on the bear's chest. She curled her fingers into its fur, feeling where the heart once had beaten. In the waning light, the fur glistened, sticky and clumped and thick with the smell of blood.

"If all of us lift," Kenny said, "she'll slide out nice and easy." His instructions seemed to puzzle Sylvie's mother, who looked at everything but the bear, even as she eased her hands underneath it. On Kenny's count of three, they heaved together until the bear with a powerful thump landed on the sheet of plywood laid out on the floor of the shop.

"Gotta get this thing out of its skin." He shut the overhead door, to keep out mosquitoes. "Meat goes bad fast from the fat."

"You girls get back to bed now," said their mother.

"We'll get it tanned for a rug," Kenny said. "You girls can roll around on it, once winter comes."

"Back to bed," said their mother. "Now."

Neither one moved—not Anna, not Sylvie. Kenny honed a knife back and forth over a sharpening stone, releasing a metallic smell that heightened the smell of the blood. He centered the blade over the bear's chest. Sylvie's mother grabbed Anna by the shoulder and spun her to the side as Kenny buried the knife in the fur. The blade made a faint whooshing sound as it sliced through the skin.

Blood poured through the fur to the floor. Anna twisted out of her mother's hands and scrunched her nose. "It stinks."

"You should smell the guts." Kenny peeled back a section of skin. A clump of jelly-like fat dripped from the knife. "Lucky for you, I dumped those in back in the woods."

"That's enough," said their mother. "It's way past your bedtime."

"Let them watch," Kenny said. "They might as well see what it looks like before it lands on their plates." He handed their mother a butcher knife. "Start with stew meat." He deposited a bloody chunk of meat on the plywood. "Cut it in cubes, like you get at the grocery."

He peeled back more skin. The carcass looked almost human, all muscle and bones. In the air hung the dank odor of fur, fat, and skin. "Better get at it," he said.

"I'll do it if you won't." Sylvie longed to touch the warm flesh.

"I was just deciding where to start." Her mother positioned herself between Sylvie and the bear. Blood pooled as she sliced the meat in half and then quarters. From each quarter, she cut small, precise cubes. With the back of her hand, she swiped away a strand of hair that had dropped to her forehead.

"That blood makes you look like the angel," Anna said. "Like in the Bible. The angel of death marked them so they wouldn't get killed." She nudged Sylvie. "See. I understand."

"This isn't a show," Sylvie's mother said. "You girls don't need to stand around watching."

"You don't have to cut the pieces that small." Kenny set another slab of meat on the board to be sliced. "Some we'll grind up. Bear sausage. Wait till you taste it." He waved his knife toward the workbench. "One of you girls want to fetch those plastic bags?"

"Me!" Anna rushed to the workbench. Sylvie sat back against a sawhorse, watching as Kenny maneuvered his knife around the bear's ribs.

With the bags, Anna leaned over the plywood. "My hands are a mess," said their mother. On her face was the same grim determination as when she hauled the over-filled gray-water bucket out back to dump it. "Set them down over there, on the other side of the meat."

Instead of going around, Anna reached across and let go of the bags. A splotch of blood spread across the front of her nightgown.

Their mother set down her knife. "Look at you." She held her hands out, bloodied and useless for anything except butchering.

Anna's face crumpled as she looked down at her chest. "My favorite nightgown."

"We'll wash it." With her knee, their mother nudged Anna's leg. "Get going. Inside. We've got to get that rinsed with cold water, or the stain will never come out."

"Looks like it's up to you, Sylvie." Kenny nodded at the knife her mother had abandoned.

The flesh was warm, entirely as Sylvie had expected. So big, so feared, the bear was easily diminished. As she sliced its flesh, her hands turned sticky and wet with blood. What would Karen think of her now, and Rick?

As Kenny carved at the bear, he pointed out which parts made the best steaks and which were good only for stew. What Sylvie wanted to know was whether the bear had seen him before he pulled the trigger. Whether it had been alone or in the company of some other bear, some companion.

She sliced and sliced, steel on flesh, piling chunks of bear on the plywood as outside the twilight deepened.

"Better start wrapping." Kenny went to the workbench, blood splatting from his hands to the floor, and tossed her a rag. "Be sure to press the air out."

She wiped her hands and with the tips of her fingers eased open a bag and dumped in a load of chunked meat. She tried to think of something to say, something to show that she was worthy of his attention.

Outside, a truck door slammed. Steven came in through the man-door. "I'll be damned." He circled the plywood, peering over the bloodied bones and the rumpled fur. "Cleve told me you hauled out a big one."

"Pushing three hundred pounds." With the back of his hand, Kenny nudged the brim of his hat. "Told you. Sugar, not fish."

"If it weren't for Scott Prince, I'd have had mine by now. Bastard moved in on my stand. Best spot in the valley. He don't know who he's messing with."

"He knows." Kenny wriggled his hand between the bear's ribs and extracted a glistening lump that he held out to Sylvie. "The best part," he said. "The heart." He let go, and with a splat the heart landed on the board.

Steven laughed. "You'd think it was still beating, from the look of her."

Sylvie's face flushed. Steven shoved his hands in his pockets. "Scott Prince'll be sorry he ever laid eyes on my bear stand."

Kenny nodded at the heart, still oozing blood. "Better double bag that."

"I'll get him good. Gonna hook his bait barrel up to my tow truck and drag it out to the road."

"He'll know who did it," Kenny said.

"Course he'll know," Steven said. "That's the point."

Sylvie nudged the heart with the back of her finger, then using both hands scooped it up, slippery and soft, and stuffed it into a big plastic bag.

"You watch," Steven said. "Scott Prince will be sorry."

For breakfast, Kenny fried up the bear heart with onions. Her mother cut her slice into tiny pieces and ate each one with a forkful of onions, swallowing fast. Sylvie ate cereal.

Steven made good on his threat, dragging Scott Prince's bait barrel out to the road. Scott wasn't sorry the way Steven predicted. He was pissed. When he discovered his bait barrel tipped on the side of the highway, dented and dinged, he called the troopers.

To sort everything out, the troopers set up a meeting at the school. The classroom was put up for summer—paper taped over the shelves, the teacher's desk empty, the shades half-drawn over the glacier. Like every school out of season, it felt weighed down by routines that could be interrupted but never put completely to rest. The building was tiny, a quarter of the size of the grade school in Pine Lake. There were only three classrooms, one for kindergarten through fourth grades, one for fifth through eighth, and one for high school, because Resurrection Valley had only forty-three students.

The middle-grade room was half full by the time they arrived, mostly adults but also kids with their families, a lot of the same ones that spent Wednesdays at church. Kenny steered Sylvie's mother toward where Lena and Walter sat, squeezed into student desks. His long face half-hidden under his NRA cap, Walter nodded as they took their seats. On the rare occasions when Sylvie had seen him, he'd been bent over the newspaper at Lena's kitchen table, and when he looked up it was with surprise, as if he'd forgotten who they were, her mother and Anna and her. Whenever Lena spoke, he gave little sign that he'd heard. This event might be worth it, just to hear him say a full sentence.

Anna scooted onto the floor near some kids she hung out with at church, her friend Mila and Kate's daughter Reagan. Sylvie slid around a cluster of desks to where Cara sat, lit by a half-blinded window, looping a long strand of hair over her finger. "You got out of work," Sylvie said.

"Closed up early." Cara nodded at Magda, who hovered by the door, her gray-streaked hair pulled tight in a ponytail. "It's not every day we get this kind of excitement."

As people shuffled into the classroom, so did the smells. Dirt. Gasoline. Fried foods. Sylvie counted thirty adults, and still they kept coming. They leaned against tables and walls, as if taking a seat meant too large a commitment. Tommy bent over Patricia's baby, who was decked out in overalls and a little blue cap, Patricia clenching the back of the stroller as Tommy—Kenny had pointed her out once, from the road—touched her hand to the baby's fat cheek. Standing wide-legged, Cleve Baker had Pastor Tom backed in a corner, pitching some scheme. Magda waved her hands, talking wild and fast at Cara's mom. Church people filed by the Prestons. They smiled and offered their hands as if passing through at a funeral.

Wearing stiff jeans and a grim little smile, Scott Prince arrived. A uniformed trooper followed, pasty and plump, holding one hand to his belt like it needed assistance. The holstered gun, the polished boots, the badge—all of it made everyone straighten. The church people flocked together in the chairs, while islanders held up the wall in the back. It was easy to tell them apart. The church men folded their hands at their waists, and their women wore make-up. Patricia, who Sylvie's mother said was a little too nosy. Thin, stooping Marie, a nag if ever there was one, according to Lena. Cara's mother, Cherise, her eyelids shimmered in pink shadow and outlined in black. Kate, who got no slack from Lena.

"Look who's headed your way." Cara only half-hid her smile.

Brody Prince slunk past the Prestons, his eyes on the floor. He hoisted a desk in the air and thunked it down next to Cara and Sylvie. He slumped in his chair, a bored look settling over his face.

"Your mom couldn't make it?" Cara asked.

"She's not feeling so hot." Brody stared at the top of his desk.

"Sorry to hear it," Cara said.

Steven nudged Kenny, who looked over at Sylvie sitting right next to Scott Prince's kid. She inched closer to Brody. His eyes flitted toward hers, his fingers tracing a spot where the veneer had peeled back from the desktop.

The trooper leaned against the big teacher's desk. He glanced at one of the glacier-filled windows like he couldn't wait to hop in his car and drive back to town. Quiet rippled through the room. "I don't know about you folks," he said, "but the last place I want to be on a nice night like this is a schoolroom. Brings back some unfortunate memories. Homework, tests, after-school detention."

There were a few smiles and nods and lots of shifting in seats. "So let's get this done as quick as we can," said the trooper. "First, a few regulations."

Pastor Tom jutted a finger into the air. "If we may, sir. I'd like to open with prayer."

Murmuring came from the back wall where the islanders stood. The trooper's face reddened. "This is state business."

"It won't take but a minute to honor the Lord," Pastor Tom said. "Those who don't want to join in can just shut their ears."

"Maybe after we're finished," the trooper said.

Pastor Tom squeezed his eyes shut. "Dear Father of fathers," he began in his preacher's inflection. "God of all gods, creator of all that is in and around us." Lena's lips raced with his words. Cara stifled a yawn, while Patricia pushed her baby's stroller forward and back, forward and back, in time with the prayer. The trooper's hands gripped the edge of the desk as he studied his boots. Brody leaned forward, hands clasped, thumbs rolling slowly one over the other, as he stared straight at Sylvie, who sat on her hands and studied a pair of initials carved in the desk. A. C. plus T. M. Someone had tried to scratch out the T and the M.

"We lay ourselves down before you," said Pastor Tom. "We submit to your will. Let your keen sense of justice prevail. In your wisdom and mercy, we pray. And all God's people say it."

Amens skidded over the room. "Not so painful, now, was it?" Pastor Tom asked. He looked away from the trooper as he eased into his seat.

The trooper scanned the faces the way a teacher does after someone acts out, like line of sight was all he needed to regain control. "There are several points to consider when it comes to bear-baiting," he said, though from the awkward way he held up his hand, it seemed he was daring himself to recall even one.

Steven tipped back his cap. "That spot off Mile 84's been mine for years," he said.

"Understood," said the trooper. "But our records show—"

"How many god-damned years does a guy have to file the same crap," Steven said. He pulled a paper out of his pocket. "I got this permit."

"A permit isn't enough," said the trooper. "You must also file your location."

Steven jabbed the folded square. "It says right here on the back, how one guy can't squat in another guy's spot."

Brody shifted so that the edge of his boot touched the side of Sylvie's foot, bare in her sandal. She glanced at Kenny, but his eyes were on Steven. Scott Prince fisted his hands at the front of his belt. "The simple fact is that I got there first." Scott looked directly at Steven. "And I filed with the state."

"You know that spot's mine." Steven jabbed the air with his finger. "You know that's where I get my bear every year."

Cara ducked her head, smiling. "That location wasn't registered." Scott spoke each word distinctly, as if Steven was too dim-witted to string together his meaning. He pulled a paper from the front pocket of his shirt and unfolded it ceremoniously. "This is what you were supposed to file with the state. It gives me full rights to that spot. Which means you had no business destroying my property."

Kenny slapped his hand on his desk. "Steven did what had to be done."

The trooper held out both hands. "Let's take this one step at a time."

"There's no need for steps," Kenny said. Like poured water, the light soaked his beard. *You could pay more attention to your mother.* That's what he'd said over his plate of stinking bear stroganoff. *She's only thinking of your best interests.*

"Those papers don't matter." Around the room, heads turned toward Kenny. "It's a plain, simple fact. Scott moved in on Steven's spot."

Steven shifted as if to gather his weight beneath him. "We all feel real bad about Darla." The calm in his voice was slick, like veneer. "But that don't give you the right to set your bait where you want."

"This is not about Darla," said Scott.

Lena panned the room, as if in the faces she might read who sided with whom. "You could have put that barrel any number of places." She looked past Scott to the door. "You could have moved it when Steven first asked."

"He didn't ask," Scott said. "He left me a note. A godda..." He glanced at the pastor. "A note."

"A reasonable way to let you know you'd made a mistake." Lena's tone was smooth as winter's first ice, sharp and unclouded.

"Nothing reasonable about it," Scott shot back.

Lena turned her finely shaped hands. "You boys used to sit next to each other, right here in this room." Her voice faltered. "There's no need for this fuss."

"It's a matter of a few simple rules," said the trooper. A line of sweat trickled down from his temple.

Walter drew his folded hands across the desk, then tipped back his hat. "My boys can get a little hot-headed." It was in fact the first complete sentence Sylvie had heard him utter. "They've screwed up more than once."

Lena's lips formed an uneven smile. "Thanks, Dad," Steven said. "But right's right, and it's got nothing to do with papers and permits and rules. All it takes is a little respect."

"Punching a hole in my barrel and dragging it out to the road like it was some broken-down car—you call that respect?"

"You two aren't kids anymore," Tommy said. "Admit you're both wrong. Shake hands and let's get on with something that matters."

"This matters," Scott said. "The Prestons think they own this whole valley."

"No one owns anything except what we pay taxes for," Kate said.

"Don't we know it," said Marie's skinny husband. "They're about to tax us right out of our homes."

Steven grinned. "There you go. Calling this trooper out after hours only makes your tax bills go up."

The trooper clasped his hands in front of his chest. "We're getting away from the subject."

Kate stood. "This is the subject. Some people act like they're above everyone else. That's when the law has to step in."

Magda pointed to the trooper like he was one of the stuffed heads that hung on the wall of the lodge, a dumb conversation piece. "What I want to know is how come nobody ask before they call out this guy," she said in her broken, fast-talking way. "This guy, he bring law we don't need. No offense, sir," she added with a tight smile. "You do your job. But you got plenty more places to go than out here, over a pile of old food. Maybe somebody got a new barrel, they give it to Scott."

"Scott can get his own barrel," said Lena. "Steven wants some assurance there will be no more squatting on his spot."

Brody shifted. His knee touched Sylvie's, bare and browned by the sun.

"The only spots that are taken are those that are properly claimed," said the trooper. "There are two permits. One that allows you to bait, and one that says where you'll do it."

"Why's the state gotta make everything so goddamn complicated?" Cleve Baker asked.

Pastor Tom rose. He pressed his fingers together at their tips. "Perhaps we should start with the points we agree on."

"It isn't that simple," said Kenny. Sylvie's leg felt warm where it touched Brody's, and from the way he pretended it didn't.

"Despite our differences, this community has come together to support Darla and Scott in their time of trial," Pastor Tom said. He reached one hand toward Scott and the other toward Steven, in a way that brought to mind the portrait of Jesus that hung in the church foyer. "We all go through rough times. We need to lift up our brothers and sisters. So I ask you. Consider. How you can support one another."

"Killing a bear," Tommy said. "That's one thing they agree on."

"That's a start," Pastor Tom said, like it wasn't a joke.

"You let me out of this meeting and back on that stand," Steven said. "I'll get the job done."

"I've got a new barrel in the back of my truck," Scott said. "Me and my boy, we're setting it out as soon as this meeting is finished."

The trooper held up both hands. "We're getting ahead of ourselves."

Brody pressed his leg tight against Sylvie's. In his dark eyes she saw hope. She slipped her foot from her sandal and ran her toes over the worn leather edge of Brody's boot. Flecks of gray silt sifted to the floor. A piece of her, held tight since Pine Lake, dissolved into the space between them. When she looked up, Kenny was watching. With her bare foot, she teased the leather, then slowly drew back.

Kenny's gaze shifted to Scott, flanked by the pastor. "It's not fair, the way you people have two sets of rules," Kenny said. "One for yourselves and another for us. Steven got his truck down there once. He can do it again."

"If a regulation gets violated," said the trooper, "that truck gets impounded."

"God has graced us with a beautiful land," Pastor Tom said. "It's our duty to respond in kind. To extend a hand to our friends and our neighbors." He turned to Steven. "Knowing the trials of our brother, I ask you to act out of grace. Two can hunt from one station." He turned to the trooper. "Isn't that right?"

The trooper rubbed the edge of his chin. "That's one solution."

Steven's knuckles went white. "There's plenty of country out there. Scott can get his own stand."

"Plenty of country where you can file your own permit." Scott waved his paper.

"With all due respect, Pastor," Tommy said. "Not everyone shares your beliefs about God and our duty."

"With all due respect." Lena's chin shook. "It's for each in his heart to ponder what's right."

"Nobody asked you to take sides." Steven glared at Tommy.

"I only suggest we admit there are sides," Tommy said. "If indeed we aspire to truth."

There was some tittering over *aspire*. "You should talk," Kenny said. "The way you let that dog run."

The trooper held up both hands, palms facing out. "You people aren't any closer to settling this thing than you were when I walked in the door." He tugged up his pants by the belt. "I'm setting that bear stand off limits till you reach some sort of consensus."

"So now it's your stand," Cara's dad said.

"It's on public land," said the trooper. "I've got jurisdiction."

"State's got its hands on way too much of our land as it is," Cleve Baker said.

"I can tell you this much about Steven," said Walter. "He doesn't take kindly to threats."

"This isn't a threat. It's an action. I'm revoking all permissions and permits on that piece of land." The trooper wrapped his hand over his fist. "For two weeks. Or till you folks cool off."

"Bear will have moved on by then," Steven said.

Brody glanced at Sylvie. She felt how his hands would be on her face, chapped and rough. His lips pressed against hers, his tongue searching her mouth.

His father stared at the trooper. "You're saying we can't hunt at all. Not Steven or me."

"Hunt all you want," said the trooper. "Just not from that stand."

"You can't do that," said Kenny.

"I just did." The trooper turned and walked out. The sound of his boots echoed down the empty hallway.

The room erupted in voices. Cara slapped her hands on the desk. "That was exciting," she said. Scott motioned for Brody, who looked down at the floor.

Kenny reached for her mother's hand as Sylvie slipped out of her chair. She could in fact get stuck here all winter.

Her bare legs brushed desks and chairs as she passed. The hem of her shorts caught the edge of Patricia's big stroller. "Sorry," she said as she flicked them loose. She ducked past Marie and her twins, taking the long way around Scott Prince, his hands shoved in his pockets as he half-listened to Cleve Barker, looking for Brody so he could get to his truck and make good on his threat to reclaim the stand.

But Brody had slipped out the back, to the woods, where Sylvie would let him touch her the way that he wanted.

Kenny held tight to her mother as he watched Sylvie move toward the door. He watched, and he saw, and he knew.

Cirque

A depression eroded in ice

When Scott couldn't find Brody, Steven reached the stand first. In defiance of the trooper's orders, he set out his bait barrel, determined to prove himself Kenny's equal by getting a bear while at the same time rubbing Scott's nose in it. There was no sneaking around. Steven bragged to anyone who would listen how his bait got hit again and again. It was only a matter of time.

Much as Ruth told herself that Resurrection was no different from any small town back home, the rift between the churched and unchurched as well as this flagrant disregard for the law took some getting used to. At least since the meeting, Kenny had stayed mostly out of the fray. His eight-wheeler consumed him.

He nailed the magazine plans to a wall in the shop and then he went scrounging for parts. From Joe Pleary he bought two black bucket seats stripped from a crumpled sedan, ten dollars each. Shocks he got from a truck Roger Fleen had stashed in his yard, one of the beaters that according to Kenny he kept for this very purpose, raiding by neighbors and friends. Ruth admired Kenny's resourcefulness and enjoyed hearing about his transactions, from the back and forth with Joe to get the price from twenty to ten to the trouble he'd had extracting the shocks out of Roger's truck.

Suspension and gears he got from Cleve Baker, who ran a regular junkyard and made a killing off of it. Ruth waded behind him through Cleve's tall grass, past piles of headlights, steering columns, tires, and bumpers, while

Kenny bantered with Cleve over prices. They were friends from way back, but that didn't mean Cleve cut any deals, and Kenny left empty-handed. It was highway robbery, he said, the way Cleve took advantage. Only last week he'd charged Scott Prince twice what a tranny should cost, even though Scott needed the truck for Darla's appointments in Anchorage. But in the end Kenny decided it was cheaper to pay Cleve's prices than to search through the junkyards in town, and he went back and bought what he needed.

His prize came from Kim Fong, who kept to himself behind his tall fence and was so rarely seen that people spoke about him almost as if he were dead. No one seemed to know exactly what had brought Fong to the island. There was speculation about a card house in Anchorage and talk that he'd gotten the land from a man who couldn't pay what he owed, and it was also rumored Fong had come to hide out when his partners turned ugly and the card house went down. Kenny was one of a select few Fong allowed behind his tall fence. He swore to Ruth that Fong had more stuff piled back there than there was in the rest of the island yards put together.

Before going to bargain with Fong, Kenny took a small bag from the freezer. Inside was a dark organ the size of a thumb, brown with blood, like a small misshapen heart. On the black market in Asia they paid big bucks for a bear gallbladder, owing to its aphrodisiac properties, Kenny said. Apparently Fong had a freezer full. Kenny assured her that everyone in the valley sold bear parts to Fong, and what he planned wasn't even a sale but a trade, and besides the bear had no use for the gallbladder now. Ruth sat in the truck while Fong let Kenny into his compound, thinking how easy it was in her old life to assume a righteous stance about such things. She thought of it that way now, her old life.

When Kenny finally came out, it was with four axles, all matching, that he and Fong loaded into the bed of the truck. Fong drove a hard bargain. He'd demanded the gallbladder plus three hundred dollars in exchange for the axles, but to order them and pay for the shipping would have cost twice that, and Kenny needed the rest of his cash for the engine and tranny, specialty parts that couldn't be had in the valley. The transmission was to be a transaxle automatic. He explained to Ruth how special drive discs allowed it to function as both a differential and clutch. By shifting two sticks, the driver could run through an infinite number of gear ratios. One set of wheels could even turn forward while the others turned back. Though Ruth appreciated his explanation, she couldn't see the advantage in wheels that went different directions. To her it seemed anything that insisted on coming and going at the same time was bound to get stuck.

After running up to his mother's house to call in the order for the trans-axle automatic transmission and the four-stroke engine and the chain drives, Kenny set the axles and wheels on the floor of the shop. He gathered plywood from stacks in the yard and collected steel tubing from Steven and went to work on the chassis. Ruth perched on a stool, watching. How it would have shocked Richard, to see how she learned the names of the tools and the parts Kenny asked for, the Allen wrench and the drill extension and the steel straps. When he concentrated on a task, Kenny's tongue slipped between his lips, only the pink tip of it showing, and that was all the reward Ruth needed, to see that.

Anna appeared in the shop, wanting to know why this bolt went here and not there and what kept the chains from falling off. Kenny pointed at parts and used his flat carpenter's pencil to sketch out the chassis on a square of paper towel, patient with Anna and her questions in a way Richard would never have been.

At the shop door, propped to let in a breeze, the dog showed itself. Anna dropped the wrench she'd held out for Kenny and dashed to the door. Tess leapt to one side, head low and wary. "Damn dog," Kenny said. As Anna patted its neck, the dog swished its tail slowly.

"It's a beautiful day, and Tess wants to play." Anna spun a circle, arms out, then stopped and staggered dizzily toward the dog.

"Not in our yard, she's not." It wasn't that Kenny didn't like dogs. He just didn't like dogs running wild. Hard on the wildlife, he said.

Ruth intervened, suggesting Anna take the dog back to Tommy's.

"Tell Tommy she'd better tie that damn thing up," Kenny called after her.

"Stay on the road." Shielding her eyes from the sun, Ruth watched as Anna and Tess disappeared around a bend.

Kenny knelt on a big piece of cardboard and peered under one axle, then lay back and tightened a bolt that joined two metal bars. The under-carriage, that's what he'd called it. Ruth leaned against the door and watched, feeling wistful for, of all things, the little dog they had kept when the girls were young, the way it had padded behind her, afraid to let her out of its sight.

And now here she was, padding along after Kenny, feigning interest in his eight-wheeler project as if she feared the thing, once fully formed, might somehow replace her.

"Guess I'll get going," she said. Kenny murmured something, either to the bolt or to her, she couldn't tell which.

The house smelled of bear steaks fried with bacon, bear chunks in chili, bear chow mein. Ruth heaved at a swollen wood window until it half-opened, then called up the stairs to Sylvie.

On the floor near the table were the plastic canisters of flour and sugar and coffee that Ruth had cleared off the counters so she could stain them. Kenny had said she'd gotten the color too dark, that come winter she'd want something lighter, but she liked the contrast with the walls and the cabinets. Another coat, and they'd be perfect, considering that they were only plywood, and temporary, until they got tile.

She pried the lid off the Werther's wood stain and wriggled rubber gloves over her hands. The vapors burned the back of her throat as she dipped her rag, which had dried stiff from the last coat. She rubbed hard until the plywood turned the same shade as the antique walnut desk she'd let go at the yard sale for forty-five dollars, a little desk that for as long as she could recall had accommodated stacks of bills and receipts and papers the girls had brought home from school. The desk was nothing she'd thought she would miss, and yet she had to sit back on her heels and peel off her gloves to wipe her eyes with her wrist. Foolish, getting teary-eyed over an old piece of furniture, when she had Kenny's love and the girls could run free and the possibilities were endless here. Still, she wished she hadn't let Anna go off with the dog.

Sylvie came downstairs finally, wearing cutoffs and an old gray sweatshirt so relaxed at the neck that it hung off one shoulder. "Anna's gone off with that dog," Ruth said. A neutral topic was best, to feel out Sylvie's mood, though at her age any subject was a potential minefield. Comment on the beautiful day, and you'd get a sarcastic retort about how there was nowhere to go. Ask about friends, and she'd be angry all over at how she'd left hers behind. "Pretty good" and "okay" were the best Ruth could get when it came to the books she was reading.

Sylvie tapped the end of the cereal box, and when the contents rushed out, she shoved a handful back. Even as a child, she had insisted on set amounts of food, filling mugs and bowls only to certain levels, wary it seemed of abundance.

"You can take Kenny's bike," Ruth suggested. "Go see Cara. Or Brody." It was a good sign, Sylvie's budding relationship with Darla's boy.

"No thanks." Sylvie reached across the table for an apple, one from a bushel Lena had insisted on sharing, and brushed it on the side of her jeans.

"You can wash that," said Ruth. "There's water."

"What's Kenny up to?"

"He's in the shop." Ruth dipped her rag again in the stain. "He's working on the eight-wheeler. Getting ready to attach the wheels."

Sylvie wiped a trickle of juice from her chin. Through the window, sunlight shimmered her hair. "That stuff smells like turpentine."

"The color's nice, don't you think?"

"Kinda dark."

Ruth stepped back, eyeing her work. "That's what Kenny said. But I like it."

Sylvie chewed a little more on the apple and tossed the nibbled core in the trash. "Guess I'll go see if he needs any help."

It could be an answer to prayer, this rise from self-pity. Not that Ruth had been praying. She didn't have faith like the others. But her thoughts did wander to Sylvie when prayers were circulated around the Ladies Circle.

She rubbed hard with her rag, only half looking up as Sylvie slipped on her sandals and slid out the door. She'd seen it often enough at the high school. All Sylvie needed was a little attention.

She leaned back and studied the color. If you were going for dark, you had to go all the way. Otherwise they'd look unfinished, with too much of the grain showing. Though her arms ached, she rubbed even harder. Had she been such a puzzle at Sylvie's age? She recalled being fundamentally steady, her desire to please her parents and teachers broken only by an occasional crush on some boy, affections that were rarely returned. That had all changed in college. Ruth had cut loose. She'd thought somehow she might be an artist—the idea made her father crazy—and so she'd run with a crowd that smoked and drank late into the night. Richard had saved her, or so she'd thought at the time, steadying her with his good looks and his charm and his reassurance that the family they'd make together would be different from the one she'd grown up in.

Finally she achieved a shade that made the countertops look like they'd soaked up strong coffee. She stuffed the staining cloth in the plastic bag and with the heel of her hand pushed the lid tight on the Werther's can. The stain had soaked somehow through her gloves, discoloring her fingernails. She washed as best she could with water left from the morning dishes, but the color remained.

Almost an hour had passed, and still Sylvie was out in the shop. A good sign, Ruth reminded herself. Mindful of not hovering—Sylvie had taken the initiative, after all—Ruth took the Bible in her lap and with her stained fingers turned to a chapter written by Paul, finding it quickly with the help of the tabs. She uncapped a pink highlighter, one of the ones Lena had loaned her. *But now I have written to you not to keep company with anyone named a brother, who is a fornicator, or covetous, or an idolater, or a reviler, or a drunkard, or an extortioner—not even to eat with such a person.* The way Paul had each sinner neatly pegged made her recall with some longing her desk outside Mr. Scranton's office, where the attendance counter set her apart from the wildness that went on in the halls. From there, she could sort students into the good, the mediocre, and the incorrigible, knowing for certain her own girls were good.

For what have I to do with judging those also who are outside? Do you not judge those who are inside? Ruth hovered the marker over Paul's tricky questions, herself neither outside nor in. Returning with Lena to the Church of New Beginnings, she had greeted Marie and Patricia and Roxanne and Trish and Cherise like they were old friends. She'd smiled kindly at Darla the way they all did, not that Darla needed their smiles. Still Ruth felt like an imposter.

But those who are outside God judges. Ruth thought as she often did of Hugh's wife. How lonely she must have been. How cold, once winter came. She might have had friends, but Ruth didn't think so. Maybe the boy had outgrown the rocking horse, but Ruth didn't think that either.

None of this was the sort of thing you jotted in the margins of scripture. With a thud she shut the Bible. She set down her pen and stepped outside. White light oozed from the sun, making distinct lines of the shed and the house and the steps and the shop, where she wandered as if unintentionally. She stomped her shoes on the steel grating in front of the door and let herself in. With its high ceiling, the room felt cavernous. Her gaze fell naturally on her daughter, bent at the waist in front of the eight-wheeler frame, shoulder to shoulder with Kenny.

"Hey, you two," Ruth said.

Sylvie turned, and then Kenny. "Hey, babe." Kenny wiped a grease-stained hand on his pants.

"Just checking on two of my favorite people." Her voice sounded high and tight.

Sylvie followed Kenny to where a sheet of plywood leaned against a wall. Each grasped one edge as Ruth hurried to help.

"We've got it," Kenny said as they maneuvered the plywood in slow, even steps, Sylvie moving gracefully backwards like a swan gliding, effortless. When they reached the frame, they tipped the plywood, Sylvie handling her end as easily as Kenny did his, in perfect balance.

"I see you've got the chassis together," Ruth said, pleased to use a word that showed she'd been paying attention.

"Uh huh." Kenny centered the plywood over the chassis and reached out his hand. Sylvie dropped a bolt into his open palm. Kenny rolled it between his fingers, then offered it back. "Smaller," he said.

Sylvie dug in a pile of bolts. "This one?"

"Yup." Kenny flashed a smile.

"Sylvie." Lifted to the sharp sound of Ruth's voice, Sylvie's face conveyed surprise, as if she'd forgotten her mother. A flush spread from Ruth's chest. "You've pestered Kenny enough."

"She's no trouble." Kenny tightened the bolt to the wood. "She's been a big help, actually. How about one of those screws?"

"Phillips or standard?" Sylvie asked.

"Phillips. Inch and a half."

Sylvie handed it to him. Kenny held it up, matched it to a drill bit, and then, drill squealing, drove it into the wood.

Ruth stood as if in a dream, acutely aware that her eyes sat a little too close and her face was a little too wide at the chin and her nostrils flattened unattractively near the base of her nose. She believed she was smiling, but she couldn't be sure, so great was her sense of how she would fail to compete with something so fresh and newly formed as Kenny's eight-wheeler, once it was finished.

When she opened the door to let herself out, neither Kenny nor Sylvie looked up. The cold would come soon. Everyone said so. But Ruth felt at times that it was already here, that it couldn't get any colder, though the sun shone urgent and warm as she paced the yard, searching for clues as to where Hugh's wife had worked her magic with the garden.

Though Ruth had mowed, the jagged grass scratched against her ankles. It had to be somewhere, that patch of dirt. She crossed and recrossed the yard, becoming agitated in her determination to lay claim to something.

Finally she went to the shed. From on top of the wood stacked inside, she hauled out the old rocking horse, a pale faded specter against the bright day. She dragged it across the driveway to where the fireweed and the goldenrod and the yarrow bloomed and hoisted the horse in her arms, heavy and unbalanced, then heaved it into a cluster of shiny-leaved willows. It landed short of the bushes, sideways against a pile of tires. There you go, Cynthia. Rest in peace. It made her feel better, to think this, even though Hugh was the one who was dead.

From her palms she brushed ancient dust. She should be glad Sylvie was busy, and that Anna had occupied herself with the dog. Busy was what they all needed. She dug in the shed for a spade and a hoe, then returned to the house and from the drawer of the nightstand extracted Kate's seed packets with their bright, hopeful pictures, carrots and onions and sugar peas and zucchini.

Choosing a sunny spot beyond where the aspen leaves fluttered, she arranged the packets in neat rows on the ground, then chunked the spade in the grass. Hard and unyielding, the dirt wouldn't give. Moving in a wide arc, she stabbed again and again at the ground, her efforts met by the crunch of small rocks, resistance that ran up the wooden handle through her arms to her shoulders, which were beginning to ache. In all her years in Pine Lake, Ruth had never planted a garden. But she'd expected it would be simple enough, involving only seeds, water, and soil, intention being the beginning of all things.

Kenny might know right where the garden had been. If he didn't, he at least had weight for forcing the spade. But he had his own project. She couldn't hold that against him. She was getting to know him all over again, this Kenny who hunted and built things, whose mother wanted only the best for him.

Sylvie would lose interest. She'd get in the way, and that would aggravate Kenny.

Ruth wedged her spade in the dirt. Heart thumping, she went to the shop and stood in the doorway and in her firmest voice said, "Sylvie, I need your help in the yard."

"In a minute." Crouched beside Kenny, Sylvie held the plywood as he drilled a hole.

"Now," Ruth insisted.

Sylvie stood slowly and brushed off her hands as Kenny set a level and squinted at the bubble that floated innocently in the yellow liquid. "Nailed it," he said. With the back of his hand, Kenny nudged Sylvie's leg, and it appeared to Ruth that Sylvie jumped a little, as if a charge had surged through her, like what you got from carpet on a dry winter day, not completely unexpected but still a surprise.

"Sylvie, I said I need your help."

Sylvie's mouth twisted in an ugly way as she moved toward the door. "Thanks," Kenny called after her.

People only want to be appreciated, Ruth reminded herself. She handed Sylvie the hoe. "I've been circling this yard, but I still can't find where Hugh's wife had that garden. It's like I've got some sort of blind spot."

The wind rippled Sylvie's hair. "You really think stuff's gonna grow here?"

"Lots of things do. Look at the wildflowers," Ruth said. "It will be a tribute, to the woman that lived here before. Hugh's wife. Cynthia. To start her garden back up. Imagine, fresh lettuce and carrots and peas. I can't think why we haven't grown them before."

"Because they sell vegetables at the store," Sylvie said.

Ruth forced a laugh, pleased to have suppressed her first impulse, which was to scold Sylvie's tone. She pointed toward the shed. "Try over there."

Sylvie dragged the hoe through the grass and made a half-hearted strike at the ground. Ruth stomped on the shovel but managed to loosen only a thin layer of gravel. "Good to get out in the sun, don't you think?" Sylvie's hoe clanked, striking the earth. "Sure can tell the glacier was here," Ruth said. "All this rock." Sweat beaded over her forehead, as much from the effort of trying to draw Sylvie out as from trying to force the spade into the ground. "I've always thought peas would be fun. Those little tendrils that grab hold of things."

Sylvie only whacked at the earth. The aching spread across Ruth's shoulders and down her arms to her fingers as the breeze shifted and settled, typical for early afternoon. She tried to think of what else she might say, something that might make Sylvie look up with anything other than contempt. She thought of Cynthia chopping at the ground, the sound endless as the flowing water. Sheer, bitter determination. That's how she must have managed.

Ruth punched the shovel again at the dirt, throwing her full weight against it. When she looked up, she saw Tommy approaching from the road, her arms gangly, loping almost, not in an awkward way but in a rhythm that seemed to run counter to the river. She wore carpenter jeans, with loops to hang hammers and narrow pockets for tools, the legs rolled to the knees, exposing tight-muscled calves, her breasts bouncing under a thin cotton shirt.

"Sorry not to have gotten here sooner." Tommy hurried toward Ruth and Sylvie like the three of them were already old friends. "You know how it is in the summer." She threw her face to the sun and laughed. Freckles dotted her cheeks, and though her hair was the same light brown as Ruth's, it was so curly and thick that the band holding it back seemed barely able to contain it. "You're getting a late start. Short season." She extended a knobby-fingered hand. "Sorry. I saw you at the meeting, but we haven't been properly introduced. My mother accused me of having the manners of a horned toad, and the older I get the more I think she was right. Don't you hate that?" She nodded at Sylvie. "I'm Tommy. No doubt Lena's warned you."

Ruth grasped her hand lightly. "Frank's ex," Tommy said. "That's what they generally say. God, I hate that, too. No one identifies men by the women they used to be with." She grabbed the shovel out of Ruth's hands. "Let me save you some trouble." For a hopeful moment Ruth thought Tommy was going to tell her to give it all up.

"If you're going to dig, you'd better do it where Cynthia did." Tommy clomped through the grass, then stopped halfway between the driveway and the shed. "Right about here." She sank the spade in the dirt. "See how it's a shade greener? There was a big fight with Hugh, but Cynthia got herself a whole truckload of dirt. Black topsoil, hauled in from Palmer. It's the only way to get stuff to grow."

Tommy's eyes were a translucent blue, the kind that might seem empty if you failed to look close enough. "That woman was spunky. She gave Hugh what-for. I admired her that. But she was a little mouse around everyone else." Tommy tilted her head, looking off at the river. "Like if she started talking she might not ever shut up. But she never did. Start talking, I mean. I expect she was overjoyed to get out of here, under the circumstances. Just packed up and left, so fast everybody wondered why she'd waited till Hugh was gone."

Tommy stomped on the spade and brought up a load of dark, loamy dirt. "She'd have liked you making an effort. No one gave her much thought except for her garden, least of all Hugh." Tommy's arms were skinny but hard. Sweat built on her face as she dug. The wrinkled skin near her eyes led Ruth to think they were close in age, but she worked with the energy of someone much younger. Sylvie leaned on her hoe, half-smiling as Tommy dug.

"Might be the name," Tommy said between breaths, as if she sensed their admiration. "Boy named Sue, girl named Tommy. Makes you think you've got something to prove. When I'm feeling generous, I figure that's what my parents had in mind." She glanced at Sylvie, who nodded slightly.

After digging out three sides of a rectangular plot, Tommy stabbed the spade in the dirt and leaned over the handle. "There. That should get you started."

She tipped the shovel handle toward Ruth, who caught it on its way to the ground. "I didn't mean for you to do all the work," she said.

"Course you didn't." Tommy swatted a slow-moving mosquito. "You could dig for a week around here and not find one spot worth planting." She glanced at Sylvie. "I don't guess this is your idea of fun. Your sister at least had the good sense to run off."

Anna. Impossible that Ruth hadn't thought of her since they'd started digging. "She's with your dog."

Tommy laughed. "Let's just say she and Tess will both sleep well tonight. That dog's got more energy than a fox on a rabbit. Should have seen her before she came to live with me. Shrank way the hell back if you went anyplace near her. No trust at all. Got her from a kennel in Palmer where the dogs were mistreated. Dozens of them, skin and bones. Animal control cleared it out, tossed the owner in jail. If you ask me he ought to be shot. But Tess has a good life now. She earned it."

"Where'd you see her and Anna?" Ruth asked.

"Running down by the river."

"Mom's scared of the river," Sylvie said.

"I'm not scared," Ruth said. "I just don't think your sister should be down there alone."

"It's safer there than the woods," Tommy said. "This time of year anyhow. Moose drop their calves there, and that brings out the bears. You don't want her coming up on a kill, with a bear standing over it." She lifted her ponytail off her neck and rubbed off the sweat. "Me, I'd rather eat from the garden and leave the bears be."

"I don't know why Kenny didn't say anything. About the moose calves and the bears."

"You'd make Anna stay in the house," said Sylvie.

"Kenny knows me better than that."

"Kenny is Kenny," Tommy said. "And kids gotta get out."

"I'll keep that in mind," Ruth said, a little crossly, since she didn't see how Tommy would know the first thing about kids, or for that matter about Kenny.

"You stir-crazy yet?" Tommy asked.

"Lena's got me…" Ruth started, but then she saw Tommy was talking to Sylvie.

"Magda's looking for help at the lodge," Tommy said. "Fresh blood. She's already run off half the girls around here."

"I heard they were hiring," Sylvie said.

"You did?" Ruth said. "I wouldn't mind working."

"No offense," Tommy said, "but you're way too old. Magda likes kids. Figures the tourists will cut them some slack. Tip more, so she can pay less. I'm the old maid of the bunch. Supposed to keep the young ones in line." She jutted her hip in a way that said she did nothing of the sort.

"Go talk to Magda," Tommy told Sylvie. "Tell her I sent you."

"Thanks." Sylvie looked so much prettier when she smiled.

"You two need anything else, I'm just up the road," Tommy said. "Little shack with a truck and a sno-go out front. No blue tarps. Won't have 'em in my yard. That was the final straw between Frank and me."

Mating songs filtered out of a clump of spruce trees, and the cold smell of dirt rose from the earth. "She's a free spirit, all right," Ruth said once Tommy was out of earshot. "I'll bet it was a lot more than blue tarps that came between her and Frank."

"You don't know." Sylvie's hoe grated, slicing the soil.

"It's obvious she likes things her way. Relationships, they're give and take."

Sylvie's lips pressed together. She was measuring her mother up against Tommy, anyone could see that, and of course Ruth would come up short. She flung a chunk of sod at the weeds. "Why don't you run get your sister?"

Sylvie hacked harder with the hoe. "She'll come back when she's ready."

"I didn't ask your opinion. I asked you to run get her."

The hoe clanked as Sylvie tossed it aside. "Actually, you asked why I didn't run get her. And I told you." Unsmiling, she strode toward the river, head up, loping a little the way Tommy had. An impressionable age. With her gone there was only the sound of the river, plus an occasional too-whit and chick-a-dee-dee, and no one to judge her.

As Ruth turned the last of the dirt, Anna sprinted across the gravel. "I thought I made clear not to play by the river," Ruth said when she got close.

"Tommy says it's better down there, to stay away from the bears."

"Kenny will tell us if we need to worry about that."

"You have to make noise, Tommy said. So you don't sneak up and surprise them. But don't worry. Tess will protect me."

"Tess isn't yours," Ruth said. "You don't need to be hanging around her and Tommy."

"Tommy says we can play whenever we want."

"She's not your mother. And don't give me that pout. Sister Jean says your smile is your crown." Ruth felt fraudulent, invoking language about sisters and brothers who were no relation at all, but the mention of Sister Jean got Anna's attention. "Where's Sylvie?"

"She went for a walk." Anna toed the dirt. "Planting seeds would count toward my Helper badge."

"That's right. You read out loud from the packets, and we'll decide where to plant them."

By the time Sylvie got back, they were molding hills for zucchini. "Don't go bothering Kenny," Ruth said when Sylvie glanced at the shop. "Get cleaned up, and when we're done here I'll drive you to the lodge, if you're serious about that job."

"I can drive myself," Sylvie said, "if Kenny lets me take the truck."

"No," Ruth said firmly. "We're not starting that." Sylvie glanced again at the shop, then ran up the steps to the house. Ruth hoped Tommy hadn't set her up for disappointment.

When she got up from planting, her knees were stiff. Anna helped haul buckets of water that they poured gently over the dirt, taking care not to wash away the seeds. Kenny would be pleased at her resourcefulness. Lena too.

Ruth scrubbed dirt from under her nails and cut up potatoes and carrots, then drained blood from thawed bear meat and dredged it in flour. As the stew started to boil, Kenny came in, grease streaking his forearms and neck.

"You're dirty," she teased. "Me too." She showed him her fingers. "You see the garden?"

"Sure did." He slipped out of his coveralls and hung them on a hook by the door. "How's the project?" she asked.

"Coming along."

"Are you done with the chassis?"

"You don't get done with the chassis. You add stuff onto it."

"What else did you add on, then?"

"A bunch of parts. More than you want to know."

Sylvie came down, a fresh shirt tucked into clean jeans, her hair pinned up. "Someone sure cleans up nice," Kenny said.

Pink tinged Sylvie's cheeks. "Tommy said Magda would give me a job."

"Maybe," said Ruth. "She said maybe Magda would give you a job." For Kenny's benefit, she explained how Tommy had stopped by and shown them where to dig.

"That's Tommy," Kenny said. "Into everyone's business."

Sylvie stared at her hands, clasped at her waist. "Well, kiddo," Kenny said. "Let's get you to the lodge, before Magda changes her mind."

Ruth rubbed a chunk of dirt from under her thumbnail. "We hilled the zucchini. Planted carrots. And endives."

"Lettuce," Anna said. "Don't forget lettuce, and peas."

Kenny cuffed gently at the back of Anna's head. "No, we won't forget lettuce, or peas." He bowed a little at Sylvie and gestured toward the door. "Hope that nice outfit survives a ride in my dirty old truck."

After they'd driven off, Ruth resisted the urge to go out to the shop and sneak a look at his project. Instead, she poured a kettle of water and set it to heat on the stove. She slipped out of her shirt, then loosened her belt as the water began to steam.

"You can't wash right here," Anna said.

"I don't see why not. There's no one to see."

"Someone could come," Anna said. "They could look in the windows."

"No one's going to come way out here," Ruth said.

"Tommy did," Anna said.

"I'll take my chances," said Ruth. A bath was what she craved, a long hot bath in a tub laced with petals picked from wild roses, without having to think of Lena hovering outside, worrying over how much water she was wasting. She stripped down to her underwear. The legs she'd once thought attractive ballooned large and white as she scrubbed them with water from the basin. As she washed, she thought of Tommy's pale skin, the freckles dusting her face. A free spirit, not so different from the art students Ruth had run with in college, brash and lively. It was important to align yourself with the right sorts of people. She'd tried to impress this upon the girls, not the way her own mother had, by finding fault with anyone whose friendship might not land you in the right social circles, but through plain common sense, in that like attracts like and trouble searches out company.

It was hard to rinse off the soap. Ruth dipped her wash rag over and over in the basin, and with an old towel, she soaked up the water that puddled under her feet. She rubbed herself all over with the towel, but her legs still itched and the dirt remained under her fingernails and the smell of bear seemed infused in her skin.

Kenny came home smelling of Lena's fresh soap. "Stopped at Mom's for a shower," he said. He set a hand on Sylvie's back. "You gonna tell your mom?"

"I got the job."

"Good for you." Ruth swung her arm around Sylvie's waist and pulled her close, though Sylvie held herself stiff. This would make what the Ladies Circle called a good report, an unexpected but hoped-for turn of events.

Ruth returned the toaster and the spice rack and the cooking utensils to the countertops and wiped the yellow-sprigged vinyl tablecloth. Anna and Kenny ate the stew heartily, but Sylvie only nibbled at the carrots and potatoes. "I see you're too good for my bear," Kenny said. "Just the idea of eating at Magda's has got you spoiled. That's okay. More for the rest of us."

"Tommy said I better watch out for bears," Anna said. "While the moose babies are little."

Kenny mopped his bowl with a torn hunk of bread. "Bears are as scared of us as we are of them."

"She says till the babies get bigger we have to be careful," said Anna.

"Tommy thinks Anna should walk by the river, not through the woods," Ruth said.

Kenny set down his spoon. "I see how this is." His eyes went from Anna to Ruth. "You girls, all siding together." He nodded at Sylvie. "Go on. Don't be shy. Tell me where else I've been wrong."

He was teasing, of course. Ruth reached under the table and curled her fingers over his hand. "I can see how Tommy didn't stay married," she said. "Hard to live with someone who thinks they know everything."

Kenny extracted his hand and reached for another slice of bread. "Frank was one of those guys that come out from the city, thinking they can live off the land. They never last long."

"I got half my memory badge," Anna said. "Listen. A foolish son is the grief of his mother. A pray... prating fool will fall. He who dili..."

"Diligently," Sylvie said.

"Diligently seeks good will find favor," Anna said in a rush.

"Not bad," Kenny said. "And what has Sylvie been up to, besides setting a chassis and digging a garden and getting a job?"

Ruth braced for a half-mumbled reply.

"I read a book," Sylvie said. "*The Life of Pi*. Last night."

Kenny whistled, low. "All in one night. Keep that up, and you'll run out of books. Just as well. There's life to be lived."

Sylvie set down her fork. *I'll read if I want. Nothing better to do here.* Ruth waited for the retort. But Sylvie only looked at Kenny the way Anna had looked at the animals that hung on the walls of restaurants and motels as they'd come north, staring down the sharp, snarling teeth of an ermine, studying the big furry feet of a lynx. "I don't see how you stand it," Sylvie said. "Living here. All your life."

Kenny laughed. "Stand it? I love it. Wouldn't live anywhere else. You gotta quit fighting it, Sylvie. One day you'll wake up and you'll understand this is your home."

Sylvie tucked a strand of hair behind her ear, then released it. She glanced up at Kenny like she might have more to say, then turned to Ruth. "May I be excused?"

When Ruth nodded, Sylvie pushed back from the table. "I'll do the dishes."

Ruth barely contained her surprise. "That's great, sweetie." She should have thought of it earlier, getting the girls more involved in the household, as they'd been in Pine Lake. Here she'd been hanging onto the chores herself, like ballast.

Kenny returned to the shop. When the dishes were done, Ruth suggested a card game, Crazy Eights, but Sylvie refused, and Anna gave up after one hand. Ruth hauled the gray water outside and sloshed it at the pile of tires where the upended horse stared wide at the sky. Wind rustled the aspen, carrying with it the lonely sounds of birds, calling and calling. A bank of gray clouds hovered over the mountains, seeding rain.

She set down the bucket and tromped toward the river, over purple flowers shaped like trumpets and tiny petals, pale pink that jutted up between rocks. From a certain angle, it looked like the mountains encircled the glacier, giving birth to it, which in one sense they had, since the glacier had first formed in their peaks. But when Ruth looked again, the angle had shifted, and it seemed the ice had been there always.

She stepped lightly across the gray sand so as not to spread it over the tight buds that bobbed one to a stalk, showing only a hint of their yellow blooms. Coaxing life from the ground, Hugh's wife must have thought always of winter, how soon it would come, reversing her efforts, the river turned silent and still.

When she got back to the house, the girls had gone up to their room, so Ruth sat in the big overstuffed chair. She breathed in the smell of Kenny, salt and grit, as she shifted Lena's Bible into her lap. Fate and love both came at you sideways, easy to miss if you weren't paying attention. She had no idea how you arrived at the point of actual believing, but the workbook at least offered clear instructions, which verse to turn to and what to write down.

Under Minerva's guidance, she flipped from chapter to chapter. *Where some saw a failing fig tree, Jesus saw hope.* Hope, she wrote in small print in the margin, so her Bible would look more like the others around the Ladies Circle table. Like fate, faith might mean simply an aversion to truth. That's how the cynical saw it. Of course she didn't write this down, but instead penned words from the verses in their appropriate places, pacing herself to draw out the calm, steadying work. Kenny would smile at the sight of her, one leg tucked under the other, lamplight warming the pages of his mother's Bible.

But Kenny didn't come in. While it was still light, Ruth went to bed. She lay naked with her hands on her belly as the sun's hard rays beat the curtains, thinking of Tommy and the way she'd spoken of Frank, not bitter or hurt but joking almost. *Kenny is Kenny*, she'd said. Ruth should have stuck up for him, made sure Tommy knew how much she loved him, though she shouldn't care what Tommy thought.

The sun's glow deepened and scattered. Nothing could be larger and stronger than the glacier, and yet she felt ungrounded. Time, that's all she needed. Time for Kenny to finish his project. Time for the zucchini and carrots and lettuce and peas to sprout and grow. Time for Sylvie to get settled. Time to forget the ones who'd come before her and failed. Time to get ready for cold.

She stared up at the ceiling for what seemed like an hour, then slipped out of bed. She wrapped her robe against goose bumps and slid her feet into sandals, then shut the bedroom door gently, not wanting to wake the girls, if in fact they were asleep. Sylvie struck Ruth at times as sleepless, watching and lying in wait.

Outside the air had cooled, hinting as always of winter, when the landscape would merge with the glacier. In the shop, Kenny hovered over the plywood platform he'd attached with Sylvie's help. Ruth leaned against the door, the metal cool against her fingertips, waiting for Kenny to notice.

At last he straightened and pushed his hand through his hair. His eyes drooped at the corners, and his lashes fluttered, defying sleep. He wiped his hands on a cloth. "Those spacers are buggers to mount."

He crouched again, next to the chassis. She crossed to stand near him. Spread on the cardboard was a mess of bolts, nuts, and sprockets. "Looks complicated," she said.

"It's a bitch." This assessment pleased her more than it should have. He swung a mallet and a rod sprung loose, metal twanging. "I've set and reset them twice." He glanced at her, his mouth set hard, then studied a diagram on a crumpled sheet of paper. "Once I get this first one, the rest will go easy."

He waved her out of his light. She stood abruptly but recovered her balance by setting her hand on one of the salvaged seats. With the toe of his boot, Kenny nudged a bolt. She scooped it off the cardboard and handed it to him.

He tossed it back in the pile. "Thanks. But I was just moving it out of the way."

"Oh," she said. "There must be some way I can help."

"Not unless you've set spacers before."

She bent to kiss him, barely catching the top of his head as he ducked to retrieve the mallet. She adjusted her robe, a whisper of silk against silk that made him look up.

His face softened, and he set down the mallet. "Careful," he said as with a surge of delight she wrapped her arms over his neck. "I'm dirty." Then he kissed her, hard like she liked, and ran his hands up the back of her robe. Her knees touched the edge of the plywood, fastened across the eight wheels. He kissed again, harder, as he lowered her onto the platform and unfastened his grease-stained pants.

"We'll break this baby in right," he said, his breath warm against her throat, his voice low and only for her as he maneuvered her onto the plywood. It was her that he wanted. Only her.

Crevasse

A crack or a series of cracks developed in response to differential stresses

Even at midday, Brody's basement was dark, though not musty like their basement in Pine Lake with its tumble of dirty laundry and outgrown toys and chemicals too hazardous to store under the sink. Here it smelled mostly new, a cavern of thick-carpeted floors and maroon-colored walls and track lighting on dimmers, a carved-out space that held its own against the elements, with the help of large furnishings that included a big-screen TV and fat brown leather sofas.

At youth group, Brody pretended not to see her at all. But in Magda's kitchen where Sylvie cut pies and brewed coffee and balanced plates on her arm, his eyes tracked her from under his white dishwasher's hat. The back of her hand swiping a stray hair from her forehead. The flick of her wrist, dumping coffee grounds. Her lips pressed in concentration as she sliced into the pies.

Brody wore his hair longer than his parents approved of; when he blinked, his lashes got caught in his bangs. In the back, the splayed ends of it brushed over his collar. Sylvie ran her fingers along the place where it curled. "Don't," Brody said.

"I like your hair," she said as he worked his hands under her shirt. "How it curls in the back."

He flung back his bangs and there were his eyes, dark and ambitious like his father's, but his mouth was his mother's, and hard as he tried to set it, there was a tenderness there that moved Sylvie, though she didn't know him, not really. She would be gone before that happened. She had to be. His fingers slid under the band of her bra and over her breasts, and she felt herself slipping as she had since she'd first let him kiss her, so unlike Rick, his longing desperate and strong. Already she regretted what they'd begun, with their separate but equally impossible desires.

She sank in the corner of one of the sofas, pinned down by Brody, the snap of his jeans cold on her belly, his hands urgent, bunching her shirt under her armpits and pushing her bra to her neck, exposing her chest. He saw nothing Rick hadn't, but the way he saw her was different, like he knew things about her that she didn't yet know herself. She shivered as his tongue wet her nipples. "Anna will come down any minute," she whispered. "She can't wait to watch some TV."

She ran her fingers along the waistband of his jeans, to show she wasn't making excuses. In his eyes was a question, a challenge, a dare. He was falling into a place he couldn't climb out of, and she wanted to hold him up, to steady him. But he scared her with his deep and unstoppable longing, as if Sylvie weren't there inside of her clothes. He seemed to hear nothing, see nothing, feel nothing but her. His need felt bigger than anything her body could give him, but her body was all that she had.

Only last Wednesday at youth group, he'd sat as he always did, looking bored as Nick droned on about the promise of heaven, the streets of gold and the jeweled crowns. Under the table, Brody had slipped her a note, which Sylvie had unfolded between her legs and glanced at when Cara wasn't looking. When youth group was over, an infernally long ninety minutes, Sylvie had tucked the note in the back pocket of her jeans, then left with Brody.

"I see you're a couple," Cara had said, smug but a little wistful.

"Brody seems like a nice boy." This from her mother.

"Watch yourself." That was Kenny.

In the dark of the basement, Brody pressed into Sylvie's chest, his shirt rough as he sucked the skin at the base of her neck, his hands feeling for the clasp of her shorts.

She shifted out from under him, wedging herself sideways against the back of the sofa. He breathed in soft little pants, and she felt his eyes, taking her in. She brushed the back of her hand across his chin, the skin smooth and taut, and tugged her shirt over her chest. "Where'd it come from?" she asked. "What you wrote in that note." She'd expected some smart-ass remark about the gates of heaven, the angels, the clouds. *Nothing gold can stay.* That's all the note said.

Brody leaned on one elbow. "It's from a poem. Robert Frost."

"I know that," she said. "You know the rest?"

His fingers shivered the side of her neck. "Maybe." He leaned to kiss her.

Footsteps creaked the floorboards above. She nudged him away. "Not here," she said.

"Not here." Hair hid his eyes. "You mean not with my mom upstairs dying." He rolled from her and hit the remote. Color filled the TV, a dance of bright shapes and voices.

She smoothed her shirt, glad for the sound of footsteps on the stairs, for the switch that washed them with light. Clutching the banister, Lena ducked to where she could see them. "Brody, your mother needs your help."

He flicked off the TV and without looking at Sylvie he got off the sofa. They followed Lena up the stairs, her breath heavy, her flesh smelling like dishwater left too long in the sink. "The sofa needs moving," she said once they reached the landing.

"There's no need." In purple sweatpants and with a bright purple scarf wrapped around her head and knotted in the back, Darla spoke from an overstuffed chair, the upholstery splashed with red and blue flowers, something you might find at a yard sale, impossible to match with any other piece of furniture, especially in this house, where the sofas were smooth leather like the ones downstairs, only creamy white. The skin around Darla's eyes and at the tops of her cheeks had lately turned puffy and soft, like air had leaked from her face. Sylvie's mother said this was the result of a new treatment, an experimental one, a last-ditch effort.

Like Lena, her mother had not let Scott's feud with Steven keep her from Darla, who needed their help, or so the church women thought. Kindness couldn't hurt, Sylvie's mother reasoned, and it was hardly Darla's fault, the way Scott behaved.

"Why is it that when you're feeling under the weather, everyone wants to mop your floors and scrub out your tub?" Darla seemed to direct the question at Sylvie, who could only shrug. "It's already way too clean around here. It's unnatural."

"Nonsense," said Lena. "With the dust bunnies under that sofa I know you can't rest."

Sylvie's mother handed her dust cloth to Anna. "You do the table," she said. "Don't use too much polish. I'll get one end of the sofa and you get the middle, Sylvie, and Brody, you get the other end." Her mother at least hadn't lost her knack for giving directions.

"Suppose I've got something stashed under there I don't want you to see," Darla said. "Some secret, and you people go and expose it." But when they hoisted the sofa, all it revealed was carpet that had seemed to have never been walked on, a cream color that wouldn't last two minutes at Kenny's.

"That's enough," Darla said when Lena shut off the vacuum. "I mean it." She shifted in her chair. "If I was feeling a little more perky, I'd boot you all out the door. Including you, Brody. Conspiring with these women." She twisted at the waist and resettled herself on the splayed floral print.

"The sofa's a lot more comfortable than that old chair," Lena said. "I don't know why you don't get rid of it. It belongs in the burn pile."

"Lena Preston. I've seen the things you hold onto." Darla grabbed Brody by the hand. "If you really want to do something for your mother, be a sweetheart and raise those blinds. I want to look at the glacier."

"That old thing," Lena said. Brody tugged a cord, and the glacier filled the window, icy humps that in the sunlight cast shadows over each other.

"All these years, and I've never been up on top of the ice," Darla said. "Can you believe it? Brody's been, though, with his father."

Brody shook his bangs, like it was no big deal. *Nothing gold can stay.* So unlike Rick, whose truck said pretty much everything you could know about him.

Darla relaxed into the chair. "Brody says when you get up on top, you can hear the ice crack and shift."

"You're in no condition to climb," Lena said.

Darla reached for Ruth's hand. "Don't wait like I did," she said.

Anna looked up from running the rag back and forth on the table. "Can I watch TV now?" she asked.

Lena's lips tightened. "We're not here to play. We've still got the kitchen."

"Patricia did the kitchen last week," Darla said. "Stop now and pour some iced tea." She waved a hand in the air. "Let the kids do what they want."

Sylvie's mother climbed on a chair and wiped the top of the blinds with her rag. "I'll do the glass too. So you'll have a nice view."

"If you must," said Darla. "I do like looking out. That glacier's got all the time in the world. You've got to give it that."

"Hogwash," said Lena.

Sylvie followed Brody through the kitchen and out to the garage. Blood. Even before he pressed the button and the overhead door lifted, she smelled it. The flood of daylight revealed a dark lump of fur in the back of the truck. "You never said your dad got a bear."

"Not my dad. Me. I shot it this morning. Don't say anything. Mom doesn't know." He brushed his hand across the fur. "It was kind of a rush, killing something that big."

"Why the secret?" Sylvie asked.

"My dad's idea. He's gonna drive it to the butcher in Palmer, have it ground up for sausage and burger. Surprise Mom."

In Scott's garage, tools hung on pegboards, hammers and hand saws and wrenches, the workbench clean as a kitchen table, nothing like Kenny's shop, where parts for the eight-wheeler were strewn everywhere. He'd been in a bad mood, bewildered at how the idler sprockets fit wrong and the cleats wouldn't mount as he'd planned. One axle shimmied, and he couldn't get the drive sprocket tension adjusted.

The girls were supposed to stay away from the shop, so Kenny could focus, though it seemed from the hints her mother dropped now and then that what she'd really like would be for him to abandon the eight-wheeler altogether. Once in awhile, when her mom wasn't looking, Sylvie snuck in the shop. Through her father, she'd learned to pay attention to the way things fit together, and she enjoyed handing Kenny the parts he needed before he could ask, breathing in the smell of gaskets and rubber and metal, and him treating her not as a child but an equal.

Beyond the Princes' garage spread Scott's lawn, plush and tidily trimmed, a rare thing in Resurrection, where any grass except the stuff that grew wild meant a big fight start to finish: hauling in topsoil and rolling it flat, working in powdered lime to balance the pH, aerating to encourage worms that were sluggish with cold, pumping fertilizers into the dirt. It looked like a golf course, or a cemetery.

Brody tossed her a helmet. "Wanna ride?"

"Sure." She climbed behind him on the four-wheeler, pressing her knees to his legs as his hand gripped the throttle, the hand he'd run under her shirt, the hand he'd set on the trigger and pulled.

"Hang on," he said, and as Sylvie clung to his waist, they rolled down the driveway, the lawn blurring as the wheels gathered speed. Without saying why, she'd told him she wouldn't be staying, then made him swear not to tell it to anyone else. It seemed not to affect him, or if it did, he didn't show it, and she was tempted to say more, about how there were places where the landscape didn't own you, where the cold didn't call to you, where there were limits to what you could want.

They hugged the highway, riding the shoulder, the wheels spitting gravel and dust, the sun warm on her legs. The helmet lacked a shield and the wind hit her face, so she ducked behind Brody's back. The wide tires floated as if the rocks were a river. The road dipped, launching her a few inches off the seat. She hugged Brody tighter, his muscles tense under her hands, and felt how nice it would be to hold on like this always, to never let go.

Brody turned wide and fast off the highway, dust billowing out from under the tires, Sylvie's knees digging into his legs as they hurtled toward the river. Her father had loved this kind of speed. The right front tire caught on a rock. The handlebars jerked, but the forward momentum steadied them.

Spinning gravel and dust, they hit the wide place between the cliffs near where Tess had cornered the porcupine. They traveled so fast that the river seemed slow. There appeared no end to where those four fat tires would take them. Nothing gold, nothing gold. Maybe Brody didn't need her after all. Out here, he seemed to need no one.

Worn and tossed by the river, a gray twisted log loomed ahead. Brody jerked the machine to the left, but it was too late. In a flurry of dust, the wheeler launched sideways, airborne, a suspension of motion and time that ended with the clunk of her helmet, the scraping of rocks, the thud of her body hitting the ground.

Sylvie's hands lay still at her sides, like they belonged to someone else and had landed there only by chance. She stared at the sky, blank with blue, her shoulder throbbing, her thigh stinging, hurt but also angry at how she'd clung to him, how she'd trusted.

She listened, but there was only the sound of the river riding the rocks. Her stomach tightened. "Brody?" She pushed herself out of the gravel and pulled off the helmet.

The four-wheeler lay on its side, its cowling cracked, its fender dented. Beside it lay Brody, his legs bent. He rolled slowly to one side and with a low mewing sound he sat up. Gray silt dusted his jeans and his shirt, and his helmet was crooked. He crept across the gravel toward her. "You okay?" His voice was small compared to the river. He wriggled out of the helmet, the side of it scraped, along with his face and his hands. "Your leg." He reached to touch the raw stinging place on her thigh, floured gray from the silt.

She pushed his hand away. "You could have killed us," she said.

"I'm sorry," he said. "Really sorry." He stared at her leg. "We should wash out that dirt."

Because there was no other way, she leaned against him and limped toward the river, where he helped her over the rocks to the water. But she refused his help with the washing. Her hand went numb as she splashed river water over her leg and rubbed at the dirt, the big raw patch gaping ugly and red. The more she rubbed, the redder it turned.

She sank on a boulder and cradled her head in her hands. She sobbed, violent and heaving, Brody hovering close. Through her tears, she waved him away. He paced the bank, glancing back as she wiped her face on her sleeves.

"Get me out of here," she said. "I want to go home."

"We have to set the wheeler upright. You have to help me."

She didn't want him to need her, for that or anything else. She wanted only for the river to tumble and turn her like one of its rocks. The shock of the cold, the rush of the thick, grinding water would smooth the hard jagged places, making everything new.

Downwasted

Thinned from ice, both moving and stagnant

Kenny said she worried too much, about Darla, about Sylvie—and who wouldn't, after that accident—even about Steven and how he might retaliate, now that Scott's boy had gotten his bear.

She needed a break, Kenny said, laughable when Ruth thought of how hard she worked to fill up the days. But when he offered to leave his eight-wheeler project—so close to finished, but a steering cable had him stumped—and take her dip-netting in the Chitina River, four hours' drive from Resurrection, she'd quickly agreed.

As Kenny predicted, once they got there, Ruth forgot all about Darla and Sylvie and the trouble over bears. Chitina was a wild place among wild places, where the river rocketed willfully, carving a steep-walled granite canyon that funneled an endless, whipping wind. The mountains felt sharp and new, as if they were still being thrust skyward; it would be no surprise to wake in the morning to find they'd doubled in size. Though flowers struggled out of the dirt, scotch broom and paintbrush and arnica, the wind-stirred dust and sprayed water covered over their scent.

Kenny helped her into the waders. Take it nice and slow, he told her. Feel for rocks with your feet. Stand firm, you have to stand firm. If you slip, the current will carry you off. He handed her a metal pole twice her height, the net on the end so wide you could use it to scoop up children were they to bob from the water, so dark and turbulent that it would hardly surprise her if a leg or an arm did flail up. Ruth struggled to balance the pole, heavy on the net end, while Kenny waded into the water, using his pole like a tightrope.

When he was waist deep in the river, he lowered his net. Take it slow, he urged. Nice and easy. She steadied her feet, shuffling over the rocks, her waders cold as water rushed past them, her feet and her ankles and her shins and her thighs. "You gotta get out where the fish are," he'd yelled over the roar of the water. "You'll feel the fish when they hit."

Below there was only gray water, beating and chopping and foaming. She looked up, staring straight ahead like a blind person, feeling with the rubber soles of her waders for a flat place to stand. Her foot slipped, and she wobbled with the pole, the net bobbling. This was how people died. She recovered her balance, planting one foot and then the other to root herself against the current, determined not to let the river carry her off. Her girls needed their mother. That was all she could think.

She dared to turn her head ever so slightly, and there was Kenny smiling real and full, at the way she planted her feet and scrunched up her forehead and stood her ground against the current. Right then, a fish hit her net, a mysterious thunking that upset her balance, but she somehow kept her feet underneath her as she tugged hard, up, up, and up, to hoist the thrashing king salmon into the sunlight, twisting and dripping and heaving.

The dip-netting wives from the church complained how sand blasted every corner and pocket of their tents at Chitina. But not Ruth. She loved the sound of the tent flapping in the wind that blew through the canyon, drowning their rustles and sighs, hers and Kenny's, and she was sad once they'd caught their limit and had to pack up for home.

The church women also grumbled about the work that came out of Chitina. Slimy waders and nets. Sand tracked through their kitchens. Sinks stinking of fish. But the Chitina couldn't give up enough fish to satisfy Ruth. The slicing and freezing and canning and smoking—she felt purposed by all of it, especially when Kenny bragged to his mother about all she had done.

In the canner was the last of the salmon, soaked in brine, patted with brown sugar and cloves, smoked outside over smoldering wood chips. For three days she'd tended the fish, rising each night to refresh the wood stacked on the hot plate, poking the slow-cooking flesh with her finger, rotating racks in the plywood smokehouse Kenny had built with scraps left from the eight-wheeler project. She'd boiled jars and packed them with fish and processed them in a pressure cooker borrowed from Darla, till the whole house smelled of fish and smoke, like water dumped on a fire. It steamed into the red tablecloth she'd sewn to replace the flower-sprigged vinyl, and into the striped curtains she'd made from some old fabric of Lena's, to replace the towel that hung on the door.

She leaned against the swollen kitchen sash and got the window to crack a few inches. The needle of the pressure cooker hovered barely under the red zone. One time Cherise had neglected the gauge, and her canner had spewed fish and glass all over her kitchen. Even with two batches behind her, Ruth didn't trust that sort of pressure. One hour and fifty minutes of watching and fiddling with the heat and not standing too close proved a very long time. Yesterday Anna had hovered beside her, wanting to know exactly how steam could cook air out of jars. All Ruth could see was the cooker exploding and shards of glass piercing Anna. Today Lena had come to the rescue, taking Anna to church to help with the safer task of baking cupcakes for the big church barbeque.

The timer dinged. Ten pounds, 110 minutes. Ruth shut off the gas and sat at the table to wait for the pressure to drop. The whole room looked brighter since Lena had loaned them two crocheted afghans to tuck over the chairs. The walls were still bare, but Kate had talked about starting a group to do quilting at church. Ruth envisioned bright fabric, snipped, shaped, and stitched, to hang over two spots near the furnace where smoke smudged the wall.

Though the house was coming along, the garden was a disappointment. Ruth lugged water daily and fussed with the weeds, but only half of what she'd planted had sprouted. The seedlings that did come up looked spindly and weak, like they'd shot up too fast. They were too close together, but by the time Kate mentioned thinning, Ruth feared pulling one seedling would remove the whole clump, and she felt an irrational affinity for each of the plants, for their struggles, and she couldn't bring herself to pull any out.

Only the radishes appeared healthy. They grew hardy lobed leaves, bristly on the underside, but when she yanked one plant up by the stem, the root was spindly and pale. She'd buried it back, thinking she'd pulled it too soon, but the radish wilted and died.

While she waited for the fish to cool, Ruth thumbed through the Bible. Though it was starting to look like the Bibles the other women brought to church, scribbled and bent at the corners, she still felt like a fraud. She'd thought of returning the Minerva Jones workbook and staying home Wednesday nights, but Lena would be disappointed, not to mention Anna. Minerva Jones had moved on to explaining Paul's first letter to the Corinthians, a hard book despite the verse about love. No matter what the Corinthians did, they were a disappointment to Paul. Ruth understood they had flaws. Pride. Bickering. Lusts of the flesh. But Paul's standards seemed high. He nitpicked and nagged and then made a point of saying how humble he was.

As the lids sealed, the jars of smoked salmon popped one by one, a pleasant sound like slow-cooking popcorn, as the air contracted inside. With a dish towel Ruth blotted the puddle of water from each concave top, careful not to disturb the subtle shifting that had gone on inside, the vacuums created. A broken seal meant failure. From the first batch of smoked fish, there had been five broken seals. From the next batch, there'd been three. She'd stacked the faulty ones in the back of the fridge to make salmon loaf, salmon patties, salmon spread.

When she determined that each seal in this last batch had stuck, she wiped her hands and admired the jars, gleaming on her coffee-brown counters. With this tangible success, she could overlook all the unreasonable situations that continued to present themselves in her imagination. Tommy scolding her for her failure with the garden. Cynthia returning from wherever she'd gone to, derisive and angry. Kenny driving off on his eight-wheeler, once it was finished, and never coming back. The glacier descending, dooming them all to the cold.

Sylvie came home, looking grown-up in the black pants and white shirt Magda made all the girls wear, her hair pulled back and her cheeks flushed from riding Kenny's old bike. Ruth asked in a casual way how work had gone. If she tempered her interest, Sylvie was more apt to answer. Ruth loved the gossip from the lodge: the squabbles, Magda's high-handed attitude, Tommy's flippant remarks.

"I made a whole bunch in tips." Sylvie emptied wads of bills from her pockets onto the table. She sniffed. "Stinks in here."

"It's the last of fish," Ruth said.

"Praise the Lord," Sylvie said, though not in a tone Paul would have approved.

Ruth lifted a warm jar to the light. Smoked, the fish turned more red than pink, its skin bronzed by the heat. "You'll be glad for it once winter comes."

Sylvie's mouth tensed. Slight, almost imperceptible. From a young age, she'd seemed to take pleasure in her own reticence, forcing Ruth to guess what was wrong—heat, hunger, cold. With the heel of her hand, Sylvie flattened a crinkled twenty-dollar bill. "Look what some old guy shoved in my pocket," she said. "When his wife wasn't looking. And all they had was coffee and pie."

Ruth wiped her hands. "You'd better watch yourself, flirting."

"I wasn't flirting. I just poured him coffee."

With a bottle opener, Ruth pried off one of the just-sealed lids. With a fork, she stabbed a chunk of salmon, pleased at how firm it was, colored like the sun filtered through smoke, a deep orange-red. "Try some." She hovered the dripping fork, offering the fish to Sylvie.

"No thanks."

"It's delicious warm." Ruth pushed the chunk onto a saucer and set it between them. "All that oil." The fish was smoky and salty and sweet on the tongue. She nudged the saucer toward Sylvie. "Come on. Try it."

The fork hung between Sylvie's fingers, top-heavy like Ruth's Chitina net, her eyes dark with sorrow or perhaps suspicion or maybe even joy, they were that unreadable.

Back home, people would kill for this abundance of fish. You'd pay a fortune for it in the Lower Forty-eight—she was learning to say this, like everyone else, instead of *back home*. But points like those never moved Sylvie, so instead Ruth said, "It's thanks to Kenny we've got all this fish," which convinced Sylvie to wedge a morsel onto the fork and play it around in her mouth and declare it not too bad.

Ruth screwed the lid on the jar. "Better than bear, by a long shot."

"Yeah. Bear smells like old gym socks."

"Or damp leaves," Ruth said. "On the ground, in the fall, after a hard rain." She tried to think of what else to say, to make the most of a moment when Sylvie wasn't hedged up against her. "How much did you make all together?" she asked.

Sylvie shuffled the money. "Eighty-two bucks." She stacked up the bills. "We'll need it, for when we go home."

Ruth reached her hand across the table. "Honey, this is our home now."

"God, Mom." Sylvie pulled her hand to her lap. "You're so unrealistic."

"Sylvie. Watch the way you say God."

"If God's so big, he won't care how I say it."

"It's not just God," Ruth said. "You could offend someone else." She felt on sure footing, having learned this from Paul.

"Like Cara, you mean? Or Brody? Hate to tell you, Mom, but they say God all the time, and it's not like they're praying."

Ruth pushed away from the table. She had one minute, maybe two, before Sylvie stormed up the stairs. "I don't care how your friends talk," she said. "I care about you." No matter how Sylvie frowned or how her forehead tensed or how her eyes defied understanding, her soft mouth was a reminder of the child she'd once been, full of wonder and eager to please. "You seem awful touchy," Ruth said. "Since you broke up with Brody."

"We didn't break up. We were never a couple."

"It's not easy for him," Ruth said gently. "With his mom sick."

"Like I don't know that," said Sylvie.

"All I'm saying is you could be nice."

Sylvie flattened her hands on the table. "The way you're nice with Kenny?"

"Kenny's part of us now." Ruth sugared her voice as she'd coated the fish, rubbing even and slow. "We're not going back."

"You're no better than Anna," said Sylvie. "Playing pretend with your fish and your jars."

"I know you miss Karen and Rick," Ruth said. "I know it's not easy, adjusting. You're bound to be—"

Sylvie shot her an accusing look. "You came for that glacier," she said. "And now you can't even face it."

Ruth folded her hands. Hands that scooped fish from the river. Hands that sliced off heads at the gills. Hands that stuffed flesh in jars. "That's not true," she said.

"Brody would take me whenever I want," Sylvie said. "To the ice."

"Don't do that, Sylvie. Don't use Brody to prove something."

"You're jealous," said Sylvie. "Because Kenny's all caught up with his guns and his fish and his eight-wheeler."

"This is not about Kenny." Ruth infused her voice with calm.

"You think I don't see it." Sylvie's voice quivered. "You think I don't see how he looks at me."

Ruth forced a breath of salmon-smoked air. "Kenny does no such thing."

Sylvie shot up from the table, glaring down at her mother. "You never learn, do you?" She scooped her cash in her hands and trounced up the stairs.

Ruth stared at the fish, neatly processed and packed. In her mind there were hordes of them flapping and thrashing, sexed and spent by the water, icy and cold, unmoved by the hovering net, a world apart.

⁓

The chilled air felt more like Thanksgiving than July, but Ruth was determined that nothing, not even Sylvie's outrageous accusations, would spoil their Sunday. They'd slept late and, to fend off their grogginess, they drank strong coffee with their pancakes. Soon there would be blueberries, Kenny said, to add to the pancakes. He'd show Ruth where to pick them, the Prestons' secret spot.

Clouds pressed thick and gray, hiding the mountains so that only the glacier was visible, sprawling white. Though Lena had prayed hard against it, rain splatted the ground, stirring up smells that brought to mind time itself, pressed down and compacted. Rain had been one of several objections when Kenny's mother had proposed that the church host its annual picnic on the island. Others included the overall hassle and the break with tradition. There was a general feeling that the islanders knew right where the church was and could show up for picnics whenever they wanted. But Pastor Tom held with Lena. After the fuss over Scott and the bear baiting, divisions had deepened. Healing was needed, and that was the call of the church. With some grumbling, the elders had nailed up a shelter in a wide space near the river that was normally used for target practice.

In her role as picnic ambassador, Lena had recruited Ruth to stuff mailboxes with fliers. She quizzed every person she saw about their plans and extracted promises from both her boys that for once they'd attend. Bad feelings, suspicions, mistrust—Lena was sure they'd dissolve if folks came together under the banner of God.

Sylvie of course wanted to skip the picnic, but Ruth insisted she attend. As they approached the newly built shelter, the rain let up. Maneuvering between the clouds, sunlight glinted off water beaded on the windshield. They got out of the truck to the smell of charcoal. Behind them, Lena's car crawled reptile-like over the dips and bumps in the dirt road. Nosing close, she hit the brakes and heaved herself out, then leaned against a wobbly table as she steadied her breath. "I've got the cupcakes," she announced.

Shoulders hunched, Sylvie watched Brody and Cara toss a Frisbee with the Markham kids, a game of keep-away from Tess. Ruth was done indulging her daughter. Sooner or later, she was going to have to quit feeling sorry for herself. From the back seat of Lena's car, she plucked a flat of cupcakes and handed them to Sylvie. The frosting looked hideous, blobbed thick in spots and scraped thin in others. Several of the cupcakes were badly smashed.

"I took the corner a little too fast," Lena said. "It always sneaks up on me." Sylvie thunked the cupcakes on the nearest table and wandered toward the game of Frisbee while Ruth put Anna to work fixing the frosting. Out loud, Lena counted heads from the island. Tommy and Cleve and Cleve's wife. The Markham kids, all seven, along with their parents. Plus twenty-three more. Not as many as she'd hoped for, but it was early, and island people often came late.

"There was more grumbling than the children of Moses when it started to rain," Kate informed Lena. "People looked ready to leave."

"I don't see that anyone did," Lena said. "It was only a shower. A cleansing."

Anna displayed her cupcake repairs, and in a burst of affection, Lena swooped her under her arm. "A real Glory Girl in the making," Lena said.

A line formed before the hot dogs were ready, and soon plates were loaded with buns and potato salad and coleslaw and beans. Lena picked at chips and burnt bits of hotdog as she went from table to table, extending her hand to each of the islanders. *So glad you could join us. Be sure to stay for the real food that follows.* Once she'd worked the crowd, she eased onto a bench next to Kenny and Ruth. "I hope your brother gets here soon," Lena said. "Before the hot dogs are gone."

"Mind if I join you?" Before anyone could answer, Tommy set down her plate. Her breasts jostled under her shirt, a soft cotton tee the color of fireweed. "Wish there was salmon," she said. "Hot dogs are loaded with nitrates and salt."

Ruth licked a spot of ketchup from the edge of her mouth. "I'm having two," she said. "It's been ages."

Tommy laughed. "You'll die already pickled."

Ruth peeled the paper back from a cupcake. "I might just have two of these, too."

"Don't get me started on cupcakes," said Tommy. "All that sugar."

"Nothing like frosting that melts on your tongue," Lena said.

"Those kids zipping around," Tommy said. "That's sugar."

"Their mothers don't mind," Lena said. "It's a picnic."

"How's that garden coming?" Tommy asked Ruth.

Ruth snapped a potato chip. "Growing," she said. "Slowly."

"I'll stop by for a look," Tommy said. "Summer's already on its way out. July, that's the tipping point. The slow skid to winter."

"It's too soon to think about cold," Lena said firmly.

Scott Prince parked next to Lena's car. He hurried around the front of the truck to help Darla out, but she waved him off, the wind flapping her scarf, sheer and red.

On the road behind Scott came Steven. He steered his truck to the far end of the parking area, where he shut off the engine and leaned over the steering wheel as if deciding whether to get out.

"Don't you look cheery," Lena said as Darla approached.

"I love picnics," Darla said. "And look how this came together. All these people from the island."

Lena's hands fluttered. "Kenny, go see about your brother. I don't want him missing out on the food."

"And those cupcakes," Darla said. "Such cute decorations."

"No matter what anyone says, you know they all love that frosting," said Lena. "The thicker, the better."

Tommy touched a bruise on Darla's arm. "From the chemo?"

"Darla doesn't want to talk about chemo," Lena said sharply.

"I fell," Darla said. "Lost my balance. Feet went right out from under me. Not that I ever was graceful. And it felt like just too much work to get up. Brody found me, poor kid."

"You can't be worried about Brody," Lena said. "You've got to think of yourself."

"Ha. As if you haven't always, in every circumstance, put your boys before yourself."

"That's different," Lena said. "We're talking about your health."

"I used to pray, Lord, help me hang on to see my first grandchild. Then, help me hang on till Brody gets married. Then graduation. Lord, let me see graduation. But there's no point to the bargaining, is there?" This she aimed directly at Ruth. "I just want him to be happy, you know?"

"Brody's young," Lena said. "He'll be fine. Look at my Kenny. You'd never guess it, how sick he was way back when with rheumatic fever, and us out here with no doctor."

"Kenny was sick?" Ruth asked. He'd never mentioned it.

"Deathly sick," Lena said. "I stayed right by his bed, day and night. When he went back to school, he was too weak to play. Rheumatic fever's hard on the heart. Kids made fun when he sat on the sidelines at recess. One day I could tell he'd been crying. So the next day I went to school with him. I went back the next and the next, every day till the school year was over."

Darla's eyes wavered toward Brody, who'd gone off to eat by himself. "Then there was Steven." Lena seemed compelled to keep talking. "I had to step between him and his friends more than once."

"I suppose it gets better with time," Darla said.

"Kenny's weak spot is women." Lena seemed to have forgotten that Ruth was there. "They've gotten him in all sorts of trouble."

Darla looked kindly at Ruth, who smiled a little. "That must be the speaker from Fairbanks." She nodded at the only person Ruth didn't recognize, a slender man in a suit who was talking to Scott.

"Brother Engells," Lena said. "A real man of God."

Waving a photo, Steven stepped between Brother Engells and Scott. Behind him was Kenny.

"You stole my bait." Idle chatter ceded to Steven's loud accusation. "Got your bear. But that wasn't enough. You had Crowley Air take this picture, so I'd get a citation."

"Who's to say Fish and Game's not flying surveillance?" asked Scott. "You heard that trooper." His voice rang off the roof of the shelter. Pastor Engells set down his plate. Ruth stared at a half-eaten cupcake. Next to Brody, Sylvie looked down at her feet.

"No one but you would narc on a neighbor," Steven said.

Scott balled one hand in a fist. He jabbed a finger at Steven. "Don't provoke me," he said.

"That's real neighborly, Scott. Real God-like." Steven began to pace.

"Boys," Lena said. But the tone she must have used on the playground back when they really were boys sounded ineffectual, laughable even. "Scott. Think of your wife."

Scott swung around. "You leave Darla out of this. You people. You," he pointed at Lena. "And you." He pointed at Ruth. "Always up at my house." Ruth's pain at this, the turning of her best intentions, was large and physical, a shearing off within her chest.

Pastor Tom approached. "Scott, these women only mean to help Darla."

"That's what I hoped." Scott's face took on a wild look, his mouth large, his nostrils inflated, the furrows between his eyes dark and angry. "But I might be dead wrong."

"Scott." Darla was working her way to him, reaching from table to table. "Don't be a fool."

Scott hiked up his shoulders, rejecting the Prestons and everything they stood for as Steven stuffed the photo back in his pocket. Lena's shoulders slumped, her flesh folding in on itself like a box that had sat too long in the rain.

Scott grabbed his wife's arm. "Don't know that we can stay for the message," he said to Brother Engells. His voice trembled. "But I'd be much obliged if you'd lay hands and pray for my wife."

The tension broke as churchgoers swarmed, circling Darla, none of them seeming to notice as Ruth did when Darla shook her head and tried to step back.

"Sorry, Mom." Steven leaned over his mother. "But that bastard—"

"Enough." Lena held up her hand as she moved toward the circle of prayer.

His eyes squeezed tight, Brother Engells cupped his hand over Darla's head. Hands rested on her shoulders, on her back, on her arms. Those who couldn't get close set hands on those who could reach, and the prayers began, voices low but building like a wave. Ruth felt conspicuous, holding back. But when the prayer ended with murmurs and hugs, no one even looked her direction.

Scott took Darla's elbow. "Let's get you home."

"No," she said. "I want to stay."

Several islanders had left while the church people prayed. The Markhams. The Hanleys. Cleve Baker.

Sylvie approached her mother. "Can we go now?"

"We're staying," said Ruth.

"I've gotta get home," Kenny said. "Finish my wheeler."

Irrational, the way this filled Ruth with dread, the prospect of him being finished and able to ride away on the wheeler, wherever he wanted. He had a truck. But this new thing was fashioned of his single-minded devotion.

"I'll go with Kenny," said Sylvie.

"No," said Ruth. "You'll stay for the message. Honey, you could stay, too. It would mean a lot to your mother. You can finish another day."

"Sorry, babe. I'm this close." He held his thumb pressed to his finger.

"Please." This Sylvie directed at Kenny. "I won't be any trouble."

Kenny crossed his arms over his chest and stepped back like he was sizing her up. "Sure looks like trouble to me."

Sylvie nudged a toe in the dirt. "That's exactly right," Ruth said in the forced, cheery tone that resulted when you told yourself to buck up, to quit thinking and feeling outlandish things and go about the everyday business of living. "You're staying right here."

"You don't understand," Sylvie said. "You never understand."

A fly was buzzing the cupcakes. From behind, Lena grabbed Sylvie's arm. "Be a dear," she said. "Tuck some plastic over the food."

With a sullen look, Sylvie did as Lena asked. "The best cure for a self-centered child is a task," Lena said to Ruth.

She watched as Kenny drove off. It was nonsense, to think she could lose him.

Brother Engells opened his Bible, and Ruth realized that she'd left hers in Kenny's truck. "Now to the faithful." The visiting pastor smiled as if God had ordained the disappearance of everyone else. "You all know what Paul wrote to the believers at Corinth. How he saw through their pretense. How he noted their flaws, which were many. Strife. Envy. Immoral behavior. But you know what the biggest one was? The one that took the cake, so to speak?"

After a weighty silence, Brother Engells answered his own question. "Rebellion. That's the sin that clobbered those Corinthians. And do you think they recognized it? No sirree. The roots of rebellion run deep." He spread his hands in the air. "Picture a lawn. Big. Beautiful. Green." He pointed at Scott. "Like the one our brother here grows. I do believe I've heard talk of it all the way up in Fairbanks. Like he's rolled up all of God's goodness right there in that spot."

Scott looked down at the dirt. "I'll bet a few of you are nursing some envy." The preacher's voice surged. "Me, I'd give a lot for a lawn like that.

But a lawn that perfect takes work. The worst of it's yanking up weeds. Dandelions. Scourge of the earth. Am I right, Brother Prince?"

Scott nodded, knowing and resigned. "I understand those roots can reach down three feet. Impossible to tear out something that deep. And that's how it is with rebellion. It's got roots long and tough as those nasty old weeds. Break it off without getting the roots, and back it comes with a vengeance. And oh, does it spread."

Ruth watched as Lena penciled "rebellion" next to Paul's first letter to Corinth. *Deep roots*, she wrote.

"I know what you're thinking." Ruth blushed, feeling the preacher's gaze had fallen directly on her. "From rebellion, you think you know where I'm headed. Obedience, right?" Brother Engells cocked his head like a weasel poking out of a wood pile, a wrong way to think of a preacher, though the way his sharp brown eyes darted from one side of the shelter to the other encouraged it. "You're saying, this guy's traveled from Fairbanks to preach another dang message on how we've got to obey. But you're mistaken. I'm here today to talk about secrets. Our secrets, you see, are the greatest rebellion from God. The roots of the weeds that crowd out all the good God has in store."

He flipped a page in his Bible and began naming the secrets the Corinthians tried to keep from each other and Paul. Divisions. Pride. Fear. He swept a hand toward the river. "Think of that water," he said. "Gallons and gallons rush by every second." His voice mounted toward a crescendo. "Loaded with silt. Carving through rock. Crashing and rolling. You hear how it roars. And no one but God knows what's beneath it."

Sylvie looked up from her sandals, head tilted toward the river. Brody had sat down beside her, away from Darla and Scott.

"Paul says we see through a mirror thick and dark as that water," Brother Engells said. "To be free, we must know and be known." He clasped his hands in front of his chest, his forehead lined as if with the weight of their collective sorrows. "We're called to set ourselves free. To reach for true independence."

At the next table, Marie was wiping furiously at her eyes. She bent her head and her shoulders began to shake as her tears turned to sobs. Kate and Roxanne scooted close, whispering comfort, but this only encouraged her weeping. Brother Engells steepled his fingers. "Yes. Yes," he murmured. "We walk through the valley, but the Lord is with us."

Marie smiled weakly at Kate and Roxanne and then stood, sniffling and brushing tears from her cheeks. "Brother Engells, I know what you say is the truth." Her voice wobbled like a rain-pelted puddle. "These children." She glanced at them, cross-legged and vacant-eyed. "I know they're a blessing." Her voice caught. "But sometimes I just lose my patience."

Brother Engells fisted one hand. "Yes, sister." His voice rose over the sound of the water. "Let go of that secret and you're free, truly free."

Marie sank to her seat and collapsed into tears. Brother Engells paced in front of the benches and tables, staring at his fingertips, a prophet consulting his God. Beyond the shelter, the sun had made a full break from the clouds, turning the old riverbed into a patchwork of shadow and light, the lichen and rocks smelling of water dissolved into air. Above a small plane droned, dipping one wing as it banked and turned.

Break free. Soften your heart. These were things you said to prove you belonged, plastering over the cracks between what you'd intended and what you'd become. The pastor looked straight at Ruth, but all she could think was of what Sylvie had said, that she didn't understand, that she never had.

Darla stood, the ends of her scarf fluttering in the wind. "You've all been so kind. Your prayers lift me up. They give me strength." She hugged her waist. "I believe in God's healing. I do." Marie sniffed and nodded. Roxanne patted her leg. Scott looked at the smoldering charcoal like it might need his attention. "But deep down..." Darla's voice trailed off.

Beside Ruth, Lena uncrossed her ankles and stared at the back of her hands. "God says the truth makes us free." Darla appeared not to notice as Lena pressed her hands to the bench and raised herself up.

"See the freedom," Brother Engells said. "It's written all over her face."

What Ruth saw on Darla's face was resignation, defeat. "It's not fair." Darla blinked hard. "It's just not fair."

Lena maneuvered around Sylvie and Brody, past Marie and Kate. As she reached for Darla, her hand caught the edge of a full flat of cupcakes, tipping it so that three of them slid out from under the plastic, splat, splat, splat.

"It's the devil!" Lena wheezed like an old set of bellows.

Everyone stared, including Brother Engells.

"The devil." Darla wiped her cheek with the back of her hand. "The devil. Yes. Of course." Her lips turned, a thin smile. "It's the devil."

"You go on ahead now." As Darla clung to her arm, Lena nodded at Brother Engells. "Go on and preach." She patted Darla's hand. "About those secrets. It was just getting interesting."

Ablation

Loss resulting from melting, runoff, sublimation, evaporation, or wind

In Pine Lake, July meant fresh-picked corn, slathered in butter. Fireflies pricking the dark and bonfires out at the dike. The comfort of the familiar, where things went on as they always had. Where it was possible to forget.

More than halfway to winter. The downhill slide, and no closer to leaving than they'd been on the day they arrived. Her mother's attempts at homemaking, the countertops and the curtains and the jars, these would protect them from nothing, her mother growing better by the day at ignoring the obvious.

The devil. That was one way to put it.

Brother Engells closed his eyes and turned his face toward heaven. "Lord, I know there's another," he said. "Another who's burdened by secrets. Another who churns like that river, trying to hide. But you see all, Lord. The smallest pebble rolling around in that water is no secret to you."

He opened his eyes, looking to Brody, and then to Sylvie. She felt the place on her thigh where skin was growing over the silt, the grayish-pink scar. There was danger in what built up without your knowing, circumstances layered so convincingly that you attributed them to fate or faith, depending on which way you leaned, though in the end it didn't matter where you put the blame. This Sylvie had discovered with her father on that long-ago September evening, speeding over the glassy lake, cloaked in darkness.

It was not the preacher, not her mother, not the thought of Kenny even, but the slapping waves that compelled Sylvie to stand.

"There's this thing I've never told anyone." Her voice rang clear. Heads nodded, encouraging, though not her mother's.

"Back where we came from," she said. "Back in Pine Lake." She shifted to one side, to better see the ice. "We had this old house, with a big staircase." She recalled the banister, the way her father had taught her to slide down it. "We went on picnics in summer. At Halloween, we carved pumpkins. Strung lights for Christmas. The perfect family."

The spray on her face, cold assurance that nothing could ever come between them, her and her father. It made her dizzy to recall this, and she had to steady herself against the bench. "This one time I rode my bike to the place where my dad worked. Dillinger Ford. I went in through the back, where they stocked all the parts. And there was my dad. He was…"

Brother Engells pressed his Bible to his chest and nodded, encouraging. "He was with this woman." She had no words for the anger, the shock, the betrayal. "They were…" Her voice trailed off. Her mother stared. Lena gripped the flesh of her knees. "They were kissing," Sylvie said. "Her shirt was undone. My dad had his hands, you know, on her chest."

From her mother came a small gasp, barely audible over the sound of the water. "You kept this a secret," Brother Engells said. "What you saw."

"I was eleven. By Christmas, he was gone. He left with that woman. Mirabelle." Her legs no longer worthy of trust, Sylvie sat down.

Brother Engells swayed, shifting his weight from one foot to another. He scrunched his eyes shut. "Yes, Lord," he said. "Yes. We trust in love we can't see." As he launched into a prayer, Brody glanced sideways at Sylvie, a look of affection or admiration or possibly understanding. Her mother looked ready to cry.

Once the prayer ended, the clean-up began. Her mother shoved a tray of cupcakes at Sylvie. "You will not run us off," she said. "No matter what mean thing you confess."

"You always say to be honest."

Her mother circled, gathering smashed paper plates, greasy napkins, half-empty sodas. "That wasn't honest," she said. "It was mean. I'm sorry you had to see your father like that. But you could have told me in private. You could have told me a long time ago." Her hands shook as she cinched the trash bag shut. "Of all things. In all places."

"Careful," Lena called from across the shelter. "With those cupcakes." Sylvie gripped a flat with both hands. Nick called it conviction, when you did things for reasons you couldn't explain. It came from God, he said, and if you acted on it, you were supposed to feel what he called release. But all she felt was heaviness, a weighing down caused by all the wrong that was in her.

Hauling the leftover cupcakes, she trudged toward Lena's car. Tess ran alongside, snapping at the frosting. Sylvie slid the cupcakes into Lena's back seat and slammed the door, blinking against the stinging wind.

Soon Brody would be at the glacier. His father had chartered a plane, Crowley Air, because his mother wanted to get up on the ice.

I know you're still mad. That's what Brody had said, and she'd let him believe it. There was an extra seat on the plane, and his dad had said Sylvie could go if she wanted. And she wanted, fiercely and unreasonably. But there was this difference now, since the four-wheeler tipped, of Brody wanting to know, and her wanting to be known, and that frightened her as much as anything. Still, she wished she could see Darla standing wide-legged on top of the ice, warm breaths dissolving into the cold, and the fullness of Brody's love, fierce and angry and raw, understanding what his father could not, that she had only to slide and let go.

Sylvie's father used to tousle her hair, scoop her up by the arms, swing her in circles. With those same hands he'd caressed Mirabelle's shiny blonde hair, with those same fingers he'd fumbled with her silky pink shirt, loosening one large breast and then the other. Roused by his hands, the round dark nipples had stiffened, and her father had moaned in a way that was guttural, frightening. Still Sylvie had not looked away. The wind sang his name and the river tumbled his promises, all of them gone.

Tess charged beside Sylvie through the brush. Out of the rocks pushed wooly red paintbrush, tiny pink bellflowers, twists of white tundra cotton. She tripped over a branch washed up by the water as she skirted the place where the tram had been, where the woman had died. At the water's edge she flung rock after rock, each one a memory. Karen. Rick. Her father.

Tess froze, her stubby tail erect, ears up and eyes fixed. Sylvie turned, a rock in her hand, and there was her mother, small against the broad sky. As she came close, she attempted a smile. "Look how it's blooming," she said.

"A woman died here," Sylvie said. No words seemed too shameful now. "Lena's sister."

"The tram broke. It wasn't kept up." Sylvie couldn't help herself, folding pain over pain, the same as when she'd worried the raw place on her thigh.

Dust swirled from the gravel, caught by the wind. Tess trotted up with a stick. "We don't belong here," Sylvie said. A pure simple fact.

"Of course we do." Her mother sounded false-fronted, all trim and flourish. "It takes time, that's all." She bent and scratched Tess behind her ears the way Tommy did. Tess dropped the stick, relaxing under her hand, then flopped to the ground and offered her belly. "I wish you'd told me, when it happened. About your father."

"It's not about him," Sylvie said.

"Things will look different once you get older."

There was no shimmer, no shifting. No lake and no truck. There was only the steady song of the water sprung out of ice, receding already into memory. "School will start and you'll have a routine. Things will get better with Brody."

"Winter will come," Sylvie said. "Then what?"

Her mother blinked into the wind. "What you said. About Kenny. Honey, you can't think—"

"Darla's there," Sylvie interrupted. "On top of the ice. Brody wanted me to go with them."

"It's a good thing you said no." Her mother's eyes were plain and calm and reassuring. Only if you knew her well would you see the sadness. "It's dangerous up there. All sorts of cracks and crevasses. And this time of year, it's slippery from melting."

Tess sat at her mother's feet, front paws spread, shoulders sturdy, attentive and waiting. Wind and water filled up the silence.

"I'm going to walk home," Sylvie said.

"Suit yourself." As her mother reached, Tess grabbed the stick. "Change takes getting used to. That's all."

⁓

Sylvie took her time walking back. She kicked up silt, thinking of Rick in his truck with some other girl, his hand moving from the knob of the gear stick to her knee and up the inside of her thigh. The new smell would be gone now, the thick rubber mats caked with mud, the windows smudged, maybe even a scratch on the fender.

Karen must wonder what had become of her. She'd started to phone from the lodge, dozens of times, but she'd always hung up halfway through dialing. The mittens and hats Karen's mother had bought to protect her from cold she'd stuffed under her bed. The books she'd read cover to cover, but none had brought lasting relief.

From the river she climbed the ridge, the wind at her back, the gravel dry, the rain shower forgotten. When she arrived at the garden, her mother was kneeling in the dirt, limp carrots and weeds in neat little piles near her knees. A loud pop sounded from the river. "Fireworks," her mother said without looking up. "Left over from the Fourth." Another pop sounded, then three more in rapid succession.

"Those are gunshots," Sylvie said. "It's too light for fireworks." To flaunt this small bit of knowledge only made her feel small.

Her mother sat back on her heels, the sun lighting the wrinkles at the corners of her eyes. In the dirt, the carrot tops drooped. Spindly and tall, the spinach had skinny forked leaves instead of fat round ones. The cauliflower had bolted, and the lettuce was more stem than leaf. "Pull one of those radishes, would you?" her mother asked, as if her own touch might be toxic.

Sylvie yanked up a root that dangled long and ugly and white in her hand. Shots shattered the air again, boom-boom-boom.

Ruth mopped sweat from the side of her face with the back of her hand. "Root maggots." Her lips trembled, turning the slightest of smiles. "That's what Tommy says are getting the radishes."

From the patch of flat-faced roses next to the shed, pink petals covered the ground. A woodpecker tapped on a tree trunk, an uneven knocking. Some other bird buzzed, nothing cheery like what you'd expect, but a whirring noise like a saw. "Dump those out by the shed, would you?" Sylvie's mother asked. "Before that chickweed reseeds itself."

She gathered an armful of weeds and chucked them at the pile of tires where the plastic horse stared at the sky. "Bring some water," her mother called.

What Sylvie had done, what she'd said, would be mentioned no more. They would go on as they had, which was to say in the wrong direction completely. Her mother's canned fish. Her attempts to grow food. The way she dragged them to church to please Lena. Anna's quest for a crown.

Kenny.

The handle creaked as Sylvie pumped water. She hoisted the bucket over the carrots, but her mother thrust out her arm. "The cold shocks the roots, Tommy says. Trickle it along the edge of the dirt and let it soak in.

Kenny—Kenny's going to hang a gutter to catch rainwater. It won't be so cold on the plants."

"He's out there with Steven." It was like Truth or Dare, which one of them would mention him first. "He finished the eight-wheeler. They're the ones shooting guns."

Her mother sat back again on her heels and poked at a cluster of little green bugs that scurried over the back of a spinach leaf. "Aphids," she said. "Tommy says soap and water will kill them."

"They sell vegetables at the store," Sylvie said. If only her mother could acknowledge this one simple fact.

"The growing season is short but the days are long, so it all balances out. That's what Tommy says. You just have to adapt." Her mother rubbed her face with her sleeve, streaked not with sweat but with tears.

Sylvie stared at her feet, her toes gray and dusty. "What I said before," she began. "About Kenny—"

"Your sister's with Lena." Her mother's voice turned firm. "When she gets home, we'll talk."

We'll talk preceded important events and big decisions, except of course the one to move to the glacier. We'll talk meant defeat and acceptance. As her mother knelt among the skinny radishes and stunted carrots, Sylvie felt no joy, only a dull, complicit sorrow.

An engine is recognized by its sound. A two-stroke whines, spinning out, while a four-stroke rumbles. Kenny must have told her mother that, too, because she looked up when the rumble began. Eight wheels spit and churned gravel, the transaxle transmission gearing down as Kenny turned into the driveway. He hit the brakes, took off his helmet, shook his head, and ran his hand through his hair, his face reddened with sun. "This is one bad machine." He patted the seat behind him. "Forget those carrots. I'm taking you for a spin."

Her mother looked away. "Let Sylvie ride first."

Sylvie dipped her head, alarm spiraling through her chest. *Broadsided.* That was a word you never heard in a poem. Too clumsy. Clichéd. "You go," she said.

"Which will it be?" Kenny asked. "Which one of you lucky ladies gets to ride first?"

Sylvie barely looked up in time to catch the helmet he tossed. Her mother's smile looked predatory, anticipating the inevitable while conceding nothing. Sylvie thrust the helmet at her. "Really. You go."

"I'm about to start supper." Beneath her mother's voice was an undercurrent like what you heard at the river if you listened hard enough, the friction of silt over rocks, grinding, insistent. "You go ahead. Enjoy a little ride. You helped build it, after all."

"Don't be scared by what happened with Brody," Kenny said. "I'm a good driver."

"I can start supper," Sylvie said.

"Don't be ridiculous." Her mother twisted one hand over the other. "You don't know a thing about how to cook fish."

Kenny nudged Sylvie's elbow. "If you're good, I might let you drive."

"Go on," said her mother. "Kenny won't bite."

Kenny lifted his gun and pulled the strap over his head and handed it off to her mother. "Hop on." He patted the seat.

As if suspended in water, Sylvie moved toward the machine. "Rides smooth as glass," Kenny said.

Her mother smiled, controlled and determined, a smile Sylvie had seen hundreds of times, thousands even, but in her eyes was despair. "You two have fun," she said.

"Hang on." The difference between a man's voice and a boy's, once it deepened, was a matter of capacity: a stronger neck, a wider throat, a broader chest. Sylvie settled her hands on her thighs, but then Kenny spun the wheeler and she had to grab hold of his waist, which was also strong and wide and broad. He waved back at her mother, who cradled the gun at her chest as she opened and closed one hand, returning the wave. Then Kenny punched the throttle, and the wheeler floated over the gravel toward the river.

He was right. Four wheels lifted you up, separated you from the earth. Eight wheels hugged the ground. "Independent suspension," Kenny called over his shoulder. "You helped put it together." She might have objected: she'd only handed him what he wanted, the right bolt or screw dropped into his outstretched palm, his hand brushing her leg as he reached for a wrench, his skin crinkling near his eyes when he laughed, the pink tip of his tongue sliding between his lips when he concentrated.

That's enough, take me home, she might have said. Her mother was banking on it.

Kenny punched the throttle. "Hang on," he repeated as he swung the wheeler into a wide and calculated turn. In a blur of gravel and weeds and carved cliffs and littered clouds, they bolted past the church's new picnic shelter, past the timber that had once held the tram.

"Got a treat for you," he yelled over his shoulder. Transparent and full, the air smelled of flowers still wet with rain. Or it might have been Kenny's neck, the thin film of sweat where his hair ended in little half-curls. He turned the wheeler up toward the road, where the tires spun even faster. "It won't take long," he yelled. "Not the way this baby flies."

They bounced in the ditch along the highway, past the church, past Brody's house. A semi blasted its air horn. Sylvie startled and pressed closer to Kenny. "Hear that?" he hollered. "Everyone wishes they had one of these."

They veered from the highway onto the road marked "Glacier Access." Dust flew up underneath them, proving the rain had meant nothing. The ruts here were deep, and the ride rough, and she scooted closer and hung on tighter and thought of what Nick said about sin, how it was separation from God, but you couldn't sin, could you, if you'd never been attached to God in the first place. She squeezed her eyes, to shut out the dust and also the memory of her mother's determined smile. Then there wasn't the road but a percussion, bang, bang, bang, and she opened her eyes as they rattled over the one-lane bridge and barreled past a sign that said "Preston's Glacier View."

They flew past campsites, most of them empty. Maybe Lena was right and there was a devil that tricked and cajoled and made you do what you shouldn't, a devil that had worked first on her mother and then on Sylvie. She had never wanted so much to believe in anything as she did right then in the devil.

The wheeler took one corner and then another. She leaned into the curves the way Kenny did as the road dipped and the ice fell out of sight. Then they rounded another bend and there it was, full-on, broad and white but also black-streaked and battle-scarred, worn down but obstinate.

The engine throbbed as it idled. "Take a good look," Kenny said. "You'll never see anything like it." He punched a lever, and the wheeler rolled forward, over mounds of black rocks, the moraine, until the ice filled Sylvie's vision completely. Brody and his mother might still be up on top.

Kenny drove so close it seemed they might tip straight up and ride the face of the ice, unimpeded by gravity and common sense. But then he shut down the engine.

Sylvie jumped off before he did. Sharp and black, the rocks made her unsteady, and so did the cold. She craned her neck, looking up till it hurt, and hugged her arms around her waist.

"Sorry," Kenny said. "Should have brought you a jacket."

Gravel clattered down the face of the ice. "It's melting," she said.

"It does a little, in summer," he said. Sylvie trained her eyes on the gullies and ridges, the curves and the dripping. "Thirsty?" Kenny leaned forward, hands cupped, to catch a trickle of melt. "Nothing purer than glacier water." It shimmered as he licked it from his palm.

As Sylvie stepped back, her foot slipped. Water spilled from his hands, a baptism of earth and air, as Kenny reached for her. Warm and thick, his fingers circled her skin as he pulled her up from the rocks. "Good thing you weren't wearing shorts," he said, brushing silt from her jeans. "Million ways to twist an ankle up here."

His eyes pooled blue like the ice. She felt watched. Known. Beautiful. "Pretty damn big, ain't it? Where it's blue, that's where light can't get in."

She knew this, all the facts, not that they were any use to her now. As her cheeks burned with cold, the ice went about its business, dragging rocks, jagging alongside the mountains, undoing and reforming the earth.

"Takes some getting used to," Kenny said. He thrust his hands in his pockets, thumbs out. "I forget that." He drew a breath and stared at his boots, the toes of them gray, and then looked up at Sylvie. "I know it's hard for you. Everything's new."

Not new, she wanted to say. Old. Old as time.

He shielded his eyes, to fend off the glare. She felt herself yielding, giving way, letting go, not caring even that it was her mother who'd done this, believing there might in fact be things that were fated, no matter how wrong they seemed.

Kenny turned. She heard a sigh, or maybe it was the wind, funneled down off the ice. "With your mom, you're bound to butt heads." Kenny looked not at her but at a dense, blue patch of ice, and he seemed somewhere else, though she felt him close, so close that the pulsing in her chest might have been his.

"She's got her ways," Kenny said. "But I love her like crazy. No disrespect, but your dad was a damned fool to leave her."

Regelation

Derived from ice, water refreezes, relieving pressure

R uth made excuses, when Kenny got back, about how she was too tired to go for a ride on the wheeler. The next morning, she refused him again, claiming she had too much to do. He teased and cajoled but stopped short of begging and rode off alone, a cooler tied to the place where Ruth might have sat, eight fat tires kicking dust over her sad little garden.

She listened until the sound of the engine faded. She'd let go. Trusted fate, which in fact might be no more than one event following after the other, and she now trusted no one, least of all herself, for what kind of mother tested her daughter as Gideon had, a fleece spread before God.

She scrubbed out the gray-water bucket and rearranged jars of fish in the cupboard and wiped down the counters, so easy now with the varnish. Like a pioneer woman, that's what she'd thought herself, the sort of person who set off for adventure with no thought of winter. She sensed the mocking of Hugh's wife, borne of the garden dirt, her eyes round and green like Mirabelle's, her hands plump and white like Lena's.

Kenny joked that it must be the hot dogs, loaded with nitrates and salt, that had Ruth feeling off. He didn't see how she'd punished them all. Sylvie was right. Ruth's selfless love was a sham. The fresh start, the promise of love and adventure, the hand of fate—these were for her alone, not for her girls. The glacier exposed how false she'd become, with her marked-up Bible and her scratched-out garden and her disdain for Kenny's machine, the ruts it tore in the earth, a reminder that anything, anyone, could be displaced.

From in front of the door, she gathered the rug and carried it out to the landing, where she thumped it hard with a broom, stirring dust. She had once prided herself in her ability to set anything right, knowing where to start and which concessions to make. But that was back when the glacier was only a flat, contained image.

Wheels spread wide, Lena's car approached the house under a sky staked high and round like a tent rimmed with mountains. "All this sunshine," she proclaimed to Ruth through a lowered window. "It's the wrong day for inventory, that's for sure. But you can join us if you like." She was being polite. "You and Sylvie."

"Sylvie's at work," Ruth said as Anna rushed by her and jumped in the front seat next to Lena. "And Kenny took the eight-wheeler, up to the glacier," she added before Lena could ask. "He's going to try chipping ice. To sell to the tourists, from the side of the road."

"The ice explodes," Anna said. "If it comes from down deep."

Lena patted Anna's hand. "I doubt that."

"It does," Ruth said. "I saw it in a documentary."

"You can't trust what you see on TV."

"But Kenny said so," Anna said.

Lena shifted the car into gear. "You're sure now, Ruth—you don't want to join us?"

With fresh dread, Ruth glanced back at the house.

"I suppose I could," she said. "It wouldn't hurt." A ridiculous thing to say, but what did it matter?

She climbed in and relaxed into the back seat as Lena maneuvered the gravel and the highway and then more gravel, navigating the tight hairpin curves, floating over washboards that jiggled the car only a little. Where the road narrowed, they crossed the bridge over water swollen with glacier melt. Rapids skimmed the rocks, wearing them down as Ruth herself felt worn down, not so much tired as diminished.

They turned onto the wide loop of Preston's Glacier Gift Shop and Park, and there was Walter, perched on a ladder that leaned against an elevated fuel tank. Without looking away from the bolt he was twisting, he greeted Ruth. There was a steadiness about him, the same as Ruth admired in Kenny, and though he rarely sat down unless it was at the kitchen table with a newspaper, he moved with a different energy than his wife, more deliberate and less conspicuous. They were an unlikely couple living an unlikely life, but both were happy Ruth guessed in their own ways, not that you could ever know such a thing about anyone else.

Lena unlocked the gift shop, a little enclave jammed with potholders, tea towels, calendars printed on fabric, key chains, coasters, decks of cards, swizzle sticks, tie clasps, and tee shirts, bright domestic reminders of a place you had only passed through. As Anna eyed an old-fashioned glass display case, Lena pressed a button so that the shelves that were suspended like little gondolas whirred and jerked in a circle. "Go ahead. Pick out a charm. For when you get crowned." She winked at Anna. "Just one."

As Anna punched the button next to the case, spinning rows of charms, Lena shuffled through a pile of papers beside the cash register. "That inventory list is here somewhere. It should have been done in December. But you can't imagine how cold it gets in here once the heat's been turned off."

This brought a new dread, to think of frost spreading over the charms, up the flailing arms of the sea star, over the horns of the tiny caribou, across the spread wings of the eagle. To quiet it, Ruth thumbed through postcards, shots of the glacier from a number of angles and in each of the seasons. Aerial shots. Shots from the highway. Close-ups of the place where Kenny had brought her. Sunrise. Sunset. Zoomed in. Zoomed out.

"Here it is." Lena brandished a stapled list. "We'll start with the charms. I'll read off which ones and Anna, you count them."

From outside came the sound of Walter banging on a rusty pipe with a pair of vise grips. As they began their work, Lena naming and pointing, Anna counting out loud, Ruth felt herself made obvious by exclusion, as in the tiny back room of Ray's Pawn Shop. "I can start on the next page," she offered.

"Tee shirts." Without looking up, Lena gestured toward the far wall. "You can sort them by size."

Ruth dragged a stepstool to where the shirts were stacked and gathered a bundle of them in her arms. Depositing these on the counter next to the cash register, she made piles, small to double XL, glaciers silk-screened on teal, pink, and blue.

"Nine sea stars," Lena announced. "Those sure don't sell." She and Anna moved with the list to the shirts, Ruth watching idly as they repeated their process of naming and counting. To see Kenny's mother so engaged with Anna should have cheered Ruth, but it only made her feel unnecessary.

"I might go see what Kenny's up to," Ruth said.

Lena eyed Ruth's sneakers. "You're not dressed for it."

"It's sunny," said Ruth. "I'll be fine."

"Ice to the tourists," said Lena. "I can't see what he's thinking." The accusation seemed aimed directly at Ruth. "Wait here."

She went in the back room and emerged with two poles. "We rent them to tourists. It's the only way to get past the rocks, if you're going on foot."

Ruth took the poles and slipped from the gift shop. She followed the gravel road past the campsites to the huge moat of jagged black rocks that guarded the ice. The wind kicked up, clouds muddling the sun. She wished for a storm, for thunder and lightning and the clean, fresh smell of soaked earth, taken for granted in summer back home.

She started across the moraine. Lena was right. Even with the poles, her feet slipped on the rocks, their sharp edges poking at the soles of her sneakers. Her ankles twisted, first one, then the other, as she picked her way toward the glacier. She searched for the smallest rocks, the ones least likely to turn her feet, but there was no easy path. Head down, she watched each step. Despite the cool breeze, sweat broke out on her forehead, then her arms.

She stopped to strip off her jacket and tie it around her waist. She spotted Kenny, at the face of the ice, beside his eight-wheeler, but his back was turned. She willed him to see her, to smile, to wave, but of course he had no reason to look. As she started walking again, a rock caught her foot and she stumbled, pain shooting from the arch through to her ankle. She picked herself up and unloosed a button on her shirt and pushed her sleeves up, then started forward again, her attention fixed on her feet, on the poles, on the rubble.

An hour had passed, maybe two, when she heard Kenny call out. She stopped and looked up as he started for the wheeler. "No," she yelled. "I'm almost there."

He veered toward her then on foot, moving fast, even without poles. "You sure like to do things the hard way," he said once he reached her. He took her hand, steadying her in a way that the poles did not, and led her slowly toward the base of the glacier, where the cooler sat, half-full of ice.

"Bottled water would be easier," he said. "But Steven looked into it. There's all sorts of regulations on water." He slanted a chisel against the glacier and struck it hard with a mallet.

As bits of ice clattered over the rocks, Ruth felt oddly saddened, that the glacier could in fact be so easily shattered. "Plenty more where that came from," Kenny said.

She shoved her hands in her pockets. "Maybe it's better to leave it alone."

"You sound like one of the old Native ladies. They talk like the ice is alive."

She reached toward it, slippery and yet unyielding, touching it first with her fingertips and then with the whole palm of her hand pressed flat against it.

Kenny clanked again with the chisel and mallet. "I'm thinking three bucks a bag." Near his eyes, his cheeks were wind-burned. "Quart Ziplocs. That cooler holds thirty-three gallons. One hundred bucks, once it's full. And plenty more where that came from." Ice splattered over the rocks. "I brought Sylvie out here last night. She liked it, I think."

Ruth brushed her palms on her legs. "I'm concerned about Sylvie."

"She'll come around."

They had to leave, her and the girls. They had to go back. Simple words, if only she could speak them.

Kenny took her hand in his, large and warm, and wrapped her fingers over the handle of the chisel. "You try."

"I can't," Ruth said.

"Sure you can. Give it a whack."

The metal weighed heavy and cold in her hands. "Don't stab. Just set the chisel, like this, and give it a good hard thunk with the mallet." He showed her how to stand, one foot under each shoulder, crouching a little. "That's it. Leverage your weight. Tilt the chisel, remember, so you've got an angle."

She scrunched her eyes and tightened her hold and struck with the mallet, hard and direct, the force reverberating up the handle as ice scattered at her feet.

Kenny grinned. "That's the spirit."

She clanked again with the mallet, and again, striking hard, spraying shards. The bear lured by sweets. Paul's impossible call. Her selfish desires disguised.

She beat at the ice, stubborn with the hope that anger could, by some alchemy of pressure and cold, be transformed into freedom. Her legs grew tired and her shoulders burned and her arms ached and her fingers turned numb from the cold, and still she kept chopping and hacking. "See," Kenny said as he shoved ice in the cooler. "You could do this all day and not make a dent."

When the cooler was full, she handed the chisel to Kenny and tipped her face to the wind as a pair of ravens rode a thermal, warm air colliding with cold. Kenny set his hands on her shoulders and rubbed where it hurt. She stiffened, shutting out the smell of brushed cotton, the prickle of beard, his fingers teasing her lips. She'd find some way to tell him. Not now, but soon.

Trimline

A clear boundary that indicates the maximum thickness of ice

How come you didn't go up there with Brody?" Cara asked. The noon rush was over, and they stood side by side in Magda's kitchen, cleaning strawberries for pie. Good produce was hard to come by in Resurrection, and strawberries were no exception. Sylvie tossed moldy fruit in the trash bin, one mushy berry for every two she salvaged, and that was with cutting off brown spots. One mushy, two good. The rhythm of it steadied her.

Cara nudged her elbow into Sylvie's ribs. "I see it now," she whispered. "Brody grabs for you, just as you're about to slide off the edge."

From across the kitchen, Brody's eyes followed Sylvie's fingers as she dug into a berry, large and white at the top, and peeled back the green crown. Her thumb hit a soft spot, and when she lopped off the bruise, the fruit was half of what it had been. "These things sure get beat up," Sylvie said, loud so Brody would know she wasn't talking about him.

Cara laughed. "You come three thousand miles from Venezuela or Brazil or wherever these things grow and see what sort of shape you're in." She lowered her voice. "That boy is all gone and ate up over you. But I guess it would have been weird. Up on the ice, with his mom there and all. I heard she wants her ashes dumped there. At the glacier." Cara wrinkled her nose as if the thought of this smelled like the cabbage in Magda's walk-in cooler. *Brassica Oleracea.* Latin was safer than the English of Grendel, the *fens* and *march-rievers.*

Sylvie looked down at the red-stained board. "Scattered," she said, her voice quiet. "They scatter your ashes."

"Whatever," said Cara. "It's weird."

Sylvie dropped her knife and wiped her hands on the sides of her apron, smearing it pink. Brody tipped back his hat and started toward her, his boots scuffing the floor.

She peeled off her apron and bolted through the swinging doors into the dining room, which smelled of chili and onions and cornbread, meant like all buffet food to please everyone, salty and spicy and sweet. Even before his fingers brushed against the back of her arm, she felt Brody behind her, like a ghost.

Tommy looked up from wiping the already-spotless buffet table. Despite her casual dress and her easy smile, she fussed over small things. If the register wouldn't balance, her face would knot up and she'd run the tape again and again till she found the mistake. In the kitchen, she seemed not to trust Brody, inspecting each steaming plate as it came from the dishwasher.

"Brody," said Tommy. "Get the kitchen trash and meet me out back."

The swinging doors flapped as Brody slipped back into the kitchen. "You'd think that boy had grown claws and fangs," Tommy said, "the way you look when he comes up behind you."

Sylvie stared at the wood-planked floor. No one else saw how Brody had changed since he'd been on the glacier with his mother. How he'd shifted and hardened but was also more vulnerable, his glances no longer sideways or half-hidden by hair, but full-on. No one saw how Sylvie was helpless to stop it. Brody could stare all he wanted, but he still wouldn't get that she couldn't be trusted, not in this place.

She shoved her hand in her pocket, reassured by the roll of bills. "Fill the ketchups," said Tommy. "Then either you or Cara can leave."

While Sylvie gathered half-empty bottles, Tommy delivered coffee to the man at the end of the counter, a trucker who smiled when she filled his cup and asked where he was headed. "Anchor town," he said. "Gotta load up for Prudhoe."

Sylvie watched as Tommy and Brody pulled out of the lot, trash heaped in the back of Tommy's truck. Then she went to the phone. Three rings, and a half-beat of silence.

"Oh my God. It's alive," Karen squealed. "I know you said there's no broadband up there, but I didn't know you were going back to the Pleistocene Age." Sylvie turned, her back to the trucker, the phone wedged under her chin. "How awful is it?" Karen asked.

"You don't want to know." With a little effort, any place could sound ordinary. "I've got a job waiting tables. Valley View Lodge. Coffee and pie and frozen entrees we heat up in ovens and set out for tourists that come through by the busload." It was the easiest of everything to put into words, her job. "There's a stuffed bear, six feet tall with its claws and its teeth, and a stuffed fox and a stuffed hare and a big set of moose antlers. And a guy at the end of the counter who's watching me talk. He's got piecrust stuck in his beard."

"Get out," Karen said. "Are you half frozen yet?"

"Not yet." She couldn't say how the sun shone and the air felt like summer and yet winter hovered always.

"Hot as blazes down here," Karen said. "I'm working at Jens. If I can stay out of the mall, I'll have saved half of what I need for a car by the time school starts." A pause. "Sylvie. I want you to hear it from me. Rhonda McArthur's been riding around in Rick's truck."

"I figured something like that." This didn't affect her the way she might have expected.

"If you came back, he'd drop her, pronto. Tell me your mom's seen the light and you're on your way home. My mom's sure you've frozen your toes or a bear has had you for lunch or some lumberjack's dragged you back to his camp."

The trucker plunked his mug on the counter. "Hang on," Sylvie told Karen. She set the phone by the register and grabbed the coffee pot and filled up his cup. When he smiled, you could see how his bottom teeth overlapped, the little fangy ones on the sides. With his shiny pale skin and the dark gleam of his eyes, he reminded her of a frog, not an ugly toad-to-prince frog, but the slim eager kind, all face and eyes. "Don't let me keep you," he said.

"I'm not in a hurry," she said, though the phone card minutes were ticking. Her eyes strayed toward his truck, a big black semi cab, shiny-wheeled, with white script arched on the door, "Out North Transport."

"Nice rig," she said.

He wrapped both hands on his cup, fingers chewed at the nails. "Gets me where I'm going." He brought the cup to his lips, peering over the rim with his frog eyes as he sipped long and slow. Sylvie stuck her hands in her pockets and held his gaze.

He set the cup down. "You better get back to that call, or your boyfriend will get pissed and hang up."

"I don't have a boyfriend." A calculated turn. She felt his eyes on her back.

"I can't talk much longer," Sylvie said when she got back to Karen.

"You won't believe what's happened with Ginny and Brent." Karen's voice surged with pent-up news. "You know how she dumped him. Now he—"

"I've got to go." The words half-stuck, coming out. "I'll call again. Soon."

"Tell your mom to buy you a ticket," said Karen. "You can always stay here."

"Later." Sylvie's voice was barely a whisper.

As she hung up, Cara swung through the doors from the kitchen. "I've had it with strawberries. Let them eat cheesecake. I'm going home."

"Sorry," Sylvie said. "Tommy said you have to stay. Fill the ketchups and make pies."

"She knows I hate pies," Cara said.

"You shouldn't have told her," said Sylvie. "That's why she wants you to do it."

Cara smiled like she'd just unraveled a secret. "I get it," she said. "She doesn't trust you and Brody alone. Not the way he's been looking at you. Fine. I'll suffer with pies. Just for you."

She disappeared through the doors. Sylvie brought the trucker more coffee, but he flattened his hand on his cup. "Gotta get haulin'."

She set down the pot and leaned over the counter. "You've got something caught in your beard."

He went to swipe it, but Sylvie's hand got there first, their fingers touching as she knocked off the crumb. She looked from him to the truck. "There's a guy out here that just built a big eight-wheeler." A small blush rose in her cheeks. "Off-road vehicle. You should see how it tears up the dirt."

The trucker sat back, his hands on his knees. "That's the problem with a big rig like mine. Gotta spend all your time on the road, making it pay. Long lonely hauls up to Deadhorse."

She flexed her fingers over the dull shine of the counter. "I don't guess they let you take anyone with you."

He leaned forward on his elbows, the pale skin of his face only inches away. "No one tells me who rides or who doesn't. That's why I got my own rig. Just got it, as a matter of fact. Still breaking her in. Got a load to pick up in Anchorage."

"That's funny." She held his gaze, feeling no joy or anticipation, only a strong sense of conviction that came not from God but herself, unreliable at best, but it was all she had, a familiarity of intent. "My weekend's just start-ing, and I was thinking of Anchorage. All I need is a ride."

He smiled. It wasn't only his eyes but the turn of his lips, up a little on each side, that made him look like a frog. "Your mother gets back and hears you talking like that, you'll be grounded," he said.

Sylvie smiled back, wide and pretty. "Don't let her hear you call her my mom. Tommy's my boss. I'm just summer help." She had to keep her resolve. It was best, for everyone. "First year of college. They have this thing where they place you in jobs in Alaska. It's cool at first. But it gets awful lonely. Once in awhile, you have to get out. You know, to town."

His smile relaxed. "In that case..."

She didn't wait for him to finish. She took his money and yelled back at Cara and locked up the till.

In the truck's big mirrors, the highway rolled out behind her, the glacier a shrinking white dot. She was glad when the road curved and it disappeared. No one would miss her, not at first. Later, Tommy would blame herself, but that wouldn't last. Cara wouldn't be hurt; she'd admire the way Sylvie had kept her secret. *I knew it*, she'd say. *She hated it here.*

Brody might feel somehow responsible. She hoped not. Lena would pray, naturally, but there was also the way she'd looked at Sylvie the other day at the picnic, instructing her on the cupcakes, as if she'd known Sylvie couldn't be trusted. Her mother would miss her, and Anna. But they'd be okay.

She wouldn't think of Kenny. Not yet.

Tyler, the trucker, had grown up in Texas, and he still had the twang to prove it, flattened vowels and lazy consonants. "Came north right out of high school," he said. "Uncle got me on up at Prudhoe, setting explosives. But cocky kid that I was, I screwed up."

Sylvie shifted. She hadn't counted on sitting so high, or on the smell of new vinyl, so much like Rick's truck. "You exploded the wrong thing?"

"Got drunk. Ain't no drinking in Prudhoe. Took me six years driving truck to work up to half what I made on the Slope. Only way out of that kind of hole is to get your own rig."

She told him she'd finished a year at St. Cloud. "It's a real party school," she said. "You should see the stuff that goes on. They have these bonfires, out by the dike." It amazed her, how easily these details emerged, another life fabricated. She told him about her philosophy professor, Dr. Hanklen, she named him, who shouted out facts about Aristotle and Plato and Descartes, and she complained about the cafeteria food, the overcooked pasta and the limp broccoli. Mostly Tyler was interested in the women she invented, a flaming redhead named Katrina who'd come from Russia and wore tight leather skirts, a blonde named Priscilla who wore boots that slinked up her legs. She concocted scenes in which these women gathered in dorm rooms to drink vodka and laugh about men that secretly they admired.

Tyler's frog eyes brightened. "Man, I shoulda done college."

It wasn't hard to feed his fantasies about college parties and dorm rooms and unchecked behavior. Everyone craved details of the lives they hadn't chosen. She felt grateful for once for the way her mind ran, how she could fill the spaces with talking so she wouldn't have to think of what she was leaving behind, or how she'd soon be in Anchorage, buying her ticket, her fate as it were.

The highway twisted and curved, winding out of the mountains. Tyler cursed an old truck and its driver, holding up a line of traffic on the two-lane road. "They're supposed to pull over if they've got more than five people behind them." He'd made several of these righteous comments already, about other drivers who went too fast or too slow or too close to the shoulder. Each was a personal affront, ignorant of protocol and rules, though these same qualities in the made-up college girls excited him.

Finally the road flattened and straightened. Tyler's mouth tightened as he accelerated, the truck gathering speed as he passed one vehicle after the other, and at last the old pickup, after which his jaw loosened and his lips relaxed. "Florida," he said, reading the plate on the pickup. "Figures."

Tilting toward the side mirror, Sylvie ran her fingers along the edge of her face, the invisible down of her cheek, the hairline, the curve of her ear. Tyler reached over and flipped open the visor. "Got a mirror right here, if that's what you're after."

She shut it quickly, smiling a little so he wouldn't see how she startled at her own image when she came on it unexpectedly. On the surface, it was Anna who'd changed. She was always doing some new thing with her hair, plaiting it down the side or pulling it back in a bun at the base of her neck, the way older women wore their hair when they were too vain to cut it. She sat differently, too, self-conscious and deliberate, smoothing her pants like they were a skirt, her knees pressed together and turned demurely to the side. This was the result of the Glory Girls training in etiquette, or as Sister Jean called it, charm.

In the short time since they'd left Pine Lake, their mother had visibly aged, though perhaps this was only an illusion caused by the long and unforgiving daylight. She still put on make-up, using a small mirror that hung at the side of the bedroom door, but the lighting was bad, too much glare from the window, and so she relied on Anna to point out where the liner was thicker on one lid than the other, or the mascara caked, or the lipstick smeared at one corner.

Sylvie had quit makeup altogether. It began as a deliberate protest to their isolation, where no one cared how they looked, a premise faulty from the start if you spent any time at the Church of New Beginnings. Her abstinence went for the most part unnoticed, except that Sylvie's mother had made a vague comment about her face looking fresh, and Cara complained that no one should look that good without effort. With no mascara to frame them, Sylvie's eyes appeared darker than ever, the pupils and the iris nearly one. Untamed, her eyebrows arched to dramatic effect, while her lips seemed to have swelled, shaped to new fullness by the wind when she walked by the river.

Tyler leaned forward and with a punch of air, the brakes Sylvie realized, the truck began to slow. "Pit stop," he said.

She shifted a little, toward the door. He straightened, aware it seemed of the power of what he commanded, as he turned the semi wide into the parking lot of the Royal Mountain Roadhouse. "Might as well grab us a drink," he said. "Celebrate the start of your weekend."

As the engine shuddered off, Tyler's hand lingered on the shiny round head of the gear shift. The view out the windshield was lonely and large, the river wide here and braided with gravel, a maze of channels. Sylvie dipped her head and bit the side of her lip and smiled a little, not showing her teeth. She felt like she had at the river with Brody, tossed and suspended, sensing the hard thunk even before she hit. "We could wait till Anchorage," she said. "It's not that far, right?"

"What the hell." Tyler massaged the shiny knob with his hand. "Don't tell me this is your first time. To Anchorage."

"Of course not," said Sylvie, summoning the person she'd claimed to be.

"Beauty of my own rig," Tyler said, "is I can stop wherever I want. Hell, there's a whole bedroom back there." His lips glistened, wet by his tongue. "In case you get tired."

She reached for the door handle. "Okay. One drink."

He caught her hand in his. "What's the hurry?"

She pulled from his grasp. "The thing is, I've got a plane to catch. At—at eight tonight. My friends are expecting me." Not desperate. She couldn't sound desperate.

"Your friends." His fingers went to his beard, not stroking but touching like he'd only just remembered it was there. "You never said nothing about a plane."

"The truth is," Sylvie said, "I really can't take it up here. I've got to get out."

"Well, then. Syl-vie." He drew out her name like he owned it. "All the more reason to celebrate." In a slow roll, his eyes moved from the top of her head to her feet. She felt distorted by their roundness, as if she were reflected in a bad mirror.

"You're sure we've got time?" She wished she'd said the plane left at seven, or six.

"Absolutely." He slid out of the truck.

Sylvie cracked her door. Calm and steady. She knew calm and steady. Tyler offered a hand to help her step down. She squinted against the wind-whipped dust that swirled across the parking lot. The Royal Mountain Roadhouse sat low to the ground, like a big red caboose knocked off its wheels, with tiny dark squares for windows. Sylvie shivered and tucked her hair into her collar so the wind wouldn't catch it, wishing she'd at least brought a jacket.

Inside, it was nothing like the bars she'd concocted in her college stories for Tyler, with their pulsing lights and loud music and long-legged women. The roadhouse had a low ceiling, dark-paneled walls, a dartboard, four square tables, and five bar stools. The only light came from the windows, and it was quiet inside except for sportscasters babbling from a television mounted above the bar, two men in suits arguing over a referee's call.

Tyler slid onto one of the round bar stools and patted his hand for Sylvie to sit next to him, which she did, the vinyl cool through her jeans, her back rigid, barely touching the bent metal that would hold her up if she dared lean against it. A short brown woman with straight dark hair stepped away from the blare of the televised soccer game. Without speaking or smiling or looking at them, she set two napkins on the bar, and as she did Tyler flattened his hand across Sylvie's thigh, warm and heavy. "Rum and Coke," he said to the bartender. "Two."

"IDs." The bartender held out her hand.

Sylvie shifted her leg from under Tyler's hand as she reached for her purse. There was no cause for panic. He'd believed her, with everything, and once you started believing, it was hard to stop. "Looks like I left it at home," she said after digging around in her purse.

"Ain't that a shame." Tyler's teeth were little white nubs between his thick lips. She'd seen a bat once, a photo in her biology book, with a mouth like that, and though she tried to cast him again as a frog, his eyes appeared now more dark than bulging, and his face more alert than complacent, as if he could sense her alarm even in the dark. "Just a Coke then, for the lady," he said.

The soccer ball rolled toward the front of the screen, black blurred with white, followed by a jumble of cheers and boos as the goalie thrust a leg out to block the shot. Tyler slung one arm over the back of Sylvie's stool and draped the other over the empty seat on the other side, his thumb rubbing up and down in a circle over her shoulder while she pretended not to notice. The bartender disappeared after producing their drinks, leaving them with only the TV for company. Heads stared from the wall, dark shapes livened with glassy fixed eyes, a moose and a caribou and a Dall sheep. Sylvie leaned forward, away from Tyler's thumb, to sip from her drink in what she hoped seemed a casual way.

The steel feet of Tyler's stool ground the floor as he scooted close. He flipped his straw from his glass and it skittered across the bar. He upended his drink, and when he set it down it was half gone. The white flesh of his face glowed a little in the dim light. "So the college girl's going home," he said.

Sylvie played with her straw in her hands. "My parents never really wanted me to come up here in the first place." She pressed her hand to her purse like there might be a cell phone inside it. "My mom." Her voice caught. "My mom calls every day."

Tyler leaned forward on both elbows, his lips inches from her face. It was only a truck and a ride, not so different from Rick and his keys and the wheels that barreled wherever she turned them. She shifted her legs on the vinyl and smiled, not too large. "I sure wouldn't want to wait tables the rest of my life."

He drained his drink to the ice and tinkled the cubes against the glass. "Of course you wouldn't," he said. "Gotta make your folks proud."

"Oh, they're proud." This once had been true, at least of her mother. "My mom especially. She'll call any minute. She's like that."

"Hard to let her little girl go." He leaned back. "You heard they found a body. Fox Lake, not ten miles from here. Some young girl. Now there's a mother with no one to call." His eyes shifted, catching the gleam of the jukebox.

She tried to summon the ice, its potential, its power, but it was impossible, with the jukebox and the television and the dartboard. "Can't believe you don't have a boyfriend," he said. "A looker like you."

Sylvie ran her fingers up the side of her glass, pushing back droplets of water. "Oh, you know. Boys come and go."

He leaned close, and she smelled the rum on his breath and the remnants of a stinging aftershave. "It might be, Sylvie," he said, "that what you need is a man."

She took a long drink through the straw, though all that was left was a little water melted out of the ice. "We should get going," she said. "I'd hate to miss that plane."

He sat back, lips curved at the corners. "Don't travel by air much myself. But I hear it's hell getting on without your ID. Damned near impossible. Least that's what I hear."

Her face flushed. He leaned close again. "Might not be quite so smart as you think you are, Syl-vie."

She forced a tight smile. "I can take care of myself."

"If I were your dad, I'd be pissed. My little girl running off with a trucker."

Sylvie's chest filled like a river, tumbling and splashing and grinding. "Oh, well, you know. My dad's not really around." But she'd mentioned two parents, she realized, only moments before. "Of course I know where he is," she said quickly. She stopped short of saying where, the advantage of her father being that she could place him wherever she wanted. "We stay in touch." She almost believed this herself, feeling a point of solidarity, in that he too had run off.

Tyler appeared unconvinced. "To tell the truth," she added, though it was likely too late, "my dad left. With another woman. Mom was crushed."

"I'll bet she was." Tyler pushed a stout finger against the side of his head, wrinkling the skin of his temple. She considered ways to escape. The bathroom. The back door. But from there, it would only be wilderness.

Tyler set his hands on his knees. "A free lift." He shoved his empty glass across the bar. "Guess that's all you want, huh, Sylvie? What everyone wants, something for nothing. Sometimes they get it. Sometimes they even get a little bit more."

"I can pay," Sylvie said. "For gas or whatever."

"No need for guilt," he said. "No, we can't have that. Come on, Syl-vie. Let's roll."

She froze, still and stiff as the big-snouted moose lit up by the jukebox. Once as a child she'd crouched between sheets her mother had hung to dry in the Minnesota sun, weeping self-consciously as the cicadas buzzed, at the realization—it had come as a surprise—that love wasn't dependable in the ways she'd once thought. Crouching by the river, dusty and bruised, nursing the dull spreading ache in her leg, she'd sensed this again, that you might never truly be known in the way love implied. But here in this box of a bar, pinned by glassy eyes all around, her trouble was something else alto-gether, her destiny laid open, exposed.

Tyler held the door, letting in light that revealed bits of scattered dust floating aimlessly toward the earth. "Coming?" It wasn't so much a question as a command. Sylvie tucked her toes around the bottom rung of the bar stool and stared at the bottles behind the bar, the square beveled edges, the slim necks, the distortions of liquid and glass.

"I said, you coming." His voice sounded urgent and sharp, like Tess and her barking, loud enough in fact to bring the bartender out from behind the swinging doors.

"We don't want no trouble," she said with a stern look at Sylvie, as if she were the cause, and she seemed not to notice how Sylvie pleaded back, with her eyes.

She unhooked her feet from the rungs and slid off the stool and crept across the wooden floor through the open door to the light, where Tyler's face appeared chiseled and hard. Without speaking, he opened the truck door and gave her a little shove, up and into the cab.

Fingers trembling, she strapped herself in and brushed a strand of hair from her face while Tyler revved the truck's large engine and shifted hard into reverse, then pulled forward, the tires spitting gravel the way Kenny's eight-wheeler did. He drove onto the highway, not toward Anchorage but back in the direction they'd come.

Sylvie clutched the door handle as the truck picked up speed. "I'm sorry," she said. The wheels rumbled. "You don't have to take me all the way back."

"No." He glanced at her, barely. "No, I don't."

"You could let me out here." Overhead a plane skimmed the sky, like an insect over the skin of a lake, leaving no impression. Inside the passengers were folded and strapped in their seats, tucked up safe in a way Sylvie could scarcely imagine.

Tyler gripped the steering wheel, his hands broad and large-knuckled, his gaze rigid on the road, the tires humming deeply, rum and sweat a powerful addition to the smell of vinyl.

"I have this friend," Sylvie said. "I've been saving up money to see her. This…this…" In her babbling, she was incoherent as the river. "This isn't where I belong."

Tyler tipped his chin at the windshield and downshifted, the sound of the tires expanding, then flattening. "You think you can't take it now? Just wait till the sap slows and the trees bend and all this country fills up with snow. Till it's so quiet all you hear is what's in your head, all the things you can't stand, and it's so cold the air hurts to breathe, and the snow keeps on coming, snow and more snow." He was practically shouting. "Think how desperate you'll be then."

He punched the brakes and the truck skidded to the shoulder, a turn-out shaded by a cliff. *Falling rocks*, the sign said. Quiet fell like whispered snow, the river barely audible as it braided and stretched, feeling its way to the ocean.

"Now Sylvie," he said as he let up on the clutch, a move her father once taught her. "I'd say you've got yourself in something of a predicament here." With a click he undid his seat belt.

A clutch loosened everything up. That's what her father had said. You could go forward or back, flipping one gear to the next. Like a bicycle, he'd explained, but she couldn't picture it, then or now, though she hadn't tried very hard, only trusted.

Denim brushed the seat as Tyler edged toward her, one of thousands, maybe millions, of unique sounds formed from the rubbing of one thing against the other. His jeans were a stiff awkward blue next to hers, judiciously faded with multiple washings, back when she'd taken such things for granted. As he leaned over Sylvie, she focused on the buttons of his shirt, ordinary plastic and perfectly spaced. He hooked his thumb under her seat belt, running it along the inside of the webbing, brushing her breast. He smelled of flannel, like Kenny, and weakening aftershave. "So what are you?" he asked. "Sixteen?"

He unlatched her seat belt and ran his thick-knuckled hands up the inside of her shirt. She had used up the words that could save her, and still they were all that she knew. "Please," she said as tears swelled in her eyes. "Please. I'm sorry. Please just take me home."

He pressed his flat, bland face next to hers. "But you don't properly know me. And you know you want it."

"No," she said. "No, I don't."

He flattened his lips into hers, forcing his tongue between them, flicking the hard little tip of it inside her mouth. "Course you do, Sylvie," he said, and he worked his mouth harder.

She fumbled for the door, but he caught her hand, bearing down on it. "Now Sylvie," he said. "You know there ain't no place to run to. Not way out here."

Tears blurred the trees, endless beyond the window. She struggled, gasping as her breaths turned to sobs, the kind she hadn't cried since her father left.

Tyler leaned back, his eyes lit with anger. "How old?" he demanded.

"Six—" She forced a breath. "Sixteen."

He blinked long and slow and his full wet lips parted. "And you ain't been here even one winter."

She clutched the seat.

"Have you?" he demanded.

"No." Her voice small.

He pounded the wheel with the heel of his hand. Her sobs turned to whimpers. "You ever been with a man?"

She shook her head, futile as Tess with the quills.

"Don't lie to me now."

"Yes," she said, though there was no way of telling, from his glare, which answer was best. "There's a—a boy back home. Sixteen, like me." She was in fact that kind of girl. Fate knew it, ensured it.

Tyler landed his hands on the wheel, his thumbs stroking the plastic. "Well, Syl-vie." He looked her up and down slowly, the dark pools of her eyes, her arched ragged brows, her lips pink and smooth as the wild roses that had bloomed by the shed. His gaze fell again on her breasts, exposed first by Rick when she'd thought not of Rick's hands but of Kenny's, broad and rough and calloused on the edges, teasing her skin, and she was somewhere else, anywhere else, not here, not here.

Moulin

A circular chute of ice through which water moves

From the edge of the rocks, Lena and Anna waved, arms crisscrossing the air. Ruth knew right away it was something with Sylvie. Wounded. Betrayed. Any mother could have seen it. Any mother but her.

The dispatcher asked her name and location and the nature of the emergency. Ruth stumbled over the words but finally got out that her sixteen-year-old had disappeared in a truck, a big semi, with a shiny black cab, a name painted over the door, though no one seemed to recall what it said.

When had Sylvie last been seen? With whom? Had she talked about leaving? Each question sliced Ruth open for examination, implying that had she only spoken the right word at the right moment, Sylvie would not have hung up her apron and climbed in a tall, shiny truck with a stranger.

"We only came here this summer," Ruth said. "Sylvie knows almost no one."

"Kids do these things," the dispatcher said.

An officer came on the line with more questions. Ruth cut him off. "Just find her," she said. "Please."

He explained in a patient voice that it wasn't uncommon for teens to act out by running. At least, he said, no doubt meaning comfort, Sylvie hadn't gone off in the woods. The troopers would keep an eye out for a black semi—there were a lot of trucks in Alaska, he made sure to say. If twenty-four hours passed with no word from Sylvie, Ruth should call back.

Her mouth opened and closed like a fresh-netted salmon. She handed the phone back to Lena. "They said to wait. Twenty-four hours."

Lena set down the phone and crossed one flap of a box over the other. Then she straightened, hands on her hips so her elbows jutted like wings. "Well then. We'll have to go after her."

"No offense, Mom." Kenny rubbed the base of Ruth's neck. "But we don't know the first place to look."

"We know they were headed for Anchorage." Lena took her keys from her purse. "Ruth can ride with me."

"You'll never find her in Anchorage," Kenny said. "All that traffic."

"This is what happens," Lena said, "when you don't go to church. You forget the ways that God works. Anna, you call Sister Jean. Tell her to get the church praying." Her hand fisted over her keys. "Come along, Ruth." She glanced at Ruth as she had at the smashed flat of cupcakes, not so much with judgment as with the special strain of disappointment that accompanies the failure to protect.

"I'll drive," Kenny said. "We'll take the truck."

"No," Ruth said. "I'll go with your mom."

Kenny pressed his hand over hers. "Babe. I'm just saying—"

"It's best," Ruth said. She hoped he'd see it as the camaraderie of mothers, not that Lena's assurance meant more than his.

"There's no sense you bothering yourself over this," Lena told Kenny. "Like the trooper said, Sylvie's just acting out."

"You stay with Anna," Ruth said. "At your mom's house. The troopers might call."

"All things work together for good," Lena said once they'd got in the car. Ruth wished she believed the way the church women did. But in the thin soil of her soul it seemed nothing would take hold, not even her simple and urgent prayer that Sylvie would come away from this unharmed.

Lena's car floated the road, up and away from the ice. Ruth shrank into the seat, cocooned in the smell of worn leather. "Tough to swallow sometimes." Lena steered between cliffs, strafed where the highway cut through. "All things working toward good. It doesn't seem that way, not in this life." She glanced at Ruth. "I suppose that's why there's all the fuss about eternity. Forever. Although that's a little hard to fathom as well, don't you think?" Her chin jiggled as the wheels sang like sirens, a thin whining.

Ruth rubbed the soft flesh at the base of her thumb, recalling the fat folds of Sylvie's legs, how as a baby she'd kicked the air froglike, the miracle of her small grasping fingers, the joy of her laughter.

"But there's no sense in faith," Lena continued, "if you can't call on it in a crisis." She said this with a sort of wonderment, as if she'd passed by the most familiar of places, her own driveway for instance, and now couldn't find it.

"I should have known," Ruth said. "I should have seen this coming."

"Young people have their own way of thinking. It might be that trouble with Brody."

"Sylvie never was one for boys," Ruth said. "Till Kenny. I mean, once Kenny and I decided to come up here. That's when she got her first boyfriend. A nice boy from school, with a pretty red truck." She nearly choked, recalling the easy shine of that truck, and Rick's smooth-faced adoration.

"There are all sorts of ways for a child to act out," Lena said.

"I was a problem myself," Ruth said. "That's how my mother tells it, and she may be right. Mothers know things."

Lena smiled without taking her eyes from the road. "They do. Not everything though. They wouldn't want to."

Ruth wanted to say she appreciated Lena, so different from Ruth's own mother, with her thin hands and her stooping shoulders and her yapping dogs, her biggest worry whether the gossip of her bridge circle might turn against her if she failed to show up on a Tuesday morning at ten, a fear Ruth believed kept her mother alive, death being only one more way to be absent. Instead she turned and pressed her hands into the cushioned leather. "I can't keep ignoring the obvious."

"I'm not sure I follow."

"Sylvie's at a difficult age." It wasn't fair laying blame, but it was what people could understand. "It wasn't wise, dragging her up here."

The silence that followed lasted so long that Ruth began to question whether she'd actually come out and said it. "So you want to leave," Lena said finally.

Ruth hadn't thought it quite like that, in such a crushing, blunt admission of failure. "I haven't said anything about it to Kenny. And I'm not sure where we'd get the money." It was the natural stopping point for her despair, that they had no means to get back, though Sylvie had thought of it, Sylvie with her wad of cash.

Lena drew herself up, the car accelerating out of a curve. "Judy was our problem child. My sister. She died here, you know."

"Kenny told me." Already there was a sweet sort of nostalgia in saying his name, now that she'd spoken out loud about leaving. Kenny. Kenny.

"You wouldn't know it now," Lena said. "But back then, I had some sense of adventure. And what I had, Judy had tenfold. I came up here because Walter insisted, even though I said it was too far, too big, too cold. Dad lived for golf and Mom fussed at the house, a new theme, a new room every week, and I wasn't about to live that kind of life. Judy needed no one to prod her. Wanderlust was just in her nature. She was jealous when I took off before her. It sounded romantic, traveling thousands of miles, homesteading on our own piece of land. We weren't impulsive, mind you. We studied and planned. Everywhere on the road there were young couples like us, fattened on dreams."

Her hands tightened on the steering wheel. "Of course Judy never admitted her envy. She made fun of Walter and me, how we'd turned ourselves into an old married couple before we'd hit twenty." She paused without glancing away from the road. "Rebellious isn't quite the word for Judy. Reckless was more like it. But she could brighten a room with her laugh." Her voice faltered, a tiny crack from which she quickly recovered. "Willow thin, and if you looked close at her fingers, you'd see where she'd chewed along the edge of each nail. Like a little caterpillar, munching away at her flesh. But she only did it when she thought no one was looking. It didn't fit with her image. Carefree and all."

The siren-whine of the wheels filled the space between them as the highway edged close to the river, which spilled out across a wide expanse of gravel. "It was the baby that broke her," Lena said. "She got careless, and then she got pregnant. Of course she tried to hide it at first, and she never would say one thing about the father. Finally, she sent a card to announce it, a blue-winged butterfly on the front, white space all around. We'd been up here three years already, and I was pregnant myself, with Kenny. I tried calling, but Judy could hide when she wanted.

"Thank the Lord she went through with the baby." Lena's chin bobbled. "That's what I said to the ladies at church, though to tell the truth, I don't know that in the end it was wise. That child haunted Judy like a little ghost. She held him in the hospital and then handed him over for adoption.

Years later she said she still fell asleep imagining the clutch of his hand on her finger."

She paused. "Walter built that tram, before we put in the road. We thought we'd sell tickets to tourists."

Ruth knew what came next. How Judy had hoisted herself with the pulley, the river gaping below. How the cable had frayed. The snap, and the splash. The cold, sudden and icy. "Kenny told me," she said, to spare Lena, but it was too late. Her face was already wet, and her chest heaved, holding back sobs.

"Walter quit church." Lena wiped a shimmer of tears with the back of her hand. "I couldn't blame him. What kind of God allows something like that? Or forgives it?" She pressed the flat of her thumb to each eye, but the tears kept on falling. "I'm sorry. You mustn't mind what I say. It's my fault as much as it's Walter's. I was the one who insisted Judy come up here to stay."

She drew some courage it seemed from glancing at Ruth. "The weight of that little boy she gave up was slowly crushing her, day after day. I had the idea she'd warm up to church and sell that van where she lived like a gypsy and settle down and let what was past be the past." She spoke in a tumble of words. "She fell all over herself for that ice. She wanted to touch it, to climb it, to know it. She couldn't get over its age or its strength. People smirked at the way she went on about it. 'That sister of yours,' they'd say. 'She's sure crazy for ice.'"

Lena wept again. "I'm sorry," she said. "So sorry."

Where the highway dropped off, the river spread, braiding and unbraiding. Beyond it, mountains tore at the sky. They lost speed, Lena seeming to have forgotten that she was in charge, trusting the car to move forward on its own while she struggled to recover herself. Finally she steered to the side of the road, a skinny little shoulder that dropped off toward the river. The engine puttering patiently, she fumbled in her purse, extracting a fistful of tissues that she swiped at her face. Ruth sat with her hands pressed under her thighs, not wanting to look at Lena but also not wanting to look over the edge at the river. There was a reverence in having witnessed such old, private grief, the kind over which tears had no effect. As Lena dabbed her eyes with new vigor, blotting up foundation and rouge and mascara, Ruth invoked the closest she knew to a prayer, *Sylvie, Sylvie, Sylvie.*

"Judy believed herself capable of resisting all kinds of love," Lena said, a tissue fisted in her hand, "on the grounds that it made her weak." Crying had distilled her voice into something simple and pure. "It was nonsense, of course. Judy loved harder and longer than any person I've ever known. She wore that tram out, crossing back and forth to get to the ice."

"How sad," Ruth said, though she might well have said *how brave*.

"Judy liked to think she never was sad." Lena set her mouth in a thin little line. "I'm sorry," she repeated. She reached for the steering wheel. "I shouldn't burden you, when our worry is Sylvie."

"It's fine." It was more than fine, an honor, really, but Ruth had no way to say that.

"When you get older, I expect you'll understand," Lena said. "Though I don't wish it on anyone, finding out how much there is to be sorry about." She gripped the steering wheel tighter, and for a moment it seemed she might confess more regrets. But she only shifted the car into gear and pressed the accelerator and steered back onto the road.

"Walter thinks we should charge more, to see the glacier." Indignation lifted Lena out of her sorrow. "He thinks when you charge more, they'll see how it's special. He forgets you can drive two hundred miles and see Worthington Glacier for free. Of course you can't camp there, but these days everyone wants plug-ins and asphalt and wireless internet. We get ten tourists a day. On a good day, fifteen. That stuff in the gift shop has sat there for years. Now Kenny wants to sell ice."

It felt as if Lena wanted Ruth to take sides, but in her distress over Sylvie, she couldn't see her way through to the right one. She was spared a response when Lena veered again off the road, pulling up behind a gleaming black semi that was pulled off on the shoulder.

There was no river, no road, and no mountains, no silver-backed leaves and no tiny twinflowers, only elation and dread, knowing and not wanting to know. Before the car had come to a full stop, Ruth had the door open. The shiny chrome. The tall steps caked with silt. The sun-glinted glass. She jumped out but somehow Lena was faster, halfway around the long hood of her car already as Sylvie, her Sylvie, stumbled out from the truck.

Ruth called her name, such a beautiful name, and it was the most wonderful thing, to have called it out needlessly, because Sylvie was right there, collapsing into her. She stroked Sylvie's hair as she pressed against her, limp and warm.

The truck started up. "You wait one minute." Lena leaned with one fist against the hood of her car as she waved at the driver. "You've got some explaining to do."

A pale face leaned from the window. "Your girl's the one that's got some explaining," he said. The tall, crushing wheels began to roll.

Ruth held Sylvie by the shoulders and stepped back so she could see her face. "What did he do?" Her voice was shrill, urgent, unrecognizable. "What did that man do to you?" She wanted to spit, throw, kick, maim, kill.

"We don't take to trouble," Lena yelled as the truck pulled onto the asphalt. "The authorities—"

The roar of the engine drowned her words. "Tell me," Ruth demanded. "What did he do? You tell me right now."

Sylvie's face was unreadable, her eyes dark, her mouth pressed tight, her chin tucked. "Please," she said. "I just want to go home."

Distributary

Spurred by differential melting, a section of ice separates from the rest

Glaciers move slowly, imperceptible to the casual observer. But a remarkable instability can cause the ice to bolt forward. Several theories explain these sudden surges. There is the geothermal effect, where molten rock presses close to the crust of the earth and the ice deteriorates from underneath. Another cause involves rough patches of bedrock that create friction and melting. There are also earthquakes that shift large plates of land, unsettling the ice.

But most often it's the sediment dragged by the glacier itself that causes the surge. Debris blocks the channels under the ice where the meltwater flows. As the pressure intensifies, more channels close off, and the ice shoots across the pooled water, crushing anything that gets in its way. Once the pressure has been relieved, the advance will slow, and the ice will begin its retreat, leaving behind eskers, long ridges of dumped rock that prove how far it advanced. Blown by wind, the glacial dust scatters, laying down a thin, fragile skin where life wriggles in. From dust all are said to have come, and to dust we return, dust born of ice.

Sylvie's sheets smelled of this dust, stirred by wind and deposited on the laundry her mother hung out to dry. With her thumb she stroked the scar on her thigh, dirt trapped by new skin. The beauty of a poem was in its tight, measured surprises. Here the beauty was ancient and unforgiving, nothing you could tuck away to consider some other time when you felt more ready. *Fen and foesten. March-riever mighty.* As in a poem, it exposed what you most meant to hide, and there was no escaping it.

Her mother said over and over how lucky she was, that nothing awful had happened, but then a half-hour later she'd ask again if Sylvie was sure she hadn't been harmed, never trusting her answer. They could press charges, she said, because Sylvie was only sixteen.

Kenny was angry. He blamed her for frightening her mother, and he was hurt that she wanted so badly to leave. Sylvie felt untethered, not sure any longer what home meant or where it might be.

When the sun was only a promise tucked in back of the mountains, she crept down the stairs. Outside, a pair of owls called who-hoo-hoo, back and forth in the almost-dawn. She'd seen them once, perched on a berm by the side of the road, following her with their big yellow eyes.

She straddled Kenny's bike and rode in the tracks left by his wheeler, past the shed and the horse upturned, past her mother's struggling garden and the wire fence of the neighbors. She peddled hard in the morning chill, the sky thin and gauzy, the dew thick on the grass, her calves burning as the road rose toward the highway. The planks of the bridge rattled pleasantly as she crossed over the place where the creek's clear water met the river's gray silt, the wet boundary pulsing and swirling. As the sun shot past the top of the mountains, the air began to warm, the sound of the water receding as Sylvie pedaled away from it.

As she rode the shoulder of the highway, a semi whizzed past, showering her with dust. Overhead a Crowley's single-engine plane dipped and banked, then circled back toward the glacier. When you saw a dot on a map, heard the name of a place, there were things you expected, street lamps and gas pumps and sidewalks and curbs, proof that the land had been tamed. Those must be what she missed, those simple assurances.

She rode past the church and past Lena and Walter's, sweat prickling down the back of her neck to her shirt. Though her thighs ached, she believed she might ride for hours. At a level spot, she quit pumping and let the bike coast as she lifted her face to let the wind press against it. As the bike slowed, she held out her legs and with her feet dragged to a stop. From the bottom of the driveway she looked up at Brody's house. He was the one who'd spotted her, riding high in the shiny black truck, making her escape from the lodge. When Tommy wasn't convinced, he'd found her bike stashed behind Magda's old shed, and that had set off the search.

The bike wobbled as she set her feet back on the pedals, not trusting her intentions. She got off and began pushing it up the hill, her breath shallow and strained, her palms gritty. The wide, gaping windows of the Prince house shone, reflecting the ice. Where the driveway got steep, she ditched the bike in weeds still wet with dew, and freed from its weight, she jogged up the hill.

Rounding a curve, she stopped. The great green expanse of the lawn had vanished. In its place was mud, rutted and ugly, stomped and churned, as if in some awful despair the grass had hurled itself back on the earth. She squatted at the edge of where the lawn had once been and touched the flat of her thumb to the dirt, then smudged it against the pads of her fingers. Even in the aftermath of the winds that sometimes tore through Pine Lake, winds that ripped down signs and tipped pots full of flowers, she had never seen such destruction. Ruts showed where tires had spun, pulling up grass by its roots, churning and spitting until the last bit of green had collapsed, leaving an open wound that gaped at the sky.

Wind blew from the bottom of the hill, lifting the hair on her arms and chilling the sweat from her skin. Gravel crunched underfoot as she climbed the hill toward the house. She hesitated, not knowing what Brody's mother would think, or his father, or if they even knew yet about the lawn, but they must, because how could anyone sleep through such destruction?

As she approached the steps, she stopped to examine two streaks of clumped mud that ran from what had once been the lawn toward the garage door, spaced the width of a four-wheeler's axles. The tracks weren't powdered gray silt, but dark loamy topsoil. No effort had been made to hide the evidence.

She kicked aside the chunks of mud, then climbed the wide steps to ring the bell, a series of chimes that rang like an organ prelude. It was still early. She could ride back and climb in bed and get ready for what would happen once Kenny got up, and her mother.

Brody came to the door, his face pale, his eyes tired. He looked past her toward the once-lawn.

"I thought..." She saw the raw truth of it then, that Scott's big truck was gone, and that Brody's wan face had nothing to do with the dirt.

"My mom," he said. "Last night. This morning, actually. Two forty-seven a.m."

She must not cry, must not cry. He gripped her hand, his fingers soft and cold, and led her to the sofa. He bent his head like an awkward bird toward her shoulder as she ran her hands over his back, up and down. From the kitchen came the irregular drip of a faucet, and beyond the walls, the almost unrecognizable whir of a car on the road. "I'm so sorry," she said.

"Dad's on his way home." Brody's voice fell like an early snow, wispy and uncertain, and his jaw shifted. She pulled his hand into her lap and stared at the tall vaulted ceiling, the creamy white walls edged with mitered wood, the glass-eyed bear skinned and stretched, the moose with its bulbous nose, the emptiness made self-conscious by the chair with its big red and blue flowers, the purple afghan folded neatly over one arm. "He ran her to Anchorage," Brody said. "But it was too late."

Sylvie tugged at her jeans, straightening the seams. "You wouldn't guess it," he said. "But it smells like spring, up there on the glacier. Early spring, before the grass and flowers, when it's just sun on cold. "

She reached to touch Brody the way his mother sometimes had, exposing the broad smooth skin of his forehead, then, deciding against it, pressed her hands in her lap and stared out the window, past the churned lawn to the ice. "She asked to be burned," Brody said. "She wrote it down."

An arc, almost electric, rose between his knee and Sylvie's. She shifted to break it. "My dad is pissed. He thinks it's unholy. That the—the body is sacred. But it's Mom's choice, don't you think?" His lips trembled. "She wants the ashes scattered up on the ice."

Sylvie touched two fingers to his mouth. "You don't have to choose." It was the truest thing she'd said, for a good long while.

"She's the one…" He pressed his fingers to his temples and stared at his feet. "She gave me that poem. Nothing gold. This one Christmas, when I was little, before Dad's business took off. We didn't have this big house, just one of those little places down on the island, and there was no money for gifts. I must have been three, maybe four. She held my hand out, like this, and pressed her fingers into my palm as she said each word and had me repeat it. 'Eden's first green…'"

But he couldn't go on. Sylvie pressed his head to her neck and again ran her hand up and down his back, the way she used to do when Anna had trouble falling asleep. *Forget. Don't forget.* But she couldn't think how to say it.

He sat up, wiping his face on his sleeve. Sylvie sat on her hands. "Remember how Lena made us clean under this sofa? How she said your mom wouldn't rest with the dust bunnies there?"

Brody's lips turned a weak smile. "Dust bunnies. What the hell are those anyhow?"

Sylvie shifted, her smile self-conscious, uncertain. "Stuff builds up, I guess."

"Mom could have cared less what was under this couch."

"You won't convince Lena," she said.

"No." His voice sounded distant. "It's too late for that."

She rearranged her hands in her lap. "They say it's never too late." Her father had said that once, about something she'd wanted but couldn't have, an expensive toy, maybe, or a pony, the things you believe you are desperate for and then later can't recall.

"You could have told me," he said. "That you were leaving. I wouldn't have stopped you. Not if that's what you wanted. You're not like the rest of us here." He paused. "A big fancy casket. Granite marker. That's what Dad wants." His mouth tightened. "He says the chemo messed with her brain. Screwed up her thinking." A small, bitter smile. "The way she was in the end with the glacier, that's his proof." He pressed his hands again to his temples, rubbing slow circles that wrinkled and stretched the skin of his forehead. "I wish I believed the way she did. In heaven and that."

"My mom was obsessed with that glacier," Sylvie said. "She found it in a magazine. Framed it and kept it on her desk. People gave her a hard time about it. You're supposed to have pictures of family, they said. Vacations. Your pets. Mom had her glacier, and all she'd say was how she liked ice."

Brody kept working his temples. "Every day," Sylvie said. "Every day I wake up, and I'm surprised it's still here."

He eased off his rubbing. "That's what Mom used to say. It even got into her dreams."

"I used to dream my father was drowning," Sylvie said. "In a big ocean with no one to save him, no one but me. Now I dream he's up on the ice, and it's moving and shifting, but he doesn't see it. He slips, and before I can reach him he falls, into one of those crevasses."

From the driveway came the sound of a car, the slow scrunch of gravel under tires. Sylvie got up and stood to one side of the windows, where she could see without being seen. "It's Lena," she said.

"She's probably got breakfast. It's what they do at the church. They feed you when stuff like this happens." He leaned into the cushions, white like the river flowers that twisted and opened, springing cottony seeds.

With some effort, Lena shoved out of the front seat and stared at the torn stretch of earth. She wobbled a little, then steadied herself on the hood of the car as she toed the dirt with her shoe, a white sneaker, and hugged her arms to her belly, looking like she might be sick.

"She thinks Kenny did it," Sylvie said, barely out loud.

Brody shrugged, elbows propped on his knees, hands steepled at his forehead. "Go see what she wants. Please."

As Sylvie descended the steps, Lena started toward the house. "It was good of you to come," she said. "To be with Brody."

Sylvie nodded dumbly, realizing that she'd never thanked Lena for coming to find her, and that the moment already was gone, missed like so much else she had missed.

"It's a shame about this lawn, on top of everything else." Lena's gaze fell on the driveway, on a clump of dirt Sylvie had failed to erase from the four-wheeler tracks, and then back to where the lawn had been. With her foot, Sylvie brushed aside this last bit of mud, the evidence she'd meant to hide.

"I don't suppose Brody knows how this happened," Lena said.

"No," Sylvie said. "I don't think he does."

"Whoever it was, I suppose he feels better now. He made his point." Lena glanced up at the windows. "Fixes nothing, but you can't fault it, just the same."

A car lunged up the driveway and stopped behind Lena's sedan. Pastor Tom eased out the driver's side door and approached Lena, drawing her into a tentative embrace. "We all feel the loss." He shoved his hands in his pockets. It looked like he hadn't slept.

Scott got out from the passenger side. "What the hell." He looked hard at Lena. "Damned poor timing, that's what this is."

"Now, Scott." Lena reached for his arm, but he drew back, his face red.

"As if you people hadn't done enough damage."

Lena drew herself up. "I'm sorry," she said. "We're all sorry. Darla, she was…"

Behind Sylvie, the door opened. The wind fluttered Brody's hair as he looked past Lena and Pastor Tom to his father, the small twist of his smile like his mother's, knowing and full of grace, a song, a remembrance.

"You must have heard something," Scott said. "You must have seen who it was."

Brody shifted. "I don't know," he said. "I guess I—"

Lena cut him off. "Now Scott, you know how boys sleep. Brody says he knows nothing, and that's all that needs said."

"Speak the truth, son," Scott said. "We all know who did this."

Lena looked momentarily flustered, but her composure quickly returned. "If you mean my boys—"

"Sister Lena, Brother Scott," Pastor Tom said. "A lawn can be replanted."

"Not without a hell of a lot of work it can't," Scott said.

"Nonetheless," Pastor Tom said. "We can look for blame later."

"No." Lena looked directly at Sylvie, a warning. "Let's settle this now, before any more harm's done." She heaved a breath and glanced at the glacier. "It takes a big machine to do something like this. And you know my son recently built one."

Sylvie drew a sharp, almost audible breath. "My boys are fiercely protective," Lena went on. "They come by it naturally, I'm afraid. I'm sure Kenny didn't consider the harm, and he wouldn't have known the bad timing. Scott, you have my full and humble apology, on Kenny's behalf. And my promise that we'll make it right, just as soon as we can."

Névé

Perennial snow

It was Pastor Tom's first funeral. His face looked a little too pale, his smile a little too quick, unsteady around the edges. It didn't help that there was no great oaken casket at the front of the chapel, only a small box tucked near the foot of the podium.

The church was packed full, warm with bodies. Every house on the highway was represented, as was every house on the island. Even Fong was there, looking genuinely sad. Her thin hair teased high, Trish swayed at the organ, leaning dramatically into the notes as she played them. In the back, Marie jiggled one twin on her hip while the other whined and tugged on her skirt. Cherise pulled Cara awkwardly against her shoulder, while Roxanne's Bible was splayed beside her on the pew, taking what amounted to a seat for someone else.

Kenny pressed his hand over Ruth's, her nails dirty from helping to replant lawn. At Lena's request, Kate had orchestrated the effort, calling in rollers and rototillers and bags of seed and fertilizer, plus a brigade of sprinklers and hoses manned by the Glory Girls, who took the watering on as a project unconnected to any badge.

Lena had explained to Kenny, simply and confidentially—though of course he'd told Ruth—how a rift between Scott and his son right now would have been too large to mend, that in his grief it would be Scott's last straw, to learn that his own boy had torn through his lawn, and so Lena had seen she must act as Darla would have, shifting the blame to spare Brody. She would have offered herself, but no one would have believed it, Lena Preston riding circles over Scott Prince's lawn, and so it fell to Kenny; she had, as it was said these days, thrown him under the bus.

My own mother, Kenny had said, but with a smile. Ruth only wished Darla could have seen.

At the front of the church, Scott averted his eyes, his mouth set hard. Though he'd allowed the cremation, he said he'd be damned if his wife's ashes would be scattered on ice. Brody stood at his side, shoulders slack, hair straggled over his collar, and beside Brody stood Sylvie. No one at church had said much about her running away, the timing turning out as it had.

The service began with a shuffled rising for prayer. Voices joined in hymns that proclaimed the mighty fortress of God and the rock that belonged to the ages, but no voice stood out the way Darla's had. Pastor Tom read off and on from his notes, about how Darla had found peace with God. Brody dropped his head to his hands, while beside him Sylvie sat rigid, her fingers stroking the spine of the hymnal.

In his message, Pastor Tom repeated what Paul had written about new bodies, how we must shed the old so one day all could rise perfect and whole. When he finished, people got up one by one to tell different things Darla had done—the cookies she'd baked to raise money for the school's PTA, the toddler class she'd taught in the nursery, the songs she'd sung from the front of the church. Ruth wished she could rise up and speak, but her throat felt too tight and constricted, and what would she say—that she envied Darla's courage with ice?

At last the closing hymn came, a song Darla had once sung of a sparrow and how God's eyes were on it. At this Lena gushed tears. They made a watery mess of her tissues, so that Walter had to pat her cheeks with his handkerchief.

Once the song ended, Pastor Tom looked limp with relief. Kenny huddled with Steven and Walter, their hands stuffed in their pockets, while the men of the church and their wives gathered around Scott.

Tommy slid into the pew next to Ruth. "Sylvie looks lost."

"It was one of those teenaged things," Ruth said. "She was homesick."

"Not the running away," Tommy said. "I mean up there with Brody." She nodded at Sylvie, who looked down at her hands, still clutching the hymnal. Light poured through the stained glass, purple and red, wavering over her head, Jesus in the garden, praying for the cup to pass. She twisted her head, like a bird about to take wing, and the colors kaleidoscoped over her skin.

"I hope at least she's some comfort to him," Ruth said. "When it's all said and done."

In the basement, the food was laid out with beauty. Triangled sandwiches, the crusts neatly extracted. Corkscrewed pasta tossed in a big glass bowl with crisp peppers and carrots and tomatoes. Deviled eggs sprinkled with paprika and lined up in rows. White chocolate cookies, and chocolate chunk, Darla's favorite. Wedged between them, cupcakes someone had pulled from the freezer, the frosting and the decorations restored, more or less. Lena hovered over them, then scooped the tray in her arms and hurried off with it.

At the trashcan, Anna scraped breadcrumbs off a cutting board. "Our cupcakes," she said as Lena prepared to dump them.

"They're not the same once they've been frozen," Lena said.

Anna stood on tiptoe and sniffed the frosting. "They're still pretty," she said.

Lena turned the tray in her hands, studying the sagging, drooping, sodden mess. "I suppose they've survived as best they could," she said. "I don't expect we can ask more than that."

"Darla would like them," said Anna.

"You're right about that," Lena said. "Darla would love every last one."

Impossibly, everyone ate. The women began to clean up as well-wishers flocked around Scott, acclimating themselves to the idea of death. Ruth supposed it was the same every time someone passed, the solidarity of grief when what the loved ones most wanted was to be left alone.

She was wiping the cut-glass plate that had held the egg-salad sandwiches when she saw Lena ascending the stairs, gripping with one hand the velvet bag used for the offering while with the other hand hauling herself up by the banister. The railing was loose; it wobbled each time she clasped it, as her feet teetered in her small-heeled shoes.

Ruth put the plate away and spread her dish towel to dry on the stainless steel counter, then slipped from the kitchen, up the stairs behind Lena. In the darkened sanctuary, only Lena's faint wheezing broke the empty quiet as she moved toward the altar, the pink bulging creases between her toes ballooning over the shiny smooth edges of her shoes.

She stared at the place where Pastor Tom had stood, then sank into the front pew, dropping the velvet bag to the floor next to her feet.

Ruth hesitated. It wasn't a good time, but what would be? She moved toward Lena with a soft thudding of footsteps intended to warn of her approach.

"I came for Darla." Lena nudged the velvet bag with her foot. "For her ashes. To bring them to Scott. But she's gone."

Ruth stared at the place where the box had sat, ashes to ashes, dust to dust. There was this benefit then, to a casket. It stayed where you left it.

"Now I have to get up the nerve to tell Scott." Lena rocked in the pew, her large body keening forward and back as tears streaked her face. Ruth folded her hands in her lap, pretending not to see.

As her rocking slowed, Lena wiped her face with a tissue. "She sat right here, when Judy died. Assured me she'd be with the Lord." For the first time since Ruth had sat down, Lena looked at her. "I doubt she believed it. But she said it for me. That was Darla."

There was silence, the true and natural state of a church. "Walter thinks we should go south for the winter," Lena said. "A place opened up next to where Trish and Pete spend the cold months, down in Sun City. Little single-wide trailer, not much to look at. It's not like I'd have to start over, he said. They've got churches down there." She half-smiled at Ruth. "Shows what he knows."

"I thought some more," Ruth said. "About leaving. For Sylvie's sake."

Lena stared again at where Darla's ashes had been, her large face unreadable.

"If you and Walter…" Ruth drew a long breath. "If you could make a small loan…" The walls seemed to slant in. "I'd pay it back, right away, as soon as I'm working."

Lena straightened. "What does Kenny have to say about it?"

"I haven't told him," said Ruth. "He'd never have to know. About the money, I mean. Where it came from."

Lena's face shifted in a way you might not notice if you hadn't been looking, a softening at the corners of the eyes and the mouth.

Relief.

Footsteps thumped the stairs, a one-two, one-two gallop. "Hey, you two," Kenny said. Ruth felt lightheaded with what Minerva Jones might call conviction.

"Darla's ashes," Lena said. "They're gone."

Kenny held up both hands. "Not me, I swear."

"I know that." Tears ran again down her face. Kenny slid beside her and took her hand as he produced a tissue. She dabbed her cheeks and, having no pockets in her swishing silk dress, she stuffed the wet Kleenex under her thigh.

"Not a word from either of you about those ashes," she said, her voice recovered. "Scott will find out soon enough."

Steven wanted Kenny's help with the well he was drilling, so Ruth rode home with Tommy, who hated funerals and wasn't afraid to say so. She tried to talk Ruth into stopping by her place for a glass of dandelion wine—like liquid sunshine, she said, a touch of lemon, a touch of honey. Though Ruth agreed that Darla would approve, she declined. All the way home she'd thought about who to tell first, after Kenny and the girls. Tommy at least wouldn't judge. She'd understand how fate could be something entirely different than what you'd first thought.

After Tommy dropped her off, Ruth stood in the yard, the white glare from the glacier searing her eyes as the wind danced her hair. She brushed past the weeds and lifted the plastic horse up by its mane. Things could be put back to how they once had been, the horse to the shed, the garden to sedge grass and horsetails. The curtains and the countertops would remain, but the rest would return to the way it had been, as if she'd never come, except that she now knew more ways to fail.

The horse slid from her hands, toppling back to the weeds. No one cared, she supposed, where it landed, and so she left it, knowing soon snow would come, mounding over the horse, a better fate perhaps than the shed where Kenny's cooler now sat, the chipped ice turned to water. This she dumped over her flimsy carrots, invoking Cynthia's unrepeatable accomplishment.

Packing wouldn't take long. The coming undone of a thing was easy compared to its stitching together. The frame and the photo and the glass that was cracked she would keep packed away. Once a few years had passed, she would take it out and say wasn't it something the way they'd gone north, all because of a glacier. The frame would feel light in her hands, and she would acknowledge that Sylvie was right, that there were things too ancient and large to hang onto.

She returned the empty cooler to the shop, where the wheeler sat muddy and scratched, its plywood base already nicked in one corner. She circled, studying the challenge it posted, its capacity to confound and infuriate the way Mirabelle had, and now Sylvie.

She slid onto the seat salvaged from Joe Pleary's truck, the mud-splattered vinyl cool on her legs. She hiked her skirt to her knees and straddled the sticks that jutted up from the plywood, mysteriously connecting the gears and the cables and the levers underneath. She was no good with such things. That's what Richard had said.

The seat tilted back, so she had to scoot forward to see past the windshield. Binoculars hung on a nail near the dash, and on the floor there were matches and wadded-up trash but no pedals. She tried to recall what Kenny had said about how it all worked, the engine and the torque and the transmission with its infinite gears.

He was the last one to care about locking things up, so though the engine required a key, it was right there in the ignition, ready for turning. She fingered it. Felt its promise. What was love but the building of a thing out of scrounged parts, a wisp of dream made manifest?

She slid from the seat and heaved open the shop's overhead door and returned to the wheeler, then flicked the key, simple and easy. The engine powered up. Vibrations ran up the chassis through the floor to her legs. Even with the door wide open, it smelled of combustion.

She wrapped her hand around one of the metal sticks and tugged, but nothing gave. She grabbed the second stick, but that wouldn't budge either. Nose and eyes stinging from exhaust, she grabbed both sticks and rattled them backwards and sideways and forward, and all at once the wheels spun her into the light and she was driving.

She yanked the handles and the wheeler spun in reverse, jolting her nearly out of the seat as it hurtled backwards toward the shop, spinning grit on her garden. She shoved the handles forward, and the wheels spun forward again, at a pace she could almost manage, charging past the turnips and the carrots and the tiny cabbages balled up tight.

At the end of the driveway, she pressed her foot to the floor, hoping to stop, forgetting there were no pedals. In her panic, she grabbed the closest stick, causing the machine to veer to the right in a barely controlled turn, and then all at once she was on the road at least with some semblance of steering if not braking. She sat straight up, dust billowing out from the eight wheels as she maneuvered the levers forward and back, causing the wheeler to fishtail from one side of the road to the other, skimming the gravel.

With some jerking, she steered onto the trail that went down toward the river, crossing the wide ancient place carved first by ice, then by water. The wheels churned seeds from cottony balls that had once been tight yellow flowers, the predominant color now gray, the red paintbrush and pink twinflower and blue twisted stalk having also gone to seed, leaving only the purple fireweed flowers creeping up the stalks.

Ahead the sharp-edged cliffs cast shadows like spiny-backed reptiles, the mountains behind them cushioned partway up with the green of leafed trees. She worked the sticks, steering toward a hunk of weathered wood half-buried in the weeds, Walter's tram, a tangle of rusted cable and fallen timbers. She pressed her foot again to the floor as one of the tires skittered and bounced against the big splintered beam.

The machine wobbled then righted itself as it pummeled toward the riverbank that fell off toward the water with its endless pounding and crashing. Riding a wild surge of terror, Ruth clutched the sticks, certain there had never been a time without ice and there never would be. She leaned into the air that washed over the windshield, bathing her forehead, her full weight on the sticks, the landscape a jumble of river and rocks. She should pull back, make it move in reverse, away from the river, but in the gap between knowing and doing, Ruth let go. She flung her arms wide, feeling no suspicion, no fear, and no guilt. She only wished Kenny could see her like this.

The wheels seized and the wheeler bucked up and back, slamming her into the seat. Her head thunked the windshield, and her body went limp, and she felt herself floating, floating, as the engine rumbled, low and expectant, and beyond that, the water roared.

Trembling, she sat up and wiped her palms on her skirt, streaking it gray. She touched her forehead in the place where it stung, then leaned back and shut her eyes. In her mind the sky stretched blue and taut, though when she opened her eyes it was only dull gray.

With no effort, she turned the key—such a simple thing—and the engine noise quit. She held one hand to her forehead where a lump was already swelling, then lifted the binoculars from where they hung.

She scooted to the edge of the seat so the windshield wouldn't cut her view of the glacier. Her hands continued to tremble as she raised the binoculars to her eyes, the image wobbly at first, a kaleidoscope of gray, black, and white, infinite gradations that were beyond separating. She turned the eyepiece and it came clear, the ice in its fullness, the fracture zones and the foliation and the aretes and the cirques and the seracs and the downwasting and the crevasses and the trimline. For a long time she studied the glacier, amazed at how knowing and loving were so alike, and yet one didn't always lead to the other.

She dropped the binoculars into her lap and fingered the key. She thought of Kenny's bright smile, his hands on her waist, his lips pressed on hers. If there were one thing she hoped her girls learned, it was that you didn't have to justify your desires, not the true ones.

She hung the strap over the nail, the binoculars dangling. Then she picked them back up. One more look, she told herself as she held them up to her eyes. Adjusting the lenses, she saw two black figures, unrecognizable, scaling the face of the ice.

So brave, she thought. Maybe one day she'd try it herself.

Serac

A jagged pinnacle, rising up from the ice

You feel it first in the dry, sucking wind that shivers past shadows, the air mean and low, siphoning warmth, the ice a large and perpetual testimony to cold. Two figures creep toward it, dwarfed by raw-edged mountains that chew at the sky, the illusion of ice so close you could reach out and feel the wet melt of it under your skin as you press against it as if for a pulse.

Neither child—for we are all children, awed by ice—neither is dressed for this kind of cold. Rubble sprawls between them and the glacier, a graveled gauntlet of jagged rocks lain down. The best of boots will wobble and twist. His are leather, scuffed and worn, army surplus. Her shoes are for running, utterly worthless here. Through their meager soles, rocks jab at her feet. Her right ankle twists, then her left. Like a teetering old woman, she struggles for balance as she strikes with poles clenched in her hands, clanking metal to rock. The pointed ends wedge sideways. She yanks the poles free, swings one, then strikes with the other, a slow laborious crawl.

Poleless, the boy scampers freely, arms out like a dancer's, angled and sliding, resisting the earth. Atop the sprawling moonscape of rock, he stumbles, falls, and rights himself all in one motion. Each time he falls, the girl sucks a breath. Nothing gold, nothing gold. The ice is too far, and then there is the climbing, up the impossible face of it, equipped only with spikes and ropes, the wind pitching and howling over the yawning gaps of the glacier.

It was easy, so easy with Rick. His truck gleaming next to the fire, a wild thing about to escape. The keys stashed in his pocket, ready and warm.

211

The oversized tires crunching the gravel, the prison lights pushing up at the night. But her motives were wrong. She sees this now. You don't do these things out of sorrow, or fear.

The sky is hazy, the rocks black and greedy for heat, the day more than half spent. At the church they are cleaning, the basement smelling of boiled eggs and coffee and frosting. Her sister sweeps crumbs from the egg-salad sandwiches, the bread spongy and white, its crusts neatly sheared. Lena clucks and fusses while her mother hovers, uncertain. She should be here, not Sylvie, scaling these rocks, clawing her way to the ice. Her mother, who had the courage to come here, the faith to love.

No one blames the boy for shrugging out early, for leaving the egg salad and tuna, triangles fashioned out of remembrance for his mother. No one blames him, after all he's been through, though no matter what Lena says, there is still whispered talk of the lawn. The ashes may already be missed.

Nothing gold, nothing gold. She unzips her coat to let the wind chill the sweat on her neck and her chest. The boy turns, waves her on. She wants to feel his determination, let it carry her forward. But everything changes so quickly. The putt-putt of a sprinkler refreshing a lawn, the purr of a borrowed boat on the water, her own light steps on the stairs as she listens for small puffs of breath.

He's at the ice, feigning patience, jiggling the ropes he has cinched to his waist. "Come on," he urges. "We have to get down before dark."

She maneuvers the last rocks to reach him. Resists folding into his arms. He ties a rope to her waist and it hangs limp between them. It's surprisingly warm here, the ice a shield from the wind, beaten and scarred, scored by the stones it has dragged. Some cling still, like parasites pressed to its face. Rocks skitter and fall. Water trickles and runs. The smell even here is as he promised, fresh with gouging and melting.

She straps the spikes to her boots, and he shows her how she must kick at the ice, to wedge her toes for a foothold. She kicks once, tentatively, but the glacier feels too big and alive. He makes her kick again and again till she gives it the force it requires. "Don't hold back." He hands her an ax. "Hit it hard. Like you mean it."

She swings, and the ax glances sideways off the ice. Shards splinter and scatter. "I can't do this," she says.

"Hit it straight on."

She strikes again, and again the ax slips. She lets go, the ax clattering at her feet. He bends to retrieve it, as if time isn't pressing against them, as if the day isn't waning. He wraps her fingers around the handle. "Again," he says.

"You go." Her voice sounds small. "I'll wait here."

"You have to want it," he says. "You have to keep wanting."

She shakes her head, fearful of tears. "I don't want it. I'm not meant to."

He hacks the ice, and it yields. He kicks, and the spikes on his boots crunch into the glacier. "It's easy," he says. "You've got your crampons and the ice ax and you're tied off to me."

"I can't," she says. The ice is large and uncertain, and she herself nothing more than a dizzying wave of fear and miscalculations.

He climbs, picking and scaling the ice, the rope tightening between them. He cranks his head to look down. "Kick and pick," he calls to her. "It's not hard." He tugs the rope, the ice a vertical wall, streaked with dirt, lumpy and mocking. "Come on. You won't fall."

But she sees how she'll slip. How she'll pull him down. How they'll tumble over and over, with nothing to save them.

He crunches again at the ice, kicking and picking, the rope taut. She fumbles with the small hard knot at her waist. "Come on," he urges. "You have to start climbing."

But she doesn't. She doesn't have to do anything. She thrashes side to side like a fish, resisting the rope.

"Don't do that," he yells. "You're gonna make me fall."

Exasperation, a scrambling and shuffling, and he's beside her again, feet on the rocks, forehead glistening. "This was your idea," he says.

It isn't the shifting of gears or the wobbly wheels or the yielding that comes to her then, but her mother's finger tracing the cracked glass that covered the glacier.

"You don't trust me," he says.

It's her chance to agree and be done. To untie the rope and stumble back over the rocks, to move away and away, which is what she does best.

But she has misjudged the depth of his longing. He waits, clutching the rope. His hat pressed to his head, he's all face, his father's dark eyes, his mother's promising mouth.

"Swear," she says. "Swear I won't fall," though it is not him she mistrusts but herself.

"Swearing, that's easy. It's the climbing that's hard."

She steps away as he reaches, but this too she misjudges—his hands settle on the straps of his pack, his gloved fingers tightening the yoke. "She used to stand at the window," he says. "While my dad trimmed and weeded and dusted on fertilizer and set out the sprinklers. The way the sun hit her face, you could almost see through her skin." He scans the ice, rugged, uneven. "All he cared about was that stupid lawn. Not that it matters. Not now."

In each hand Sylvie clutches an ax. He climbs like a goat, nimble and balanced, hoofs spread and clinging, defying gravity's pull to nibble on lichen that grows like some sort of miracle over the rocks. Though scrabbled and hard, a mountain nourishes. Not so the ice. It tempts and it dares, and it offers nothing beyond what the senses can hold.

She flails at the glacier. A glancing blow, then a shower of skittering ice. She swings again, a desperate, crunched hacking, and this time the ax sticks. She pulls herself up. Her arms burn with her own weight, suspended. She kicks with her shoes, demanding a hold. She teeters, perched like a high-centered bug on the sheer wall of ice.

Despite the cold, sweat builds on her neck. Twenty feet from the ground, and above only glacier and sky. It's up to her, whether to hang here or let go, to give in to the pull of the rocks and the earth.

Her breath glistens, puffed against ice. Silent. Ancient. Unknowable. A refuge against having lost and been lost. If she hangs here long enough, it will all dissolve, a gully sloshing under the heat of her hands.

She recalls her father's smooth, easy smile. *Love you, sugar.* She hacks at the frozen mass. *Love you.* Kicks to lock herself in. *Love you. Goodbye.*

Her legs shake, unsteady. She is small beyond small, the rope a thin thread. She will not look where he waits, patient and forgiving. She leans in, embracing the ice. If she only believes, her legs will quit shaking, her arms will relax. She could rest here forever, hugging the ice, letting it wrap her in cold. She could melt, and the river would carry her off.

She windmills her arms at the glacier. Hack and pull. Hack and pull. The weight of her body enormous, she heaves. Grunts and kicks. Her fear is a fire, lit by her father's hands, clutching and grasping, his enormous desire.

The spell of cold will consume her, transform her like ice at its core. She chisels, kicking and swinging, pin-pricking a trail over the wrinkled face of the glacier. She works the axes one after the other. Chop, crunch. Chop, crunch. The rope never tightens but she knows without looking: he waits.

The rocks recede as she climbs toward the wide embrace of the sky. Her arms and legs ache, her fingers gripping like death. She longs not for Karen or Cara, not for Rick or her father, but for her mother. She will do this for her, and for herself.

A subtle shift in the ice, a rounding, like the edge of the earth. Her feet dangle as she listens to the reverberations of her heart. Above, his scuffed boots. "One more step," he says. "One more step and you'll be on top." He uncurls her hands from the axes and clasps them. She kicks once more at the ice and then she's up, up on top, the whole world spread beneath her.

He slips off his pack and reaches inside. It had pleased him, to see what she'd done, slipping unnoticed into the sanctuary to retrieve what was left of his mother.

"Not here," she says. She's aware of everything now, well beyond her own breath, the ice shaped and shaping, astounding in size, like nothing she knows or will know. She sees how a person would give herself up to it.

She hobbles away from him, across the uneven surface, dimpled and crackling.

"Right here is fine," he insists. "We have to get down before dark."

She balances on the cobbled ice. Turns her face to the wind, born of cold, and spots a crevasse, gaping and black. The wind burns the tips of her ears and her nose, stings her eyes. But her legs are solid beneath her, arms swinging, running almost.

He calls out to her, urgent, but the words are lost to the wind. The crevasse looms, plunging and silent. She knows from Cara, from Tommy, from Lena, how slipping once you'll disappear, wedged forever in ice.

Clomping behind her, he jabs the back of her leg. "At least use your poles." As he says this, snow crumples under her boot. She slips, and feels herself fall.

He grabs her sleeve. Yanks her up and stares at her as if for the first time, with a sort of wonder, as he brushes her off. "That's a snow bridge. They're everywhere, snow piled over crevasses. You have to probe first. Use your poles."

She stares at the thin dark place that nearly consumed her, then starts again, feeling her way with the pole, like a blind person, testing the snow. Again it gives, but the pole finds the gap first.

"Enough," he says. "It's gonna get dark."

She wavers, but only a moment, then presses again toward the big one, the wide, gaping crevasse. She hears him behind her, scrambling to keep up. She wishes her mother could see.

At last she arrives at the dark, jagged edge. Streaked blue, the crevasse reaches to the core of the ice, where there is nothing but hardness and death. She leans toward it. Shuts her eyes tight, and lets go.

Her pole ricochets from ice to ice, clattering into the crevasse. Ten, twenty, fifty, eighty feet down, until she no longer hears it.

The first small step toward beginning, letting go of what you've hung onto, the hurts and the longings. The first small step toward home, which isn't where she'd thought it at all.

He clamps his hands on her shoulders and yanks her back from the edge. "Jesus, Sylvie." She rests her hands on her thighs, breathing thin clouds that dissolve in the cold. His hand on her elbow, he steers her as if she's an old lady at church, away from the danger to where a bit of light reaches out from between the gray clouds to the ice. He squints up at the sky, then unzips the pack.

He cradles the box, presses his lips to it, then holds it out to her, his eyes darker than any poem. "Back there," he says. "That took guts. Mom would have liked it." He swipes at his face. "Damned wind."

She understands what he wants, and though she's in no way worthy, she unhinges the lid and stares at the ashes, gray as dust ground by ice. Like silt, they feel both gritty and smooth. She curls her fingers around them, pressing them into her skin, then slides her clenched fingers over his hand and flattens her palm against his, the cold burning their fingers.

Hand to hand, as in prayer, they lift the ashes to the wind and let go, a gift to the ice that without pretense or longing scrapes everything new.

Acknowledgments

Without a band of astute readers, this book could not have found its way. My sincere thanks go to Karen Benning, Louise Freeman-Toole, Nicole Idar, Chris Lehmann, David Marusek, and Jessica Vanasse, whose insights helped shape the story. To Bill Streever go special thanks for explorations of ice that venture far beyond anything I'd ever dare, and to Kirsten Dixon, for her insistence on knowing what a photo like Ruth's might portend.

Among those who believed in this book, the encouragement of Gail Hochman, Lindsey Clemons, Anne Fontanesi, and Max Byrd especially sustained me. In gratitude that extends to the entire talented team at the University of Alaska Press, James Engelhardt and the ever-gracious Peggy Shumaker deserve special note for their vision and commitment to the Alaska Literary Series.

I owe an immense debt to author David Vann, whose fine teaching shifted the ways I think about language and story. There's no repaying that sort of influence. You can only hope to somehow pass it along.

Though enriched by my life in Alaska and my informal study of glaciers, this novel is a work of the imagination. Any resemblance of the characters to persons living or dead is coincidental, and any errors are wholly my own.